"This secret," the admiral interrupted, "is too important. We cannot afford to let anything stand in the way of keeping it."

"But firing on our own ships?" Skylarov asked incredulously. "Next thing you know, we're going to be blowing up Earth."

"Careful," Ramirez replied. "Everyone is replaceable—even you."

Is he threatening me? Skylarov wondered, horrified.

As Fleet Admiral Ramirez smiled cruelly, the look in his eyes told Skylarov all he needed to know.

I ripped the cover off a copy of this book, but it wasn't destroyed. Bummer.
—The one person who bought a copy.

Amazing. I've just discovered that a book can be self-levitating from all the hot air.
—Jacques Montgolfier

It's even better than asking yourself if you left the oven on.
—My method acting coach

You'll laugh. You'll cry. Mostly cry.
—An anonymous reviewer

Thanks to you, I lost my lawsuit for food poisoning. I told the judge what I was reading, and he dismissed the case.
—Some guy who's suing me

I've never been more bowled over by a book before.
—Victim, great book avalanche of 2023

I guess this is what happens when you make schoolchildren read Joseph Conrad. Sorry. My bad.
—My high school senior year English teacher

This is why engineers should never be allowed to write fiction.
—A reviewer under condition of anonymity

I know who you are, Jim.
—Me upon reading the previous comment

Patriots:
Beyond the Veil

A novel by
David A. Gatwood

Published by Gatwood Publishing.

Printed in the United States of America.

ISBN: 978-1-940809-05-2

For uniting an alliance, and
for free Internet without a login screen.

A Word from the Author:

This book is the third in a series of three books. Unlike most trilogies, this book does not pick up where the last one left off, but if you're reading the third book, you probably guessed that already. Instead, it starts a few months before the first book, filling in the backstory as the first story slowly unravels in the fire of truth. It continues in parallel with the first two books, and ends a few days after the first two books ended.

This book tells the story of not only the people pulling the strings, but also the people who were just in the wrong place at the wrong time.

If you haven't read the first two books, now would be a good time to get a copy and read them. That having been said, I've tried to make sure that each book largely stands on its own, so maybe you won't be *too* confused....

The first book in the Patriots series, "Traitors in Waiting," explores the great colonial war from the perspective of military officers born and raised in a loyalist Earth colony who find out, to their horror, that the military is being manipulated by traitors in high-ranking positions.

The second book, "Enemies From Within," treats the story from a different perspective. In this story, which starts a few decades before the first, we learn that the colonies were actually a dumping ground for the least desirable elements of Earth's population—the terrorists, the underachievers, the hairdressers, the lawyers, and so on.

Both the first and second books end with certain key parts of the conspiracy largely intact, however, saving the ending for the third book.

The third book, "Beyond the Veil," tells the truth behind the war.

When reading this book, you may occasionally see things repeated. Sometimes, this is done to avoid making you turn back to a previous book in the series to follow the plot, but this is not always the case. Whenever you encounter such a familiar passage, you should always ask yourself what is different this time around. Is it just a change in perspective, or did the previous perspective omit certain details that completely change your interpretation of events?

After the book, be sure to read "Closing Thoughts", where I ruin it for everybody by explaining everything you wanted to know about the story (and probably a lot of things you never wanted to know).

Special Thanks:

to my reviewers for
faultlessly catching
all the mispelled words,

to my readers for reading
the previous thank-you
and humoring me,

to my family, friends,
coworkers, and teachers for
encouraging and shaping me
as a writer,

and to everyone who
ever asked, “Why not?”
when they could have
asked, “Why?”

Prologue:

November 26, 2390

Lieutenant Pierre DesChambres could already feel the effects of the sodium thiopental as his wrist slipped free from its restraint. He struggled to release the other wrist restraint, then unbuckled the straps holding his legs.

The door opened easily when he approached it from the inside, much to his amazement.

The sick bay was not designed as a prison, he mused. *Wait a minute. Does that mean I could have walked out of here at any time for the last two days?*

His hope was short-lived, however; within moments, he found himself wishing he had a good place to hide when the doctors appeared at one end of the corridor.

He quickly ran away from them to the opposite end of the hall, turned right, ran through a door into a larger hall, turned left, and finally ran through the double doors to his right.

Once through those doors, he found himself inside the Crew's Quarter, a large eating establishment. Were it not for his medical gown, he probably could have gotten lost in the crowd, but alas, it was not to be, so all he could hope to do was to tell everyone what he knew.

"This is mad!" Pierre shouted at no one in particular. "I demand to be heard. The Alliance is corrupt!"

Suddenly, the elite security forces crashed through the doors behind him.

"They're killing us!" he screamed. "They're killing us! Their own people!"

As the security team wrestled him to the ground, he continued to try to speak. "You have to believe me! There are traitors in waiting!"

Then, he felt the familiar jab of a stunner in his back, and everything went black.

***

The next day

PIERRE awoke suddenly and glanced around the white room, its cushioned walls and padded floors a constant reminder of the state of the world around him. The creak of the giant door jostled him from his sleep as it opened slowly to reveal the hallway beyond. He glanced up to see if he could flee, but the men in white blocked his exit as they always did.

A man in a white lab coat pushed past the attendants.

"Hi, Pierre," the man said carefully. "Do you know who I am?"

"Of course I know who you are," Pierre replied in a deep Parisian accent. "You are Doctor Johnson."

The doctor nodded.

"Look, doc," he continued, "I am not crazy."

"Sure. That's what they all say," the doctor replied, chuckling.

"Zey really are out to get us."

"Who are?" the doctor asked.

"Ze aliens," Pierre replied calmly. "Zey are trying to destroy us all."

The doctor sighed and shook his head.

"There's no such thing as aliens, Pierre," he replied. "You're experiencing a paranoid delusion brought on by the stress of losing your job."

"I didn't lose my job. I'm on shore leave."

The doctor sighed. "You were fired for negligence, Pierre."

“No, it’s not true,” Pierre said, shaking his head as if to clear his thoughts. “I took shore leave because ze aliens were manipulating people. I’m not crazy. Zese drugs, they are making me crazy. I’m not crazy. I’m not, not crazy, not crazy.”

“Someone is here to see you,” the doctor interrupted. “Do you think you can keep your head together long enough to talk to him?”

Pierre nodded groggily.

“Okay, then,” he said gently as he nodded to the attendants.

A moment later, a slightly obese man entered, his toupee blowing obviously in the breeze.

“Pierre, my good man,” he said in a light British accent.

Pierre smiled. “Monsieur Jenkins,” he replied. “Bonjour, bonjour. C’est une plaisir de vous voir.”

Admiral Jenkins chuckled.

“Good to see you too, my old friend. Please. Call me Tom.”

“Are you here to get me out?” Pierre asked.

The admiral sighed and lowered his head, turned around, walked a couple of steps, turned back, walked back, then looked up again.

“Pierre,” he replied, “You know that I would if I could, but....”

“But you don’t believe me,” Pierre replied.

The admiral paused, angled his head, then replied, “I honestly don’t know what to believe anymore. I want you to tell me exactly what happened.”

“Well,” Pierre replied, “It all began when....”

Chapter One

October 30, 2390

THE command and control center aboard the small Terran Command outpost in orbit around Beta Persei barely held three people, and for the moment, Pierre was its sole occupant, filling the only non-broken chair. Once a month, he had to hold down the night shift.

Pierre wondered what the day shift would do for seating, then realized that they would probably just go down to the mess hall and steal chairs from there. Pierre could just picture Leanna hauling one of those heavy mess hall monstrosities up three flights of stairs.

Suddenly, a burst of noise from the radio woke him from his reverie.

"Thees ees...", the man's voice crackled through the radio, "of sheep Hrabrost calling Terran Command Outpost 72.... Emergency... Come een, please."

Pierre spun around in his chair.

What the...

"Yes, Her...ah.. uh... what you said.... We read you," he replied.

"Vee hev... radiation leak," the radio crackled.

He smirked as his mind drifted back to old science fiction from the late 1900s.... *So it's a nuclear wessel?*

"Do you have navigation thrusters?" Pierre asked.

"Negative," the man replied.

"State your position and we will send tow ships to pull you in."

A few seconds went by in silence.

"Please state your pos..."

"Ve hev just emairged from the folding geht et Beta Persei and are adreeft," the man interrupted.

Pierre quickly keyed in instructions for tow ships to retrieve the stranded vessel, then began monitoring the transponder screen. The disabled ship was exactly where they said it was. Three tow ships were also visible on their way out towards the wreckage. Then, the transponder signal suddenly disappeared.

"Sir," another voice crackled, "This is Captain Paulson aboard the Aenid. The Russian ship just exploded. We don't detect any life signs or escape pod transponders."

No life signs, no escape pods, Pierre noted. *They didn't know it was coming until it was too late.*

"That's not the only thing," the lieutenant continued. "Just before the explosion, I thought I saw... something."

"Could you clarify that?" Pierre asked.

The request was met with silence.

"Lieutenant?"

Then, another transponder signal went dark.

Oh, crap.

***

As dawn broke over Pierre, South Dakota, Laura Rodolfo sat motionless in a sea of cars making their way towards the Tulip Festival.

“Damn it,” she shouted to no one in particular as she slammed the palms of her hands into the steering wheel. “The one time I have a 9:00 meeting, and I’m stuck in this mess.”

The traffic suddenly started moving, and she applied the gas. Ten feet later, she slammed on the brakes again.

The very second that the clock rolled over to 9:00, her phone started ringing. She answered it.

“Where are you!?!” the man at the other end shouted.

“Stuck in traffic,” she replied, annoyed.

“You know what,” he shouted angrily, “I really don’t *care* where you are. If you aren’t here in five minutes, you can find another job.”

“Screw you,” she shouted as she threw the phone out the window.

Damn, she thought. *I should have synced my contacts before I did that.... Oh, well. I needed a new phone anyway... and a new job.*

With that, she took the first exit and began pondering what she should do with her day off.

***

Admiral Skylarov pushed the hatch open and continued up the ladder onto the ship’s bridge.

“Think you cut that close enough?” Fleet Admiral Ramirez asked him angrily. “He almost got a message off. We wouldn’t want to have to shoot down a Terran Command outpost.”

Admiral Skylarov bristled.

“Something wrong?” Ramirez asked.

Admiral Skylarov paused, then replied, “I think we may be going too far. This secret....”

"This secret," the admiral interrupted, "is too important. We cannot afford to let anything stand in the way of keeping it."

"But firing on our own ships?" Skylarov asked incredulously. "Next thing you know, we're going to be blowing up Earth."

"Careful," Ramirez replied. "Everyone is replaceable—even you."

Is he threatening me? Skylarov wondered, horrified.

As Fleet Admiral Ramirez smiled cruelly, the look in his eyes told Skylarov all he needed to know.

Chapter Two

Almost twenty-eight years earlier (January 26, 2363)

KLERN's footsteps echoed as he stepped into the ancient council chambers. The domed stained glass ceiling glistened in the morning sunlight, sending rays of sunshine streaming through the dusty air towards the white marble floor with its green and white mottled granite inlays. The dark wooden banisters still whispered memories of a forgotten era, their intricate carvings dating back thousands of years. It was against this ornate backdrop that Klern addressed the council of Ni'Utn.

"Councillors," he began, "it has been brought to my attention that you are gravely concerned about the experiments being conducted on Lenora Prime. Rest assured that we are dealing with the problem."

One of the councillors stood. "Mr. Klern, with all due respect, that is what the War Council has been saying for the past six months. Our scientists have detected dangerous levels of space-time distortion in the vicinity of Lenora Prime—distortions that, if allowed to continue, could rend the fabric of the universe as we know it."

The politician stuck out his chest as though it would somehow make him look more important than the junior councillor that he was. Klern wanted to roll his eyes more than ever before.

"So you'll forgive me," the councillor continued, "if I'm not at all satisfied to merely be told that you are 'dealing with the problem'. Tell us what you are doing, how, and most importantly, when."

"We have identified a young member of the team who is an ideal candidate to be 'replaced'," Klern replied. "His name is Cadet Mikhail Skylarov. He is scheduled for shore leave from his assignment to Lenora Prime. He is going to come down with Montezuma's revenge. He will call in sick, but the reply will be intercepted. By the time he returns, the Ackerman crystal will be long gone and the witnesses will be dead."

"Excellent," the councillor replied. "This will be a perfect test for our veiling technology. It will last long enough to confirm whether the veil will fool the Terran Alliance into believing our operative is this Skylarov fellow, but will end soon enough that our limited knowledge of their internal operations should not betray our operative's true identity."

"Excellent, indeed," Klern confirmed. "I will put one of my top operatives on the project. I will not fail you."

"See that you don't," the councillor replied, "or you will be demoted to a foot soldier."

Chapter Three

Almost twenty-eight years later (October 31, 2390)

LAURA collapsed on the sofa as the dog ran up and playfully licked at her toes and sandals. With her left hand, she keyed an access code into the data pad on the arm of her couch; then she leaned back.

"I never thought I'd say this," Laura muttered, "but unemployment is kind of fun. I just wish that rat bastard had fired me a week earlier so I could have been at Sydney's wedding. Speaking of which, let's see if Sydney sent me any more pictures from her cruise."

She quickly flipped through the images. Ooh. *Looks like they did a flyby of Beta Persei for their honeymoon,* she noted.

Suddenly, something caught her eye in one of the pictures. A cluster of ships hovered outside the folding gate, which was odd in and of itself. One ship was venting atmosphere and some sort of plasma. Its side was blackened by scorch marks as though it had been in a battle. That was also somewhat odd, given that it was so far from any disputed territories.

But what most caught her attention was a bright spot about fifty meters below the ship. In the photo before it, no spot. In the photo after it, the spot was closer. The next photo showed the ship engulfed in a giant fireball, its metal hull burning in the ship's atmosphere.

Her eyes widened. The photos were taken a few tenths of a second apart. She quickly did some math, extrapolating where the light should have been in the previous photo.

That's impossible. It just... appeared....

With that realization, she quickly copied the photos to an encrypted disk image on a keychain drive, slipped it into her pocket, then pressed a button on her data pad. Sydney's face appeared on the viewscreen a few moments later.

"This better be important," Sydney said. "We're on vacation, you know."

That's when Laura realized that Sydney had no idea what she had witnessed.

"You... didn't look at these pictures before you sent them, did you, Syd?"

Sydney's eyes widened. "I'm not naked, am I?"

Laura nearly hit the floor laughing.

"Pictures 95274 through 95279," she replied after regaining her composure.

Sydney stared at them in silence, flipping back and forth, back and forth. After nearly five minutes, she stopped and turned towards the camera, white as a sheet.

Sydney stammered.

"Wh... wh... what... w... w... was th... th... that?" she asked.

Laura shook her head.

"We have to tell someone," Sydney said.

"Who?" Laura asked. "This looks like some military secret. If we tell anyone, we could be in serious danger."

Sydney thought about this for a moment.

"Someone has an invisible warship. If we don't tell anyone, we're all in danger."

Laura couldn't argue with that logic.

"Come pick me up," Laura said.

"Where are we going?" Sydney asked.

"Where do you think?" Laura replied. "We're going to Beta Persei."

***

PIERRE stood as the station commander entered the engineering deck.

Commander Fred Ebberstein was a swarthy gentleman, his dark hair and Middle Eastern features betraying his Israeli heritage.

"What are you still doing here?" the commander asked. "Your shift ended an hour ago."

Pierre spun around and quickly placed himself between the monitors and his commander.

"I'm just going over some sensor readings," Pierre replied. "I thought I noticed a glitch earlier, so I'm just making sure all our equipment is okay."

"If you find anything, let me know immediately," the commander replied.

Pierre shivered. He couldn't place it, but something seemed very wrong.

"Will do."

"Carry on," the commander said as he stepped out.

Pierre looked down at the screen. He saw thousands of log messages. One caught his attention:

```
03:45:12.105 dev 01,35 ioctl(0x00310017):
Error 01 Operation not permitted
```

It wasn't so much the message—it was borderline gibberish to him—but he thought he had seen it before. Sure enough, five seconds earlier in the log, he saw the same message.

```
03:45:07.105 dev 01,35 ioctl(0x00310017):
Error 01 Operation not permitted
```

And five seconds before that and five seconds after. So he opened up a new terminal window and typed:

```
grep 0x00310017 /var/log/system.log
```

And he got thousands of them, but he only cared about the lines at or around 3:46 in the morning. Then, he saw it.

```
03:45:12.105 dev 01,35 ioctl(0x00310017):
Error 01 Operation not permitted
03:45:17.105 dev 01,35 ioctl(0x00310017):
Error 01 Operation not permitted
03:45:22.104 dev 01,35 ioctl(0x00310017):
Error 01 Operation not permitted
03:45:27.105 dev 01,35 ioctl(0x00310017):
Error 01 Operation not permitted
03:46:02.106 dev 01,35 ioctl(0x00310017):
Error 01 Operation not permitted
```

Pierre stared at the screen blankly for nearly five minutes trying to convince himself that his eyes were not deceiving him.

Thirty-five seconds. It can't be.... That means... someone doctored the station's system logs. Ah, how I love automatic checkpointing; it's rollback time.

***

THE sound of her front door opening in the middle of the night and the growl of her dog made Laura jump straight up in the air.

Her dog's growl was punctuated by the too familiar chirp of a gunshot through a silencer.

She quickly rolled out of bed and moved to the door so that she could see around the corner.

Three men in Terran Command uniforms stood in the foyer discussing something. She could barely make out what they were saying.

Search... upstairs... downstairs... bedroom... girl... shoot to kill.

That's when they started moving towards her.

What can I do? The closet!

She slipped into the closet, closed the doors, and ripped the cover off the large air vent. On the other side of the opening lay her bathroom. In the dim light of the skylight overhead, she could barely make out the man's shoes as he walked into the bathroom.

Seeing no one, the man quickly left. A moment later, she heard the door to her room creak open.

I am SO glad I didn't oil that thing.

As soon as he entered her room, she carefully pushed on the other side of the duct, gripping it with her fingernails so that it would not drop to the floor. A moment later, she was standing in the bathroom. She pulled the closet-side vent back into place a mere fraction of a second before the closet door opened, then closed again.

She quickly slipped the vent back off, crawled back into the closet, and reinstalled both vents.

As soon as she heard the door creak shut, she waited for about a minute, listening intently for any signs of the intruders. The creaking of the steps told her that it was safe, but just to be certain, she peered through the barely cracked closet door for a few seconds before opening it.

As soon as she reentered her room, she made a beeline for the window, unlocked it, and crawled out onto the window ledge. She knew that if she could make it to the roof, she could climb across the trellis in the garden and into the neighbor's yard.

That's when the door opened again. She had less than a second to react. She jumped straight down, grabbing the ledge as she fell. By the time the lights in her room came on, she was hanging from the windowsill by her fingertips.

Laura clung to the side of the house for what seemed like an eternity before the lights in her room went off again. From the sound of papers rustling, she thought perhaps they were searching for more than just her.

The photos!

For once, she appreciated her friend's paranoia. She never understood why Sydney insisted that Laura use encrypted local storage, but suddenly all that inconvenience was worth it. *Too bad she sent the photos in the clear,* Laura noted. *It might have saved us both some trouble. Not quite paranoid enough, I guess.*

Laura struggled to pull her weight up to the ledge again. She finally managed to get her leg over the edge and pull herself up. Then, she grabbed a shutter and pulled herself up another couple of feet.

Please don't break! Please don't break! Please don't break!

Reaching over her head, she grabbed the gutter, but it bent down instantly in her hand. She forced herself up higher on the shutter, standing on top of it while maintaining her grip on the gutter to keep from falling sideways. Slipping her fingertips underneath the bottom shingles, she got a better grip on the back edge of the gutter and slowly pulled herself up.

Suddenly, the gutter broke loose from the house. Suspended in midair, she swung out over the yard. The gutter drooped slowly downwards as it continued to swing farther away from the house, until at last it came to rest above the garden trellis.

Well, that wasn't the plan, but it will work, she thought.

As soon as she was certain she would actually land on the trellis, she let herself drop, spreading her arms wide to spread her impact as much as possible. Remarkably, though the trellis made a cracking sound, the grape vines prevented its collapse.

She quickly stood and ran across the trellis. With a running jump, she leapt across the three foot gap onto the slanted roof of her storage building. Barely managing to keep her balance, she kept running, then jumped across the next gap and landed squarely atop the neighbor's shrubs just beyond the fence.

Ouch! Holly bushes! I really didn't think this through.

By the time she reached the ground, she looked like she had been in a fight with a feral cat (and lost), but she was alive. She slipped through the gate into the next neighbor's yard, grabbed some oily rags from their carport, then ran through another gate into a darkened alley beyond it.

When she reached the alley, she collapsed onto a pile of garbage bags, covered herself with the oily rags, and slept through the night.

***

Pierre created a new filesystem view based off a snapshot from about five minutes after the explosion.

> 03:45:27.105 dev 01,35 ioctl(0x00310017): Error 01 Operation not permitted
>
> 03:45:32.679 logd: received data burst from 64:de:65:af:63:ba:6f:be
>
> 03:45:32.721 logd: received data burst from 64:de:65:af:63:ba:6f:be
>
> 03:45:32.732 logd: received data burst from 64:de:17:25:ac:19:3a:cc
>
> 03:45:32.679 logd: received data burst from 64:de:65:af:63:ba:6f:be

03:45:33.109 logd: received data burst from 64:de:65:af:63:ba:6f:be

03:45:33729 logd: received data burst from 64:de:65:af:63:ba:6f:be

Oof, he thought. *We got telemetry data dumps from the ship right before the explosion. Now where in hell did it log the actual data?*

He looked in the dumps directory and found the received files, but the data was garbage. A few keystrokes later, he began constructing probability plots of the data that was there. When the results came back, he concluded that the data was probably not from a Gaussian distribution. In fact, the data looked like a uniform distribution—every possible value equally likely—as though the data had been deliberately wiped.

We definitely have a problem, he thought. *Deleted logs could be a random glitch. Files overwritten with pure random data... not so much.*

He started thinking about possibilities—maybe the data blocks never got written because of a power failure, maybe the data files were overwritten by a computer virus or worm, maybe the data burst occurred after the explosion and the data was truly random electrical noise—but the IT guys would have mentioned it if they had seen a virus or worm in the wild lately, and all of the others should have produced decidedly nonrandom data.

He knew that electrical noise should tend to have significantly higher than random percentages of 0s or 1s unless the noise voltage range varied randomly within a very narrow band between 0V and V_{CC}, and even then, the odds of it being so random over such a small sample size were slim to none.

There can be only one conclusion, he realized. *We have a saboteur on board. Fortunately, I've been testing a comms sniffer.*

No sooner had he logged in than he realized why the logs had been deleted. They contained confidential information about a battle, ship's logs, and other information that was way above his pay grade. He carefully skipped through that information and focused on the telemetry data from just before the explosion.

Reactor: stable
Water level: 95% of nominal
Water level decay: 1% per hour
Repairs strongly recommended

Hull integrity: nominal
Shields: 65% of nominal
Pulse cannons: offline/standby

Where's the problem? Why did this thing explode? Service messages?

034549 NAV1: FAIL 075 INRTL SNS
034552 FC1: FAIL 621, 622 NAV1 NAV2
034552 NAV2: FAIL 397 PWR BUS
034554 FC2: FAIL 621 NAV1
034555 FC3: FAIL 622 NAV2
034556 FC2: FAIL 631 FC1
034556 FC3: FAIL 631 FC1
034556 COM: FAIL 631 FC1
034557 FC2: FAIL 933 CABIN PRESS
034557 FC3: FAIL 933 CABIN PRESS
034557 COM: 621,622,632,633 FAIL NAV1,NAV2,FC2,FC3

He quickly puzzled it out.

Navigation 1 failed with an inertial sensor failure, he noted. *There are any number of things that could cause that. Ignore it.*

Flight control 1 reported that NAV1 and NAV2 failed in some way, but flight control 2 only showed failure in NAV1, not NAV2. Flight control 2 and 3 reported failure of flight control 1, which may mean its messages are suspect.

By this point, his head was already hurting. It felt like trying to solve a puzzle with only half the pieces. He had to be missing something.

So flight control 2 and 3 disagree about which nav system is dead? Software bug? Cabling failure?

He began looking through the cable layout for the ship in question looking for anything that FC1, NAV1, and NAV2 had in common.

NAV2 reported a power bus failure. Obviously, that must be the main power bus, which would have taken flight control 1 offline, too, but why four seconds later? It can't be the secondary bus, because FC3 would be dead and couldn't have reported the failure of FC1, he reasoned.

But try as he might, he couldn't find even one place where all of the optical cables went through the same conduits with the power cables. He did see one conduit for both of the data cables that terminated just below a junction box where a power transformer stepped AC down and rectified it to feed backup power to NAV2.

If that failed, it would have killed FC3. That can't be it, he realized.

NAV1 and NAV2 were, however, in the same room, albeit on opposite sides.

What about a large fire? Maybe the reactor explosion melted the plastic optical cables before the glass cables? But that room is near the hull on the underside of the ship. And the ship didn't explode until nearly five seconds after that. A tenth of a second, I could believe. Five seconds? No way.

What happened on the underside of that ship?

He scratched his head in disbelief.

***

LAURA awoke in a pile of stench. For a moment, she wondered if she had forgotten to take out the trash. Then, she remembered what had happened the night before.

She slowly pulled herself out of the pile of garbage bags, looking around for any latent military forces nearby before pulling the rags off her face.

This stinks, she thought, then giggled at the double entendre.

As she rounded the corner, she looked down at her house and saw four black vans parked across the street. She shivered as she slipped back into the alley. When she reached the pile of garbage bags, she picked up the rags and covered herself with them as best she could, then rounded the corner, walking quickly away from her house.

First things first, she thought. *I need cash—lots of cash. I can't use plastic or they'll track me, so I'll have to use an ATM, then quickly catch a cab.*

She walked to an ATM next to a hotel, swiped her card, and took out the maximum daily amount—1500 Euros. She then immediately ran to the corner and flashed a hundred Euro bill at a cab.

"Taxi!" she shouted.

The cab driver looked at her awkwardly, but the cash spoke volumes.

"Wheah to?" he asked.

"Anywhere but here," she replied.

The driver began driving. After a couple of blocks, she had him make a series of seemingly random turns, eventually putting them on the freeway. They got off at the next exit and pulled up to a hospital. She got out and paid the taxi driver double the fare for his troubles.

She walked into the hospital and waited for the taxi to be out of sight, then walked back out, around the corner and into an alley. She followed the alley to the next street, walked a block, took a different alley over another block, then turned left and right again to put her on a major street several blocks from where the cab dropped her off.

She then continued walking for about an hour before she finally reached a hotel in which she had never stayed, where she checked in under a false name and prepaid in cash.

***

The shuttle Europa's manipulator arms groaned as Pierre began his preflight check.

I can't figure anything out from the sensor logs, he mused, *so let's see if we can find that black box.*

The engines screamed to life, whining like a male cocker spaniel upon catching a whiff of a bitch in heat, the slow, rhythmic hum of the scrubbers adding a bass line to support it in a cacophonic symphony that would make even Schoenberg proud.

The shuttle slowly lolled its way to the shuttle bay doors as they crept open about a quarter of the way. A low frequency radio beacon pinged in the distance, creating an occasional tiny glow in the top left corner of his heads-up display.

Pierre guided the ship in the general direction of the beacon, knowing that (at least in theory) the data recorder should be attached. When he reached the transponder, though, the black box was nowhere to be seen. That's when it hit him.

Literally.

Depressurization alarms went off like bottle rockets in January, then rapidly grew quiet. Pierre knew what this meant: outside his helmet, there was no air.

Meanwhile, the black box, having already pierced the front window, proceeded to do its best to break everything else, bouncing first off the controls on the ceiling, then off Pierre's visor, finally coming to rest lodged in one of the air vents that were useless now anyway in light of the lack of a windshield.

Pierre let out a string of obscenities in French that would make even George Carlin blush, then turned the shuttle around and landed in the shuttle bay.

As the shuttle passed through the energy shield, air flooded back into the cabin; the resulting pressure wave momentarily knocked his breath out.

After he had regained his composure, Pierre walked across the deck, entered the airlock, removed his helmet, and swore some more when he realized he'd left the black box wedged in the console, whereupon he replaced the helmet, grabbed a crowbar, and got to work.

***

LAURA stopped briefly at the concierge desk. The concierge was, true to his title, a short, balding Frenchman with a handlebar moustache and a tiny goatee.

"Bonjour, Mademoiselle," he said in an accent so thick you could use it as a couch cushion.

"Hello, sir. Would you be a dear and call me a cab?" she asked.

"Certainment," he replied. "Un moment."

She smiled.

"Zee cab will be outside momentarily."

"Merci," she replied.

"Tout de temps."

With that, she walked outside to the taxi stand. The cab pulled up in front as she opened the door.

"Airport, please," she said as she got in.

The cabbie nodded.

Ten minutes later, they reached the airport.

"Which airline?" the cab driver asked.

"Rental car garage, actually," she replied.

The cab driver drove her around to the arrivals area.

She paid in cash, then stepped out of the cab and walked to the airport's rental car pickup area. She quickly walked through it, paralleling the road in the opposite direction until she reached the terminal A taxi stand some two blocks back.

"I need you to take me to the Vanderbilt Hotel on 37th," she said as she climbed into a waiting cab, but first I need to stop at "Tech Sector Electronics."

"No problem," the cabbie said, his thick Brooklyn accent cutting like a razor.

They drove for a few minutes to the electronics store. Laura paid the fare and gave the cab driver an extra twenty Euros to wait for her.

She quickly jogged inside, picked up a VoIP adapter, paid in cash, and walked back out to the waiting cab.

About five minutes later, they arrived at the hotel, and she paid the additional fare. Then, she pulled out another twenty Euros.

"Here's twenty Euros. I want you to wait for me around on the back side of the hotel. If I'm not out in thirty minutes, call the police."

The cabbie looked at her incredulously for a moment, paused, then shrugged his shoulders.

"Whatevah. Your money."

***

Pierre connected the black box to a diagnostic station and began running system checks.

> *LENSYS SK-1072-A CORE DIAGNOSTICS*
>
> *v.1.07.216*
>
> *System storage is encrypted. Insert encryption dongle or press Escape to perform diagnostics without testing storage.*

Merde, Pierre thought. *There's no way I'll get anything from this.*

Then he saw the charred remains of a data cartridge attached to the underside with duct tape.

Can't be.... That would be like finding the root password on a sticky note under the keyboard....

He quickly reached into a desk drawer, pulled out some contact cleaner and cotton swabs, scrubbed the contacts, connected the data cartridge to the storage port on his diagnostic station, and copied the cartridge to a fresh cartridge. He then attached the new cartridge to the charred storage port on the black box.

> *LENSYS SK-1072-A CORE DIAGNOSTICS*
>
> *v.1.07.216*
>
> *Encryption key accepted. Uploading core data.*

Pierre smiled. *Jackpot.*

Chapter Four

LAURA walked into the Vanderbilt Hotel. She knew the hotel like it was family, having stayed there nearly every year for a computing conference. Again, she reserved a room, this time under her real name, and paid with a credit card.

She quickly walked to the elevator and headed to the 18th floor. As she got off the elevator, she pressed every single button all the way up to the fiftieth floor. Then, she called the remaining two elevators and repeated the process before walking to the service elevator. She called the service elevator. When it had arrived, she pulled the stop button, then proceeded to her room.

As soon as she got into the hotel room, she unplugged the phone, attached the VoIP adapter to the phone line, plugged the phone into the box, and plugged the box into a network cable.

By the time she had done this, she could already see black vans pulling up in front of the hotel.

Thank the good Lord for free Internet without a login screen, she thought.

She waited until she saw the green light appear on the device, then quickly taped it under the desk and walked down the hall away from the main elevators. As she stepped around the corner into the back hall and slipped into the waiting service elevator, she heard the familiar ding of the main elevator arriving on her floor. Laura wiped her brow.

Whew. That's cutting it close, she thought.

After restarting the service elevator, she pressed the button for the second floor, waited a small eternity for it to get there, then stepped off and walked a few feet to the back stairs, which she took down to the building's only exit door that lacked a security camera—an employee badge-access entrance on the back side of the building—then stepped out, walked to the waiting cab, and said, "Take me to the public library downtown."

A few more minutes passed. Laura periodically glanced out the back window to make sure they were not being followed, but saw no one.

Now to place a few anonymous phone calls before I go back to the hotel, she mused.

She connected easily to the VoIP adapter in the compromised hotel room, well aware that the phone would be tapped by now, equally aware that the network connection probably wouldn't be.

She managed to upload a hacked firmware to the VoIP adapter so that it could snoop on the old analog phone's microphone in spite of the phone being on the hook. She listened for a few minutes as people searched the room for her, searched for any clues about her whereabouts, and came up empty-handed.

After a while, the room went silent and the door closed. She waited a few more minutes to be sure, then placed an outbound call over the phone line.

"Hello, you've got Sydney," the voice at the other end replied.

"Hey, Syd. It's Laura."

"Laura!" I was worried about you. You haven't been answering your phone.

"They invaded my house. They shot my dog, and they almost got me! I ran as fast as I could and...."

"Whoah! Whoah! Slow down, Laura," Sydney implored. "Who invaded your house?"

"Men in Terran Command uniforms. I slipped away from them. I'm staying in the Vanderbilt Hotel," she lied. "They almost got me again, but I hid on another floor."

Sydney was suddenly very quiet.

"Look, Sydney," Laura continued. "They're probably going to come after you next. We need to meet somewhere safe."

Sydney said, "How about where we watched the big game that one time?"

Laura smiled. She knew that anyone listening would think Sydney meant a baseball stadium or at least a park, but to them, there was only one big game—the chess tournament where Sydney had met her husband. It was held at an exclusive restaurant on the outskirts of town.

"Sounds good," Laura replied.

"Meet you there at eight," Sydney said as she hung up the phone on her end.

Laura looked down at her watch. It was three-thirty.

Just enough time to get back to the hotel, clean up, nap for a couple of hours, and change into something nice, she thought.

Laura walked from the library back to the hotel, taking a deliberately circuitous path. When she reached the front desk, they smiled at her.

"Greetings, Miss Morningside," the man at the front desk said.

Laura stammered for a moment, then remembered that she was registered under that name.

"Oh, yes, yes," she said. "Sorry, I'm a little distracted. I just found out my dog was hit by an automobile."

"Oh, so terribly sorry to hear that, miss," the man replied.

"Would you be a dear and send up some clothing? I need to attend a formal gala tonight, and I don't want to look like this," she said, pointing at her torn jeans and filthy shirt.

"I should think not," the man replied.

She smiled at him.

"We have a lovely cocktail dress for a cost of three hundred Euros, if you would like," he continued. "I'm guessing you're a size four?"

"Yes, that will do nicely," she replied, nodding. "Thank you."

"And shoes?"

"Six," she replied.

"Very good," the man said. "Shall I send it up now?"

"No, that's quite all right," she answered. "I'm going to hit the shower. I'll call when I'm ready for it."

"Very good, miss," he replied, nodding.

With that, Laura stepped onto the elevator and headed for her penthouse suite.

When she arrived, she stepped briefly into the bathroom to get the water hot, then back out into the bedroom area to call the restaurant.

"Hello? Yes, I'd like a reservation tonight for two at... say, eight o'clock," she said.

"I'm sorry, madame," the gentleman at the other end replied. "The entire restaurant is booked tonight for a private benefit gala."

"For whom?"

"The University Arts Council," he replied.

Oh, yeah, that's right. That is tonight. I got an invitation to that. I declined. Maybe I can tell them I checked the wrong box.

"Okay. Thanks anyway," she said as she hung up the phone.

It's going to be one of those days.

***

Pierre paged through various file listings, none of them remotely indexed in any useful way, but all named with names that looked suspiciously like time stamps in seconds since some arbitrary epoch, so he sorted them by those strings of numbers.

The last few files in the first group contained telemetry data, which he compared against the fragments received by the station previously, but they yielded no new information.

The next batch of files were communications logs. Again, other than the message sent to the station, they were uninteresting.

The final batch of files each contained several hours of video footage from various cameras—some inside the ship, some outside. He quickly threw copies of the exterior video clips onto a data cartridge for safe keeping, slipped the cartridge into a small compartment in the heel of his left shoe, then began looking at each clip.

Most of the images were uninteresting. One showed the folding gate, then the image suddenly broke up. Another showed the Beta Persei trinary star system. Most of them showed some portion of the hull. He was about to give up, but he decided to go ahead and open the last file anyway.

That's when he saw it. A ship—the Aenid perhaps. It was too far away to make out clearly, but it was clearly headed towards the folding gate. Then, the screen broke up, but the last few frames looked like... well, he couldn't be sure, but he could swear the image was flickering and tearing and flashing white *before* he saw the telltale signs of a corrupted compressed video stream.

He slowed down playback and saw several frames with severe corruption. In some frames, entire macroblocks (large square areas) of the image were missing. He replaced those with black squares because you can't usefully reconstruct what isn't there. In other parts of various frames, a macroblock was washed out or the color was severely wrong because of garbled data. For these bits, he compared the area with the previous frame and guessed which parts of the image data were probably wrong, then painstakingly replaced those individual values with the values from the previous frame. By doing this, he was able to partially reconstruct the damaged images.

What he saw, his eyes did not believe.

***

The hot water felt like aloe on Laura's skin as she showered in the hotel bathroom. The problems of the day seemed to wash down the drain alongside the filth. She brought her clothes in with her, stomping on them to pound out the dirt, then hung them neatly over the shower curtain rod to dry before washing her hair a second time.

When she stepped out of the shower, she savored the sensation of the towel gently prickling her skin as she dried herself, the chill of the conditioned air as she stepped out of the bathroom into her hotel room, and finally, the soft comfort of the cushioned mattress as she crashed into it. Hard.

After about two hours of rest, she called room service and asked about her dinner attire. When room service arrived, she hid behind the door and accepted the clothing around the corner, paying cash with a large tip.

She smiled at the ensemble. True to their notoriously quirky sense of fashion, they had brought her a bright red cocktail dress with matching pumps. It would do for now. She had a party to attend.

***

PIERRE looked at the images. In the first image, he saw empty space. In the second image, he saw a fireball moving towards him from empty space.

Not... not possible.

Pierre looked at a nearby angle to see if he could confirm it, but there was not enough overlap to see much until he saw the edge of the approaching fireball in the final two frames. Another nearby angle was similarly unhelpful.

Pierre shook his head. *How can a fireball come from nothing?*

Pierre was so stunned that he did not even notice the camera behind him as it zoomed in on his terminal.

Chapter Five

LAURA stepped calmly off of the city bus in front of Chez du Repas Cher. She checked in at the front desk, then waited in the foyer for Sydney, who arrived a few painfully long minutes later.

"Sorry I'm late," Sydney said, panting. "I had to take three busses to make sure I wasn't followed."

Laura shook her head, then guided her towards the main floor. They made their way to a quiet corner near the kitchen and sat down in the nearest empty booth.

Hardly ten seconds later, a large bowl of salad arrived at their table, a tall, gaunt waiter nearly tripping over his own feet to ensure that no occupied table remained bare for any longer than absolutely necessary.

Laura smiled at the waiter, then served the salad—to her guest first, then to herself.

"Laura," Sydney said, "What's wrong with you? You haven't said a word since I got here."

Laura frowned. "I've nearly gotten caught by Terran Command officers twice in the last 24 hours. I really don't feel like drawing attention to myself by being overly talkative. Do you have a ship?"

"Yes," Sydney replied. "Spaceport 17."

Laura nodded. "Meet me there tomorrow at three. If I'm not there, leave without me."

Sydney stared at her in shock.

"Look, Sydney," Laura continued, "if I'm not there, I'm captured or worse. There must be somebody at the Dark Side Hotel or on Terran Command Outpost 72 who knows more about what's going on. We just have to find him or her."

"Sounds like a plan. Three in the afternoon, I assume."

No sooner had she said this than two familiar faces appeared in the doorway, flashing badges at the front desk.

Oh, shit, Laura thought. *Make that three times.*

"Change of plans," Laura said.

"What?" Sydney asked.

"Those guys at the door?" Laura began.

Sydney started to turn towards them.

"Don't look at them!" Laura shouted under her breath. "They're bad. They're the people who tried to kill me this morning."

"Are you sure they tried to kill you?"

Laura nodded. "They said 'shoot to kill'. You don't say 'shoot to kill' unless you plan to do it, Syd."

Sydney turned suddenly pale.

"Okay, we need a distraction," Laura began.

"Fire!" Sydney said suddenly.

"Good thinking," Laura replied. "We'll cause a panic and duck out in the chaos. Monsieur?"

The waiter turned towards her.

"One bottle of Port."

"Yes, madame."

The waiter slipped away and came back a moment later. He uncorked the bottle.

"It's okay, I've got it," Laura said, snatching the bottle from his hand and sloshing the contents at the candelabra in the middle of the table.

She screamed as the Port wine caught fire, then dropped the bottle, which rapidly burst into flames.

"Fire!" the waiter screamed. A few seconds later, fire alarms began blaring from nearby.

"Please evacuate the building in an orderly fashion!" the master of ceremonies said over the cacophony of screams and loud voices.

Laura watched as the exiting crowd pushed the agents out the door, then grabbed Sydney and pushed her way into the middle of a second crowd moving towards the kitchen (and, she hoped, towards a different exit door).

Seemingly three seconds later, they were on the sidewalk and pushing their way towards the subway entrance across the street. Laura and Sydney walked quickly down the steps, swiped their subway cards, and stepped out onto the platform just as a train arrived. They boarded an empty car and took the seats nearest the doors. As the train pulled away from the stop, they saw two uniformed Terran Command soldiers running down the steps.

So long, suckers, Laura thought. Then, she realized that at the next stop, more troops would be waiting for them. They needed to not be on that train, and fast.

The train passed a ghost station, then stopped suddenly, its lights flickering and dying as it did so.

Perfect, Laura thought sarcastically. *They're holding the train until they can get to us.*

Suddenly, Sydney pushed open the far doors to the train.

Laura yanked her back away from the doors as another train came whizzing by in the opposite direction.

As soon as it had passed, Sydney returned the favor by pulling Laura out onto the tracks.

"Are you crazy?" Laura shouted as the doors slid shut behind them.

"There shouldn't be another train for at least two minutes," Sydney replied, tugging Laura in the direction they came from. "There's an emergency exit about fifty feet before that ghost station. All we have to do is get there and climb a ladder up to the street level."

Laura shook her head. "They'll be watching for us. Besides, where would we go?"

"What do you mean?"

"Sydney, they didn't find me. They've had hours to catch me. They found you. They were following you to get to me."

"So?"

"So the ship rental is in *your name*. We have to assume that the ship has been compromised. We're not going anywhere. Not like that, anyway."

"What should we do, then?" Sydney asked.

"Follow me," Laura replied. "We'll hide in the area of refuge under the abandoned platform and wait them out—leave after dark."

Sydney nodded in agreement.

With that, Laura and Sydney ran to the nearby ghost station and huddled under the platform. They watched as train after train passed by on the other track. Eventually, they saw the train they had recently escaped begin to move towards its destination and the inevitable carnage that no doubt awaited it.

They allowed a few minutes to pass until another train went by going in the same direction, then climbed up onto the platform itself. As they began walking towards the main exit stairs, Laura thought she saw a spark of recognition flash in Sydney's eyes.

"Look familiar?" Laura asked.

"Yeah," Sydney said. "It's the old Kingsway Road station. It used to be the transfer station between the subway and the high speed rail line from Minneapolis to Salt Lake City, but they shut down the station when the new one by the airport opened up."

"Which means what?"

"Which means," Sydney said, drawing her words out, "that we can follow *those* tracks back instead of the subway tracks—slip into the train station near the airport using a maintenance exit from the tracks, and then take the HST. We'll be in another state before they know what happened."

Laura remained unconvinced. "Isn't that three miles... underground... on a track that's just wide enough for one train?"

"Come on! Where's your sense of adventure?"

Laura cringed. *So young. So naïve.*

***

PIERRE walked rapidly into Commander Ebberstein's office. His boss stood, startled by the interruption.

"Pierre!" Fred exclaimed. "I'm glad you caught me. I was just about to leave on a two week vacation. What can I do for you?"

Fred looked around and saw tickets to Hawaii on the desk. He smirked.

"I found something," Fred said after a few moments of thinking about his boss in a grass skirt and shivering.

His boss looked suddenly concerned.

"Define 'something'," he replied.

Fred plugged a data cartridge into the terminal on Fred's desk and showed him the pictures of the fireball suddenly appearing. Fred's eyes grew wider than a 10 Euro coin (or maybe, Pierre mused, one of those U.S. quarters he remembered seeing in an old museum when he was a kid).

"Have you shown these to anyone?" he asked.

Pierre shook his head. "No, sir. You asked me to tell you the moment I found something. I just found something."

Fred nodded, grimaced, closed his eyes, and sighed, all at the same time. When his eyes finally opened, his expression was grim.

"See that you don't. This sort of knowledge could be... dangerous."

Pierre nodded. "Yes, sir."

***

Sydney and Laura walked up a set of stairs between the abandoned subway platform and the equally abandoned HST platform. They jumped the abandoned turnstiles, walked across the platform, dropped down onto the tracks, and began running.

Thankfully, the tunnel had a narrow maintenance catwalk down one side that began about a hundred feet in from the edge of the platform. Unfortunately, it was accessible only by climbing ladders that led up from the tracks every few hundred feet.

They ignored the periodic emergency exit ladders and stairwells that led up to the surface from the far wall of the tunnel, and instead climbed up onto the service catwalk and began walking more calmly towards the airport.

About an hour (and several panicked runs between catwalks) later, they neared the station, and with it, the end of the catwalk.

"How do we want to do this?" Laura asked.

"We'll climb up onto the platform and board the train," Sydney replied.

Laura shook her head. "Too risky. If anyone sees us, we're as good as dead at the very next stop. Even if we get lucky and don't get shot on sight by Terran Alliance troops, we'll still get arrested by the transit police, which means those soldiers will know where we are, and they'll be waiting for us when we get out of jail."

"Okay, smarty pants, what's your plan?"

Laura thought for a moment before answering.

"We wait until the station closes, then we sneak up onto the platform and hide in the bathroom until tomorrow morning."

Suddenly, the train waiting at the station began moving towards them. Laura quickly yanked Sydney backwards into a darkened alcove so that they would not be seen by the train's engineer. She could only hope that they had not been spotted already.

Once the train passed, they stepped back out onto the catwalk, sat down and relaxed. A few minutes later, Sydney looked down at her watch impatiently.

"Okay, it's ten o'clock now. How long do we have to wait?"

The lights overhead gave them their answer as the station plunged into near-total darkness.

"Right about now," Laura replied.

And so, under the cover of darkness, Laura hauled her friend down the steps and along the short stretch of tracks to the area of refuge under the platform. After looking around to make sure no one was watching, they helped each other up onto the platform, then quickly ran off to the platform's bathroom and waited.

***

KLERN stood before the council of Ni'Utn. Although he had stood here many times before, the majestic hall still impressed him. As he looked up, he noticed for the first time that the carved figures around the wall were each holding letters written in Nivitian, a language he had encountered in a message from his deceased wife, Krell.

Ma sechra, i'yey mi tey inachs, ta yu yey sechra enut met.

My life, for you, I lay it down, that you your life enjoy might, he noted. *Yoda would be proud.*

Councillor Meena'i stood.

"Mister Klern," she began, "do you know why we brought you here before us?"

"Yes," he replied. "You have a special mission for me."

She nodded.

"A deep cover mission. Your instructions are on this data tablet," she said, extending her arm, tablet in hand.

Klern nodded and took the tablet.

"Should anything go wrong, you will be disavowed," she continued. "If you are captured, you must activate the self-destruct on the veil. No evidence of this technology or our existence can be allowed to fall into enemy hands."

Klern nodded again.

"Do you understand your mission?"

Klern nodded.

"Very well. Your transport will depart from docking bay 12 for Terran Command Outpost 72 at 1400 hours. Be ready."

Chapter Six

Morning came quickly. By six o'clock local time, the platform was already bustling. Laura and Sydney stepped out of the bathroom and into the crowd, purchased a ticket from a vending machine with cash, and made their way onto the waiting train.

As the train left the station, Laura breathed a sigh of relief—*no Terran Command soldiers, no police, no black vans, and no suspicious people in dark suits wearing sunglasses on a cloudy day. Life is good.*

Three stops later, they were in Seattle, where they hopped onto another train and headed down the coast to New San Francisco (which was built upon the ruins of "Old" San Francisco after it was obliterated in the great quake of 2137). When they arrived the next morning, they took a bus and a subsequent ferry out to New San Francisco West (a barrier island that was similarly pushed up from the ocean floor in the great quake of 2137), then walked up the pier towards the spaceport that covered the island.

The NSFW spaceport was unusually empty that day. On an average day, some twelve thousand transport vessels came and went on thousands of elevated platforms of various sizes that hung out over the water's edge about fifty feet up. Each platform was connected to various fenced-in areas belonging to shipping companies that transported interplanetary freight.

Most of those areas, in turn, were partially obscured by various warehouse facilities and administrative office complexes that lined both sides of the island's only street. That street, Spaceport Drive, ran lengthwise down the middle of the island, connected at one end to a series of piers for smaller vessels and at the other end to deep-channelled docks for larger, seafaring vessels.

As they stepped off the smaller set of docks into the NSFW spaceport, Laura saw the All Planets Express building and pulled Sydney towards it.

Ship All Planets Express, we'll get your stuff there safe! For the fastest service, you'll go APE, Laura sang in her head.

"What are we doing?" Sydney asked.

"We're hitching a ride to Beta Persei," Laura replied.

"What?" Sydney exclaimed. "Laura, they're a shipping company, not a passenger fleet."

Laura smiled and shook her head. "Syd, I've been dealing with APE regularly in my job for many years now. If there's one thing you can count on, it's APE employees who are willing to take a little bribe to get things there no questions asked."

Sydney turned pale. Laura ignored her and walked through the open gate into the dock workers' patio area.

"Excuse me, sir," Laura said to a dock worker who was eating lunch. "Do you have any ships heading towards Beta Persei today?"

He looked at her suspiciously.

"I'll make it worth your while," she continued, pulling out a twenty Euro bill.

"Uh, yeah," he replied, a Brooklyn accent dripping from his voice. "Lets me checks for yas."

He took the last bite of lunch, folded up the remaining mess, stood, and tossed it towards a waste receptacle, which it promptly bounced out of and onto the floor. The girls followed him into the dockyard, where he checked the manifests on a wall-mounted terminal that looked like a holdover from a bad 1980s science fiction series.

"Yeah, number 417 to Carthage Station."

"That's on the Colonial side of the border," Sydney said, speaking of the Colonial Earth Alliance, a loose confederation of worlds currently at war with Earth and Earth-allied colonies, the Terran Alliance.

"It's perfect," Laura interrupted, pulling out a wad of cash. "Have room for a couple of passengers?"

The dock worker glanced alternately between the bills and the two women for a few moments, then nodded.

Laura handed him about three hundred Euros (twenty at a time) before he began walking and motioned for them to follow him.

"What are you doing?" Sydney asked. "We can't go into CEA territory."

"Why not?" Laura asked. "We're not military, and there are no travel restrictions for civilians. And that's not a disputed region of space. Sure, it's a border zone, but there hasn't been fighting near there in... well, ever. Neither side wants to risk the shipping lanes."

Sydney growled under her breath as the dock worker escorted them into an empty shipping container roughly half the size of a semi trailer.

"Haves a nice days," the dock worker said.

Laura and Sydney smiled. Then he closed the door, plunging them into sudden darkness.

In the limited light shining through the cracks, Laura could see Sydney glaring at her and mumbling, "We can always count on an APE employee to take a bribe. We can always count on an APE employee to take a bribe. I'll show you take a bribe...."

Twelve hours later, the ship took off. It took them almost eight more hours to reach Carthage Station. They knew they had reached Carthage Station because the shipping crate they were in suddenly jerked violently, accompanied by the motorized whining noise of a forklift, followed by the sudden clunk of the container hitting the concrete deck.

They waited a few minutes for the deck to clear, then slipped quietly out of the shipping container and into the empty cargo bay. When they got to the exit door, they were relieved to find that the badge access was one-way. They exited into a service hallway, walked a few feet, and stepped through a set of double doors out into a busy concourse.

After getting their bearings, they headed straight for the first thing on their minds: *the food court.*

***

KLERN stepped through the airlock from his shuttle onto Terran Command Outpost 72. His first stop was engineering. Wearing the face of some poor schmuck ensign, he walked in unopposed.

After a quick check to make sure the access codes to key systems had not changed, he walked to his assigned quarters and waited for the right moment.

This target should be an easy mark, he thought to himself. *Sure, even engineers go through basic training, but he's not exactly special ops by any stretch of the imagination. This weekend's events should provide me with ample access and plenty of cover; I just have to be ready when the opportunity presents itself.*

***

CARTHAGE Station was the largest commercial passenger and freight spaceport in Colonial territory. Its high ceilings and open beam architecture gave it an almost military or industrial feel, its consumerism betrayed only by the rows of metal mesh chairs in large groups near the windows and the gate pedestals near each airlock.

And the central food court, of course. Like the station, it was the largest food court this side of Earth's Terran Command Station. With over a hundred restaurants ranging from fast food burger joints to sit-down Asian, Indian, Pakistani, and French cuisine, the food court gave new meaning to the word consumer. And those were just the restaurants they could see from their table.

Laura and Sydney consumed their gyros and enchiladas like they hadn't eaten in weeks. In truth, it had been almost a day. The food tasted reasonably good, but then again, Laura was pretty sure she would have eaten cardboard and tree bark at this point; she was that hungry.

As Laura looked around the room, it occurred to her that it should be safe to withdraw cash here. The Terran Alliance military couldn't follow them if they wanted to, and it would take weeks for them to convince the CEA government to do anything, by which time they would be long gone.

So while Sydney finished her gyros, Laura walked over to an ATM, withdrew more cash, and used a nearby kiosk to rent a personal shuttle.

Sydney looked up as she returned. "Rent a shuttle?"

Laura nodded. "It's about twelve hours by shuttle to get from the nearest folding gate to Terran Command Outpost 72."

Terran Command Outpost 72 was in a solar orbit around the class B8 star Beta Persei A. Because of the size and intensity of the star, the outpost was placed a fair distance away, with an orbital period measured in centuries. As the only outpost nearby, it served a dual purpose.

Officially, TCO-72 was a stationary location for monitoring the borders with Colonial space.

Unofficially, it was a restocking depot for large cruise ships. Apparently, some people actually enjoyed seeing this particular trinary star system, and TCO-72 provided a particularly nice vantage point. Sadly, the system's only folding gate sat in an orbit that provided a less-than-stellar view, with one of the stars almost completely eclipsed by Beta Persei A. Thus, ships flew from the folding gate out to TCO-72, refueled at the attached fuel depot, and then flew back.

In the event of an emergency, TCO-72 also provided docking facilities, but these were rarely used except when members of the station's crew went on shore leave...

...and for one weekend out of every Terran year, when computer geeks everywhere gathered for AlgolCon, named, apparently, in honor of a centuries-dead programming language.

Laura chuckled when she remembered the attempt to change the name of Lenora Prime to Kobol for a similar reason (*or was that COBOL,* she mused) then noticed Sydney staring at her like a madwoman and dismissed the thought.

"Shall we head that direction?" Sydney asked.

"No," Laura replied, glancing at the AlgolCon poster on the wall. "We'll have to hang around here until Friday. I think I know how we can get onto that station unnoticed...."

Chapter Seven

November 9, 2390

FOLDING technology was one of those things that happened much like antibiotics. It was theorized for a while, but almost didn't happen at all until one lucky accident brought it into the realm of reality.

The first folding experiments involved trying to transfer energy from one place to another. Scientists had hoped to put solar panels in a close orbit around the sun, soak up the energy, and beam it through a rip in space back to Earth and Mars in a form that would not light the entire planet on fire if anything went wrong. Unfortunately, dozens of explosions later, they were no closer than they had been when they started.

Then one day, a funny thing happened. A careless scientist by the name of Frank Perri left his wedding ring a little too close to the equipment.

If the rumors are to be believed, he was on his way to a bar to cheat on his wife, Laura mused, *though the history books don't actually say for sure.*

When he returned to the lab after a long lunch, they conducted another experiment. After the simultaneous explosions, he realized that he had left his ring in one test chamber, but upon entering the test chamber, he couldn't find it.

Imagine his surprise when he walked into the other lab (where he had not set foot for days) and found his missing ring. He found it stuck to the far wall, mind you—slightly charred, mostly flattened, and so hot that it left a black ring behind on the table where it originally sat—but it was definitely his ring.

At first, he accused the other researchers (one of whom, according to legend, was his soon-to-be-ex-wife) of moving it to the other lab as a prank, but when he examined the video records, what he saw left little doubt. They continued to experiment, and in a few short years, folding technology was born.

Of course, it wasn't all that useful at first. It took nearly two decades of research to develop shield technology that could both withstand the enormous shearing stress of folding and provide adequate protection from the radiation that accompanied it.

And even after they worked out those kinks, they still had to send out ships traveling at sublight speeds (about .75c) to seed the folding gates at the far end, thus limiting its useful range considerably. They cleverly used those early gates to send newer, faster gate delivery ships, allowing faster fan-out from those points, but such optimizations only went so far, and ultimately the farthest distance one could travel was still bounded by the speed of those ships.

It took another three decades before single-ended folding became practical. Early mathematical models theorized that it would take all the energy in the universe to create such a fold. Then somebody (according to legend, a high school freshman with minimal science background looking at the material for the first time) pointed out that the model failed to take into account the temporary quantum entanglement that occurs concurrent with two points in space becoming interposed. After that correction, one part of the equation canceled out another part of the equation, which meant that the extra power required for a single-ended fold was effectively almost zero instead of infinite.

After that, it took about a month. Funny how real progress always seems to come in spurts.

And so, after a quick fold into the general vicinity of Beta Persei, a three-hour tour around the dark side of the "moon" (an asteroid towed into orbit that provided a small habitable oasis of fast food restaurants and lodging near the folding gate, whose slogan was, aptly, "Give yourself to the Dark Side"), and a twelve-hour ride into the demon's lair (Beta Persei is also known as the demon star), they finally arrived at their destination.

Laura shivered as she stepped out onto the spacepad at Terran Command Outpost 72.

There is truly no sensation more disturbing than walking across a platform with no walls and no ceiling, held to that platform only by artificial gravity, breathing an artificial atmosphere held near the platform solely by that same artificial gravity—to just be standing there without any sort of space suit or protective gear in the middle of the cold blackness of empty space—knowing full well that your life is entirely in the hands of the minimum wage worker on some prison planet who built the ArtiGrav™[1] unit.

And so, it was with much trepidation that she stepped quickly across the pad, stopping only momentarily to stare straight up at the beauty of the trinary star system in glorious full view overhead.

Sydney, by contrast, never made it out the door. She just stood there, as though her feet were glued to the floor of the shuttle.

"Come on, Syd!" Laura shouted.

---

[1]ArtiGrav™ is a trademark of Artificial Gravities, Inc. Used by permission.

Sydney just stood there. Then, as the station's entry door opened, Sydney started running and didn't stop until she was in the airlock.

Laura buried her face in her hands in a classic gesture of embarrassment, then pressed the giant button to close the outer airlock door and open the inner one.

The airlock door just sat there.

Laura pressed the button again. Nothing. Then, she kicked the button with her steel-toed boot, still without success.

So they tried the next airlock, then a third. When they entered the fourth and final airlock, the button clicked and the light changed momentarily to red, then back to green. The door started moving, then abruptly came to a stop halfway open.

That's when the prerecorded announcement started playing.

"Warning: ArtiGrav maintenance in progress. Artificial gravity will be terminated in fifteen seconds. Please proceed to the nearest airlock immediately."

Laura's eyes widened. She pounded the button several times, then shook her head, squeezed herself through the door, and started running back towards the shuttle, dragging Sydney along behind her.

The moment they were safely inside, she slammed her hand against the door controls. As the shuttle's door began to close, she heard the sound of atmosphere rushing rapidly out of the ship. Without thinking, she grabbed Sydney with one arm and a railing with her other hand and held on for dear life as the door's motors strained under the force of the sudden pressure gradient. After a few tense moments, the door closed with a clunk.

"Shuttle Vertigo, this is Tay-Say-Oh-72," the voice on the comm system squawked, pronouncing the station's letters in French. "Is everyone okay?"

"We're fine," Sydney replied.

Laura slapped her hand over Sydney's mouth, but it was too late.

There was a momentary pause, and then the man replied, "This is good. Eh. I am the station's chief engineer. I have no idea what happened, but I will find out. In the meantime, I have restored the artificial gravity and I will be opening the airlock manually. Watch for me standing in airlock four. When you see me standing there, it is safe to come aboard."

A moment later, they watched airlock four close. About ten seconds later, it reopened with a man standing inside holding something that looked a lot like a cordless drill with some sort of socket attachment stuck into a hole in the wall (and indeed, upon closer inspection, it was exactly that).

After verifying the presence of an atmosphere, they opened the shuttle door, dashed across, and watched as the shuttle's door closed again.

The young man stood waiting for them in the airlock, smiling as they stepped inside. He pressed the trigger on the drill, and the outer doors slid slowly shut. Then, after a few seconds, the inner doors slid open. He released the trigger, pulled out the drill, then walked over to each of the other airlocks and, attaching the drill to a port on the interior wall, opened each of them towards the inside as well.

"Why is he doing that?" Sydney asked, confused.

"So that nobody will walk into the airlocks while they are down, I'd imagine," Laura replied.

The engineer nodded, walked back over to them, then gestured towards a door. "Please enjoy our facilities. When I figure out what happened to the airlocks and the gravity, I'll let you know. And again, we apologize for the inconvenience."

Laura smiled. "Thank you," she said.

Laura dragged Sydney towards the door and it opened ahead of them.

"Oh, yeah, what's your name?" Laura asked.

"Pierre," the man replied. "My name is Pierre."

***

Nineteen days later
(November 28th, 2390)

ADMIRAL Jenkins stared at Pierre. "Why are you telling me all of this? These girls? Who are they? Why do they matter?"

Pierre shook his head as if to clear it, then muttered, "Very important. Very important. Pictures."

"What about the pictures?"

"They had the pictures," Pierre continued. "I didn't get them right away. I'll get to that. What matters now are the airlocks."

"Oooookay. What about the airlocks, then?"

"The airlocks, the airlocks," Pierre stammered.

"What about the airlocks, Pierre?"

"They were broken."

"I know they were broken, Pierre," Jenkins replied gently. "Your commanding officer says that you broke them and disabled the five-minute and one-minute safety warnings on the gravity generator, too."

"Not true. Not, not true."

"The command logs agree with them."

"I'm telling you, I did not do it."

"So do the security cameras."

Pierre turned pale. "Then it has begun."

Admiral Jenkins gulped.

***

Nineteen days earlier
(November 9, 2390)

LAURA and Sydney stepped into their assigned quarters. The accommodations were spartan. A set of bunk beds lined the right wall, and a pair of wooden desks painted a light bluish-grey sat against the left wall, with white wooden shelves hanging from the wall above them. The far wall wasn't really a wall so much as a giant floor-to-ceiling window looking out on empty space.

In the entryway, the half bath on the left and the tiny closet on the right created an intense feeling of claustrophobia, the three-foot wide, six-foot deep passage producing a marked psychological deterrent to actually entering or leaving the room. Yet in spite of this, Sydney still immediately ran in and shouted, "I've got top!"

Laura just shook her head. *She actually looks happy to be here. I don't get it.*

"Okay," Laura said after a few moments of puzzlement. "We should probably head into the mess hall. I understand they're starting with a guest speaker from MIT, and we wouldn't want to miss it and look like we don't belong here."

With that, Laura headed out the door, followed shortly thereafter by Sydney. They headed down the hall to the left, hung a right in front of the lift tubes, then walked through the double doors into the mess hall, where they found...

An empty room? No, not quite empty, Laura thought. *There are a couple of folks at one of the tables in the back.*

They walked over to the one occupied table, where a man and woman sat. The man, a portly guy with a beard and moustache, smiled at her. The woman with him—a young girl who looked to be barely a teenager—just sulked.

"First time here?" the man asked.

"Yeah," Laura replied. "How could you tell?"

"Nobody attends the opening lecture... or the closing lecture."

Laura looked at him with a puzzled expression. "Why not?"

"Half the attendees aren't here yet," he explained, "and most of them are just using the conference as a free vacation at their employers' expense anyway, so half the folks who *are* 'here' are really out on cruise ships sightseeing, and the rest are enjoying role-playing games down on the recreation deck."

Laura rolled her eyes.

"Hi. I'm Frank," he continued.

"Laura," she replied, shaking his hand. "Nice to meet you."

The next guy through the door was of average weight, five-six, with grey hair, a grey moustache, and a thick, grey beard that reached the middle of his chest. Laura stared questioningly. "Who's that guy?"

"Oh, him? That's the wizard," Frank said. "He's great with magic tricks. I can't remember his name, but everybody just calls him the wizard, or occasionally Gandalf the Grey."

Laura laughed.

As the hour approached, a few more people wandered in, including three guys who looked like they had just bankrupted a pizza eating contest (all the way down to the stains on their 8XL shirts), two thin guys wearing thick black plastic glasses (one pair of which had a piece of white cloth tape across the bridge of the nose), a guy with a hot pink mohawk that stuck up almost a foot above his head, three guys dressed as Klingons, one particularly odd looking fellow in chaps with holes in the buttocks, and one guy whose shape could only be described as a flying saucer—normal build on top and bottom with a gut that stuck out three feet.

Laura had never seen such an odd, ragtag collection of nerds before in her entire life. Of course, there were plenty of normal people, too, but the weirdos were the ones she noticed—the ones who stuck out in her mind.

One of the pizza eaters began walking towards their table. *I put on my robe and wizard hat,* Laura thought, barely stifling a laugh as he approached.

"Hello," the morbidly obese man said with a sneer. "I wondered if you'd be interested in a little AD&D later on."

Laura looked at him incredulously. "No thanks. I have all the insurance I need."

"Oh, ha, ha," the man replied sarcastically. "You could have just said no. You didn't have to be all snarky about it."

As the man walked away, Sydney looked at Laura. "What the heck is AD&D?"

Laura grinned.

A moment later, someone tapped the microphone on stage. It squealed for a moment, then went silent.

"May I have your attention, please?" the bespectacled, elderly, balding gentleman asked. "I am pleased to present our opening speaker for AlgolCon, Mr. Sergey Yevseyev from the Massachusetts Institute of Technology. Mr. Yevseyev?"

The man who walked up on stage was not at all what Laura expected. He was a young man in his late twenties. His face radiated confidence. Laura's face began to radiate drool.

"Mine!" Sydney said, nearly shouting.

Laura burst into laughter. "Sydney, you're married!"

Sydney blushed. "Can't a girl have a little fun?"

"Speaking of which, where is your husband?"

"I left him at the altar," Sydney replied.

Laura did a double-take. "You what?"

"I left him at a casino on one of the moons of Mu Arae b... in the Ara constellation. You know, the altar?"

Laura relaxed and laughed. *Clever girl,* she thought. *Too clever.*

"And does he know you're gallivanting around the known universe?" she asked, smiling.

Sydney chuckled. "What he doesn't know...."

Laura just shook her head.

"Hello, gentlemen and," he said, pausing to switch into a sleazy voice befitting a used car salesman, "a-ladies."

Everyone chuckled. Sydney and Laura slid lower in their seats.

"My name is Sergey, and I am here to change your view of the universe."

Laura rolled her eyes. *Yeah, that'll be the day.*

"For centuries, scientists have wondered if we were alone in the universe. Now, for the first time in history, we have the answer."

Aliens? Could it be?

"A survey mission on Tau Ceti IV discovered *this,*" he said, clicking his presenter remote to advance to the next slide.

The next slide showed an image of what appeared to be a fossil of some sort.

"This is a trilobite fossil, or something very similar," he continued. "Given the depth and lack of surface disturbance, we can rule out a hoax, and given the distance, it is unlikely that any natural collision with Earth could have brought the material to the planet."

Sydney stood up suddenly. "You're an idiot."

"Excuse me?"

"Can't you do math? Tau Ceti is only 12 light years out. Trilobites went extinct 250 million years ago. In that time, a trilobite fossil could reach Tau Ceti at a little over thirty miles per hour."

The room chuckled.

"But the odds of it going that direction are," the man pointed out, "astronomical, if you'll pardon the pun."

Sydney nodded. "But not less likely than parallel evolution of trilobites on two planets 12 light years apart."

"Unless the theory of exogenesis is correct," the man replied. "Besides, that's not the only fossil we found."

The room went silent, and Sydney sunk slowly down into her chair. The next slide showed something vaguely hominid in shape, but with a larger forehead and with a wider skull at the top.

"Notice that this species is substantially different from any species that has ever lived on Earth," he continued. "Unless, of course, you believe in the Roswell greys."

The crowd chuckled again.

"What is particularly interesting was that the trilobite fossil was in the same layer of rock as the... hominid."

The room was suddenly filled with people speaking in hushed tones. He paused for about ten seconds to allow the murmurs and occasional gasps to die down to a dull roar.

"Yeah. You get it," he continued. "There was no evidence of advanced evolution anywhere. The upper layers of the planet were dead, and the lower levels showed even more primitive life. The planet, for all intents and purposes, *died* at a primitive stage of development. Yet there it was, staring at us—a fossil that very much did not belong."

"So I propose a theory. It may not sit well with some of you," he said, looking directly at Sydney, "but the most likely explanation is that the hominid-like creature came to the planet from somewhere else. Not the fossil, the actual creature. So at some point in the past, there *was* an alien species capable of space travel."

"Do they still exist?" he continued. "Are they still out there? We can't say for certain. They might have died off millions of years ago... or they might be in this very room."

Sydney looked at Laura. Laura looked at Sydney. The look of horror on Sydney's face was one that Laura would not forget for a long time.

"All we know," he concluded, "is that they existed at some point in the past, which means that the answer to the question is 'No. We are not alone.' There are other advanced races out there. We just have to find them. Thank you, and good night."

Chapter Eight

His mission was simple: kill the engineer. The girls were both an unexpected bonus and an unexpected nuisance, but they were of little consequence.

Civilians are easy to extinguish, Klern mused.

Klern knew what he had to do. Kill the girls, kill that pesky engineer, and launch the bodies into space without anyone noticing.

It is unfortunate, Klern thought, *that the girls survived the loss of gravity; but no matter. They will be easily dispatched. They are staying in a room with only one exit. At midnight, I will pump hydrogen cyanide gas under the door while holding it closed. They will not struggle for long.*

The engineer, however, posed a greater threat. He carried a radio on him at all times. If he smelled the gas, he might call for security, in which case there would be questions, and that would not do.

No, I must dispatch the engineer with haste, he thought. *A bullet to the brain would do the job nicely; but the mess, ugh. There must be a cleaner way.*

And so, Klern arranged for a "malfunction" in the navigation thruster control system during lunch. Everyone would be eating, so the engineer would probably come alone. When Pierre turned right at the T-shaped intersection near engineering, Klern would come up to him from behind and slit his throat.

It was settled, then. Klern knew what he had to do.

First the engineer, then the girls, he thought. *That way I can take my time with the ladies.*

***

PIERRE sat down for lunch at a table across from Laura and Sydney.

"I thought you'd like to know," Pierre began, "that I have some disturbing news."

Laura frowned. "News? What is it?"

Pierre smirked. "It's timely information delivered in an information-dense format, but that's not important right now."

Laura rolled her eyes.

"It was not a malfunction," Pierre continued. "Someone deliberately tampered with the control system, disabling the five-minute shutdown warning and modifying the display screens in the flight control booth so that they would lie about the status of those systems."

"Come again?" Laura replied.

"Someone tried to kill you."

"Oh."

Suddenly, Pierre's data pad began beeping at him. He flipped open the cover and frowned.

"What's wrong?" Laura asked.

"The navigation control computers are showing multiple faults," Pierre replied. "Probably a power failure. I have to go down and check it out. In the meantime, it's not safe for you to be here. Go back to your ship and go somewhere safe."

"Nowhere is safe," Laura replied. "We saw pictures from October 30th."

Pierre turned pale.

"You know, don't you?" Laura asked.

Pierre nodded slowly.

"Talk to us."

Pierre shook his head as he quickly scrambled to his feet and started backing towards the door. "Not here. Meet me in my quarters in half an hour, deck 12, section 7, room 113."

And then he was gone.

Laura turned to Sydney. "Wait, isn't that in the restricted section of the ship?"

Sydney looked at the map on her own data pad and nodded. "There's no way to get there without being a member of the crew."

Laura thought for a moment. "Maybe we should try to catch up with him, then."

Sydney nodded.

Laura ran. Sydney followed.

***

KLERN waited in the short hall that led to a maintenance tube along the outer perimeter of the landing pad—a tube that, in turn, led to the port weapons battery.

Klern brandished the machete, running his finger gently along the length of the blade, carefully checking its sharpness without drawing blood. The trap was set and baited, his breath bated, his bloodlust nearly sated.

It would only be a matter of time before Pierre came around the corner. Klern could hear his footsteps in the distance.

Yes. Yes, he thought. *Come closer. Closer. It will all be over soon.*

***

"WHICH way?" Laura asked, frantically.

Sydney swiped and poked at the map on her data pad, but got nowhere. "I'm not sure! Maybe engineering, maybe one of the computer closets, maybe...."

"Engineering it is," Laura interrupted. "Which way?"

"Down that hall, hang a right at the T-crossing, then another right, then...."

"Lead the way."

Sydney started running, and Laura followed. As they left the mess hall, they turned right. After a few steps, they entered a long hall with a glass wall overlooking the landing pad that lay two stories below them. In the middle of the right wall was a doorway to a much longer, glass-walled bridge that extended out above the pads. At the far end of that bridge, they saw Pierre turning the corner to the right.

"Pierre!" they shouted as they ran down the hall and started across the bridge. "Pierre!"

Laura and Sydney watched through the glass alongside the bridge as Pierre turned around to return. Then someone else ran across the end of the hall.

Laura's eyes widened when she saw the knife. Pierre jumped out of the way as the man struck at him. The attacker stumbled, thrown slightly off balance by the miss, then recovered and squared off, putting himself between Pierre and the exit.

Sydney pressed the "emergency call" button on her data pad.

"Beta Persei 911. Please state the nature of the emergency."

"There's a man with a knife trying to kill Pierre."

As she said this, Pierre dove and rolled to evade another swipe of the machete.

"Okay, stay where you are," said the voice on the other end. "Where is the man?"

"He's right in front of me. Across the bridge."

"Security is on its way."

About three seconds later, the lights in the distant hall turned suddenly red, and huge metal emergency doors slammed shut between the girls and the ongoing fight. Through the glass, they watched as five soldiers armed with pulse rifles ran in from somewhere off to the right and pointed their weapons at the attacker.

The man dropped his knife and ran, threw open the access door to the maintenance crawlspace, dove inside, and closed the door behind him. As he did, the soldiers fired several shots that apparently missed their mark.

Within about a minute, security forces came barreling out of the service tube. The security people in the hallway looked like they were shouting at the people who came out of the tube. The leader of the new arrivals simply shrugged his shoulders.

A few seconds later, Laura saw a puff of escaping atmosphere from a torpedo tube and watched the soon-to-be meat popsicle fly rapidly away from the ship towards Beta Persei A. She couldn't be certain, but she thought she saw the man flipping them off.

Creepy.

That's when the corpsicle caught Pierre's eye. He turned his head, his jaw dropped, and he pointed in horror.

The security forces turned and looked out the windows. After a moment, the first team's leader picked up a walkie talkie and began speaking into it. The doors opened a moment later, and suddenly Laura could hear the conversation.

"Well shouldn't you follow him?" a voice asked through the walkie talkie.

"No, I don't think you quite understand me," the leader said. "He... *left*... the station."

In the moments that followed, the silence was deafening.

"No ship?" the radio squawked.

"No ship."

"Oh," the voice said, then paused momentarily. "Carry on, then."

Laura and Sydney ran down the hall and caught up with Pierre.

"Thank you both!" Pierre exclaimed upon seeing them. "If you hadn't seen him, I would be dead right now."

"Uh," Laura stuttered, "actually we *didn't* see him… or at least not until *after* we shouted."

"But we did call 911," Sydney offered.

"Not to sound ungrateful or anything," Pierre cut in, "but why were you following me?"

"We can't get to your quarters," Laura replied. "Locked down area."

Pierre grinned. "Truth be told, I was trying to get rid of you. I wasn't sure if I could trust you."

Pierre glanced out the window at the small, human-shaped comet hurtling towards the star, then glanced back at the girls.

"Still think you can't trust us?" Laura asked.

Pierre sighed. "Someone tried to kill the two of you, and now someone tried to kill me. I don't know if I can trust you, but it looks like we're in this together, for better or worse."

"We need to get away from here," Sydney suggested. "Far away."

"Where?" Laura asked.

Sydney shrugged.

"I know a place," Pierre offered.

Laura nodded. *Probably better not to say anyway.*

"We'll blend in with the crowds and get dinner," Laura suggested. "Pull together all the information you have and meet us at the airlocks in a few hours—say 1900 hours?"

Pierre nodded, and they went their separate ways.

***

KLERN began to swear the moment his eyes began to flicker.

Those bastards backed me into a corner and I had to space myself, he thought. *What will the council think?*

Oh, sure, they'll praise me for my ingenuity in having a fold-hidden ship ready to scoop me up from the vacuum of space, but in their minds, they'll be thinking very different thoughts. Before too long, somebody will start to make comments comparing me to my wife. That's when the fist fight will start, and then they'll have me shot.

No, this incident will not appear in my report, he thought.

As he set the dial on the healing chamber to two weeks, he mused that no human could have survived for two or three minutes in empty space, much less the hour that he had endured before the ship picked him up. *Sometimes, it's good to have a rebreather implant.*

And a temperature regulation suit.

Still, an hour in space is a long time even with the suit, he realized. *I can't feel... anything. Maybe I'd better let the ship work on me a little longer.*

Klern dialed it up to four weeks and added a full dermal reconstruction pass for good measure. With that, he stepped into the pod, pressed the button, and closed his eyes, to sleep, perchance to dream.

Chapter Nine

Almost twenty-eight years earlier (February 13, 2363)

KLERN examined his wife, Krell. The veil was perfect. She was perfect. She looked like Cadet Skylarov. She sounded like Mikhail Skylarov. She even smelled like Cadet Skylarov. Klern was amazed at how perfectly she imitated a man, all the way down to the mannerisms.

"Are the preparations made?" Krell asked.

"Yes, mi'lady," Klern replied. "Skylarov is hopelessly delayed, and the message to that effect was intercepted and destroyed."

"And my arrival? Is it expected?"

"We sent a message to Skylarov's CO that he was returning a day early to help supervise the large-scale test."

"Excellent. Then I shall take my leave of you."

Klern smiled, for he knew there was no one better to infiltrate a Terran Alliance base than his lovely Krell.

***

DONOVAN Jenkins began his final preparations for the test. Everything had to be perfect, he knew, or the test would fail miserably like the last twelve. It was particularly awkward because he had taken on a new member of his team, Vladimir Rejndorv, just a week before. Ordinarily, he would have refused, but the man's background was almost too good to be true. It wasn't particularly unusual to find a graduate of MIT with a Ph.D. from Cambridge—unusual, yes, but not exceptionally so, what with all the electronic classroom programs—but to find one with actual experience working with quantum lensing and Ackerman crystals (admittedly, much smaller crystals, unlike the flawless, two-thousand karat crystal they had obtained, but Ackerman crystals, nonetheless) was staggeringly unlikely. So Donovan had agreed to give him a chance.

Thus far, he was doing a good job. He seemed particularly eager to reverse time and reverse the environmental damage done by the accidental cutatox release two years earlier, though, which was a little disconcerting. *No one should be that eager to mess with the past,* Donovan thought, *but at least his heart is in the right place.*

Donovan checked over all the calculations for what seemed like the twentieth time, checked all the safety systems for what felt like the fortieth time, and inspected the crystal for seemingly the hundredth time. Everything looked normal.

Well, in just a few hours, we'll know for sure, won't we?

***

Cadet Skylarov né (or is it née?) Krell landed on the pad outside the underground base. He (she?) approached the entrance to the cave and walked through the open outer doors. After walking for what seemed like forever, he finally reached an entrance door marked simply "Section 1". He then acted as though he were checking his pockets for a key card (which, of course, he did not possess).

After a moment, a holographic projection of a woman appeared just outside the door.

"Forget something?" she asked.

"Yes, Tessa," Krell-Skylarov replied. "I seem to have left my keycard in the hotel room... sadly, along with about five hundred Euros."

Tessa chuckled. "Come on in."

The door opened.

I love this place. It's so easy a kid could get in... or at least a kid with an anthropoveil.

He walked through several long halls, took several elevators and one set of steps, and eventually arrived at the door to Section 13, which promptly opened for him.

As he walked in, he saw Donovan.

"Hey, Sky," Donovan said.

"Hey, uh..." Krell stumbled.

"Donovan," Donovan replied, a look of mild concern on his face. "Wow, I've heard of shore leave amnesia, but this is ridiculous."

Krell laughed and Donovan relaxed.

"It was a long two weeks," Krell noted.

"And you came back early. You're a regular glutton for punishment."

Krell smiled. "Hey, I couldn't let you do the next round of testing alone, D."

"Oh, well, we brought in a new guy while you were gone."

Krell was taken slightly aback. "Anybody I know?"

Donovan shook his head. "Some local who was educated on Earth and knows about ACs."

Krell nodded. "Anything you need? I'm gonna crash."

Donovan shook his head. "Just be ready at 0800 tomorrow."

Krell nodded and headed out into the hall towards section 11 and his quarters, which were between there and section 10.

Like taking candy from an unborn fetus.

Chapter Ten

Almost twenty-eight years later (November 10, 2390)

Pierre stepped onto the rental shuttle behind Laura and Sydney. The shuttle was small and cramped, with seating for two up front, and bench seats along the sides in the back. Pierre sat in the back and threw a large rolling backpack full of gear into the aisle between the two benches.

"What's in the bag?" Laura asked.

"Evidence," Pierre replied.

Laura looked at him questioningly.

"Sensor logs, security camera footage, communications logs, data burst logs, and so on, all scraped out of various backup systems after someone tried to delete them."

Laura frowned. "I know you said you knew a place, and I know you didn't want to say anything while you were on the ship, but..."

"Are you sure you want to do this?" Pierre asked. "You might be safer just going back to Colonial space and hiding in plain sight. I can't cross the border. I'd be arrested on the spot."

Laura nodded. "Your friends are our friends. But I need coordinates."

"Head for the folding gate. I'll enter my access code and fold us where we need to go."

The ship lurched awkwardly as it left the pad, leaving one of its landing struts behind. Laura was horrified.

"Did I just..."

"...rip off a landing strut?" Pierre replied. "Yes. It looks like someone did not want us to take off."

Their ship then began its long, slow orbit around the star towards the folding gate.

The twelve-hour journey back to the folding gate passed in silence. As they approached the gate, Pierre asked, "Do you have any food in this thing?"

Sydney giggled, stood, walked back to the back, and opened the refrigerated storage area in the back.

"Let's see, we have sodas, ham, turkey, cheese, bread, and... something I can't quite identify," Sydney announced. "Laura, what's this?"

Laura left the ship on autopilot and stepped back into the back. What she saw was, for lack of a better word, disturbing. It had two hemispherical metal plates that were attached by struts to a small, round pod. There were numbers on a small box that stuck out from the outside of one of the hemispherical plates.

It looks like a bomb, Laura thought.

Pierre looked at it and immediately replied, "It's a folding tracker."

"A what?" Sydney and Laura asked simultaneously.

"We use them for certain covert military operations," Pierre explained. "By using a tiny spatial fold contained within the central sphere, the tracker—that's the pod on the outside—can transmit data directly to any spot in the universe where there's a folding gate or a special receiver pod. It gets positioning information from a series of satellites that are in orbit around all of the known worlds."

"So what you're saying," Laura replied, "is that as long as we're on this ship, they can track us?"

"No," Pierre replied. "I'm saying that as long as *it* is on this ship, they can track us. I suggest disposing of it into the nearest star."

Laura shook her head. "If we dispose of it, they'll find another way to track us. Better to keep them chasing their tails."

"And how do you propose we do that?" Pierre asked.

"Can you program this shuttle's autopilot to handle folding?"

Pierre smiled. "I think so."

"Is there an extra shuttle on the base?"

Pierre nodded, grinning ear to ear, then said even more enthusiastically, "I think so!"

"Can you get us safely out of this shuttle and over to another one with only a single landing strut?"

Pierre laughed.

"I think so," he replied hopefully but noncommittally.

Laura walked up to the controls and reversed their course. Twelve long hours later, they landed (by some definition of landing, with their ship suspended about a foot off the flight deck).

Pierre ran to the airlock and disappeared for about ten minutes. When he returned, he was carrying two devices that looked suspiciously like the folding tracker. He connected a cable to the shuttle's computer, then connected the other end to one of the pods.

"Well, come on, then!" he said to Laura and Sydney.

Laura carried Pierre's bag, while Sydney carried a disposable sack filled with the edible contents of the refrigerator as they stepped out onto the landing pad beside Pierre. They followed him to a somewhat larger shuttle parked nearby. He pressed a button on the controls, and the door opened for them. Once they stepped inside, he closed the door and programmed in a course.

"Now what?" Laura asked.

"Wait for it," Pierre replied, then took out a data pad and connected it to the other pod.

"Let me guess. Communication pods?"

Pierre nodded. "My data pad will be controlling your ship. I've written a program to select folding gates at random. Your ship will fly to the folding gate, request to be sent to the first randomly chosen destination, fly to the nearest habitable world, and request clearance to land. After landing, it will wait a few hours, take off again, and repeat the process. By the time they figure out what is going on, we will be long since out of harm's way."

The airlock slowly creaked open.

Pierre turned. "Fred!"

His commander, Fred Ebberstein, stood in the doorway. Pierre reopened the shuttle door.

"Hello, Pierre," Fred said.

"I wasn't expecting you back until the day after tomorrow," Pierre said.

"I couldn't let you deal with this nerd convention without me," he replied. "Besides, I heard that you were knifed?"

"*Swung at,*" Pierre corrected. "He missed."

"Yes, of course," he replied. "Where are you going?"

Pierre gave him a concerned look.

"Did I ask something wrong?" Fred asked.

"No, no, of course not," Pierre replied. "It's just... after you've been attacked by an assassin, you get a little uncomfortable when people start asking too many questions."

Fred frowned and nodded.

"Terran Command Station," Pierre added.

"Who is running the station?" Fred asked.

"I left Charles in charge," Pierre replied. "I can't tell you what's going on, and I can't tell you why I'm going. You just have to trust me."

"Can I come with?" Fred asked. "I need to speak to someone there myself, and I still have two days of shore leave."

Pierre shrugged. "I guess."

"I just need to get my bags. Back in ten," Fred replied before running across the pad and disappearing into the airlock.

"Did he seem unusually excited to you?" Laura asked.

"No," Pierre replied. "He always acts that way. We've been friends for years—even before we were both assigned here. He's good people."

Laura nodded.

A few minutes later, Fred reappeared in the airlock, and they began their long day's journey into the Sol system.

Chapter Eleven

About twenty-eight years earlier
(February 14, 2363)

KRELL awoke. Were it not for the stench of mechlizard droppings, she could almost have forgotten that she was in a Terran Alliance lab deep underground, wearing an anthropoveil to conceal her identity.

Her mission was simple: steal the Ackerman crystal before the fools could use it in a large-scale test.

That was before the red alert klaxons had woken her from her slumber at three in the morning. Now, it was personal.

Krell quickly checked herself in the mirror to make sure she was still wearing Mikhail Skylarov's face, then stepped out into the hall.

"Mikhail! Get out of there!" Donovan shouted.

"What?"

Krell spun around and saw it: a giant mechlizard charging towards her from Section 10. She ran as hard as she could towards Section 11. The doors were already dropping. She dove under the door when it was just a couple of feet above the floor. So did the mechlizard. The crunching sound of door-on-lizard was sickening.

“What... the... hell?” Krell shouted in Skylarov’s voice.

Donovan laughed. “You’d think you had never seen a mechlizard before!”

“Not loose!” Krell replied.

“Well, there are at least a dozen more of them. We’re stuck here for a while.”

Krell’s heart sank. *Like surgically extracting an impaled candy cane next to the spinal column of an unborn fetus... while being chased by a velociraptor....*

“Military ops has sealed off everything below section 5,” Donovan continued. “They plan to send soldiers in to kill the lizards. I keep telling them that they should take their time—let us seal off our ventilation system from the rest of the base so they can pump in poison gas—but they won’t listen....”

Krell just stood there slack-jawed.

“I’m sorry you didn’t get the message to stay in your quarters until we could come get you through the maintenance crawlspace,” Donovan continued. “I forgot you were back early.”

“No worries,” Krell replied, still visibly shaken. “So now what?”

“Now, we wait.”

Chapter Twelve

Almost twenty-eight years later
(the evening of November 12, 2390)

THE shuttle Kharon settled onto the deck at Terran Command Station. Pierre reached for the button to open the door. That's when he saw the men with rifles.

"Laura," he said, "if anything happens to me, I want you to find Admiral Thomas Jenkins."

Laura stared at him in horror.

With that, Pierre raised his hands and pressed the button to open the door.

"Pierre Lafontaine?" the station security officer asked.

"Oui?" Pierre replied.

"You are under arrest," the security officer said, pulling Pierre out of the shuttle and slamming him up against its hull. "You have the right to remain silent. Anything you say can and will be used against you in a court of law. You have the right to an attorney. If you cannot afford an attorney, a public defender will be assigned to you. Do you understand your rights?"

"Oui," Pierre replied, relishing the opportunity to make the security officer uncomfortable by speaking in a different language.

Laura watched in horror as they hauled Pierre across the flight deck and out the door. She looked at Fred, and Fred simply shrugged.

"Sydney," Laura said, "I think we'd better find lodging for the night. We can find the admiral first thing in the morning."

"I'll help you find him," Fred replied.

Laura shook her head. "I'm sorry, but you are Pierre's friend, not ours. I can't trust someone I don't know. Now if you will excuse us," she said, walking to the rear of the shuttle and taking her bags along with Pierre's, "we have business to attend to that we cannot share with you."

"Why not?"

"It's classified."

Fred apparently knew when to give up and shut up; he said nothing as Laura and Sydney walked out of the shuttle, across the flight deck, and out the door.

Chapter Thirteen

About twenty-eight years earlier
(February 15, 2363)

KRELL shook her head.

This is insane. They're going to blow up the planet. I just know it.

Krell read the message again just to make sure she didn't misread it the first three times.

ATTENTION:

All personnel are to report to the test lab at 0800 hours tomorrow for a large-scale test of Ackerman's Engine. I've decided to go through with Vladimir's plan to slow down time in part of the base so that the mechlizards will slow down while the assault team up in section 5 speeds up.

If our prior experiments are any indication, this localized dilation effect should persist for several hours after Ackerman's Engine is turned off. Over the course of that time, the mechlizards will

> *progressively accelerate, and the humans will progressively decelerate, until they eventually resynchronize with normal space-time.*
>
> *This experiment is several orders of magnitude larger than the rather unfortunate test three years ago. It is very important that we get everything right. We can't afford to have an entire ship full of people suddenly go missing... again....*

Krell shook her head again. *Well, if they're going to test it, I'd better at least make sure they don't break anything too seriously.*

With that, she headed for the lab. *Maybe if I perforate some cooling hoses, they will scrub the test,* she thought. Then she looked at her watch. 0825. *Too late.*

As she approached the lab, a man she didn't know ran past her, heading towards section 15. *Must be that Rejndorv guy.*

A few moments later, through the window, she saw Donovan run into the test chamber carrying a fire extinguisher.

This can't be good.

"Warning!" Tessa's voice intoned, "Quantum lens temperature exceeds safety limits. Catastrophic failure in fifteen seconds."

Shit!

By the time Krell figured out how to get the old-fashioned doorknob to turn, things were hopelessly out of control.

"Quantum lens temperature is now at 600 Kelvin and rising. Catastrophic failure in ten seconds."

She watched in horror as Donovan desperately tried to reconnect the damaged nitrogen cooling lines.

"Failure in five seconds.... Four.... Three.... Two.... One...."

The last thing Krell saw was Donovan Jenkins shimmering into nothingness. Then, the flames came and darkness overtook her.

Chapter Fourteen

About twenty-eight years later
(November 13, 2390)

LAURA stretched her arms as she awoke, then recoiled when her left arm hit the metal bulkhead. Now fully awake, she quickly sat up and looked around the room.

The room was a very military-looking accommodation—corrugated steel walls painted gunmetal grey, with a floor that alternated periodically between chromed corrugated steel plates and steel mesh grids, with a large throw rug underneath the bed area.

The ceiling consisted of a series of metal slats with plastic panels of various colors forming a dropped ceiling. Some of the panels were translucent and had light sources of indeterminate variety behind them. Others were opaque. A few were missing; the water stain on the rug below them suggested that they were removed for good reason.

As Laura stood and made her bed, Sydney stirred on the bunk across from her. Laura glanced at her watch to see just how badly they had slept in. Then, she rubbed her eyes and looked again just to be sure.

"Get up, Sydney," Laura said. "It's almost eleven o'clock."

Sydney mumbled something about Laura's mother as Laura pulled her out of bed.

Laura quickly grabbed a change of clothes, a towel, a soap dish, and a bottle of shampoo from her luggage and tossed them into a nylon mesh laundry sack, then carried it down the hall to the communal bathroom, with Sydney following close behind.

Unlike the guest quarters on Terran Command Outpost 72, the guest quarters they were assigned on Terran Command Station were clearly designed for low-ranking military officers. Indeed, the only reason Laura and Sydney were allowed in the military portion of the station at all was that Laura's father was a retired Terran Coast Guard officer (and, Laura mused, it probably helped that she still had a high-level security clearance because of her last job).

Either way, the spartan accommodations made it very obvious to Laura that this was not the Vanderbilt Hotel. She understood that their stay was a privilege. Sydney, on the other hand, followed her down the hall, grumbling the whole way to the showers. Laura smirked.

When they arrived, they found a single set of shower stalls shared by both men and women, adjacent to a single set of restroom stalls similarly shared. Laura was more than a little creeped out—even more so when she overheard a man in one of the stalls ask his commanding officer for "permission to pee freely". She did not relax until she saw a woman exit the shower stall fully clothed.

There must be a dry place to dress in there, she thought as she entered the now-empty stall. Sure enough, the stall had a front area with a bench for your clothes, separated from the actual shower by a curtain.

Laura quickly disrobed and stepped into the shower. She turned on the water, turned it towards the hot side, and grimaced when the water pressure dropped to nothing.

Great. No hot water.

So Laura took a very cold shower. By the time she got out, every inch of her body was screaming.

She stepped out, dried off, and got dressed. As she did, she saw Sydney stepping out of her stall, fully dry.

"There is *no* way I'm showering in ice water," Sydney said indignantly.

"They you will die unclean," a voice said from the next stall.

Laura's eyes widened.

Laura and Sydney ran out of the bathroom in a hurry. As they stepped through the door, they turned left and ran down the hall, then turned left again and ran about ten more feet to the lift.

Laura pressed the button madly. "Come on. Come on."

The lift doors opened, and the girls dove in. Laura smashed the door close button, followed by the button for the top floor. As the doors closed, she could just make out Fred's face turning towards them at the end of the short hall.

They relaxed as the elevator made its ascent. Once they started moving, Laura pressed a few more floors.

Sydney looked at her questioningly.

"No point telegraphing our destination," Laura said, knowingly. "If it stops at several floors, it will be less obvious which floor we got out on."

"Which floor are we getting out on?" Sydney asked.

"Not the first one, and not the last one."

The elevator stopped and a young, dark-haired woman stepped in, carrying a large paper bag. She looked at them with a puzzled expression.

"Going to five different floors?" she asked.

Laura smiled sheepishly. "Long story."

"Where are you headed?" she asked.

"No idea," Laura replied.

As the girl eyed them up and down, her appearance took on a concerned quality. "This base is for military personnel only," she said, finally. "How did you get here?"

"I have security clearance, and my father is retired military," Laura replied. "I'm well within my rights to be here."

"Yet you're running from someone," the girl replied, clearly unconvinced. "Security?"

"Not even close," Laura replied, seeing Fred's face in her mind, then imagining that face on the body of the assassin on TCO-72, flipping her off as it flew through space. She shook off the image. "Do you know where we could find Admiral Jenkins?"

The girl seemed taken aback.

What, is he dead or something? Laura wondered.

The girl blinked. Once. Twice. Three times. After a few seconds pause, she shook her head, then regained her composure, her expression growing once again concerned.

"Why... are you looking for my father," the woman asked cautiously.

"And you are..."

"Amanda Jenkins," the young woman replied.

"I wish I could tell you that," Laura replied, "but it's..."

"Classified?" Amanda asked.

Laura shook her head. "It's dangerous."

"Dangerous?" Amanda replied incredulously. "How could information be dangerous?"

Sydney stepped up at that moment. "Look, do you know where to find him or not?"

Amanda smirked, obviously amused at the previously silent girl suddenly growing a spine. She shrugged. "Yeah. I was just heading up to bring him some lunch," she replied, pointing at the bag of food. "Follow me."

The elevator stopped at level 12. They waited, and the doors closed again. This act repeated itself several times before they reached the uppermost floor for this lift, level 5. Then, Amanda pressed its lowest floor, level 32. Laura and

Sydney held their breath as the lift passed the floor where they got on, then relaxed when they reached the bottom.

As they stepped out, Amanda pushed every floor, smirking. Laura smiled. Amanda then led them down a hall to another lift.

***

FRED grumbled as he slunk back to his quarters through the winding halls.

At least they were too far away to identify me, I think, he thought, *and even if they did, they can't prove that I threatened them. I'll get another opportunity soon enough.*

And so he began planning his next move.

Step 1: Find out what Pierre knows.

Step 2: Find Klern and ask him why Pierre is still breathing.

The girls can wait.

***

PIERRE blinked his eyes. The bright, white lights overhead made his head scream in agony.

The girls!

He looked around and saw nothing but white, padded walls and a white, padded floor.

No, he thought. *They came for me. Maybe they don't even know that the girls exist.*

Pierre considered this for a moment, then shook his head.

No, if they were not being hunted, why would the girls have come looking for me? And why did they say that no place was safe?

Pierre knew that he had to get out. It was just a question of when. Eventually, the doctors and the guards had to make a mistake. When they did, he would do what he had to do.

***

AMANDA stepped into her father's office, only to find her father sitting at his baby grand piano, tickling the ivories. When she entered, he paused.

"Dad," she said, tossing the food on his desk and hugging him, "I'd like you to meet Laura and Sydney. For some reason, they're looking for you. I think they're in trouble, but they won't tell me why or how."

Thomas Jenkins sighed, stood, walked over to his desk, and sat down.

"Business as usual," he muttered.

Amanda shrugged off the remark.

"I hate to interrupt your lunch with your daughter," Laura began, "but this is urgent... and private."

"If you trust me," Thomas replied, "you trust my daughter as well."

Laura opened her mouth to speak, closed it, bowed her head for a moment, then looked back up at him.

"Honestly," she replied, "we don't trust you. Pierre trusts you... or at least he did before you arrested him."

Admiral Jenkins shook his head. "He was arrested for kidnapping the two of you and his commanding officer. Apparently, Fred Ebberstein fired him for negligence that nearly led to your deaths when you arrived at the station. He couldn't handle being fired, and he went nuts. He took a gun, held you all hostage, and forced you to get on a shuttle with him."

Laura just stared at him.

Sydney was slightly less reserved. "What... in... hell... are you talking about?"

Admiral Jenkins sighed. "I didn't want to believe it myself, but that's what the communiqué from the station keeper on TCO-72 said—a Charles somebody or other. He said the Commander had scrawled a note on his desk."

"Fred threatened to kill us," Laura replied.

"I see." Thomas replied. "Why should I believe you?"

"Because it's the truth?" Sydney replied angrily.

Amanda Jenkins snorted. "Okay. Tell us what happened."

With that, Laura and Sydney spent several hours recounting highlights of the tale, starting from when Sydney first sent the photographs and ending when they met Amanda in the lift.

"Amanda," Thomas said, pulling her aside, "what do you make of this?"

"Well, I don't know if they're telling the truth," she replied, "but they certainly seem genuinely terrified. Is there anywhere safe we can send them?"

"Safe from whom?" Thomas replied. "That is the operative question."

Amanda shook her head and frowned.

***

ADMIRAL Candy Sinclair looked around her office. They hadn't fully rebuilt it after the fire, and it never was the nicest office in the universe to begin with, but it was hers, and that's what mattered. Her glass desk reflected an austerity that mirrored life on the station to a great degree, the cold, metal construction of the walls, floor, and ceiling giving the perpetual sense of being out in the cold, desolate, barren wasteland of deep space.

She was just standing up to walk to the cafeteria for lunch when the viewscreen chirped.

"Viewscreen on," she replied.

On the screen, she saw the face of Admiral Thomas Jenkins.

"Tom!" she shouted. "So good to see you, old friend."

"Likewise, my dear," he replied, smiling. "Still married to that old jackass, Ralph?"

She laughed. "Even to this day, when he gets started talking about your days in the service together, you can't get him to shut up."

Thomas laughed. "He always was quite the talkative one."

She smiled.

"So how is the old coot?"

"He's doing well," she replied. "Enjoying his retirement. I'll be joining him soon."

Thomas's expression grew grim.

"What?" she asked, obviously troubled.

"We have a bit of a situation here at central command," he replied. "There are two girls here who are in a bit of trouble. They're being chased by unknown hostiles, some of whom are uniformed Terran soldiers and officers."

Her face grew dour. "So you need to arrange a six-twenty-seven."

He nodded.

"What's a six-twenty-seven?" Laura whispered.

"He delivers and rescues and works wonders in heaven and on Earth; he has delivered Daniel from the power of the lions," Amanda replied. "It's when they make you... disappear. Protective custody with a death certificate and no paper trail."

Laura's eyes widened.

"Consider it done," Candy replied. "A 'specialist' will arrive within the hour."

"Don't worry," Amanda said. "It only hurts for a little while."

"But... once we do this, we'll be... dead," Laura replied incredulously.

"As far as the rest of the universe is concerned, yes."

"Sydney," Laura said, "Aren't you worried about your husband?"

Sydney paused.

"Sydney?"

"Okay, the truth?" Sydney replied. "I caught him having sex with the maid of honor in the back room of the church the morning of our wedding. Apparently it had been going on for almost a year."

"I thought your little sister was the maid of honor."

Sydney nodded.

"She's fifteen!"

Sydney nodded.

"So no wedding."

Sydney shrugged. "Maybe for them someday. Not for us."

"And the honeymoon?"

"I decided I wasn't going to let that spoiled brat ruin all my fun, so I packed my bags that night... preflight...."

Laura looked at her in horror. "This isn't going to turn into an awful spoken word song and dance number, is it?"

Sydney smiled wryly. "You know the weirdest part?" she asked.

"What's that?"

"I don't even miss him."

"I guess that's good," Laura replied.

"How's that?"

Laura grimaced. "He won't miss you, either."

***

DOCTOR Johnson stepped into the white room. Pierre blinked as the doctor shined a flashlight into his eyes. When his eyes finally came back into focus, the white padded room looked as dismal as ever.

"Pierre Lafontaine, I understand you've been telling the nurses some rather... colorful tales," the doctor said.

"Not colorful," Pierre replied. "It is the truth."

"Let me see if I understand correctly. You say that someone sabotaged the artificial gravity system using your access codes?"

"Yes."

"But how would someone have your access codes?" the doctor asked.

"I am not sure. But they did."

"And then you picked a fight with one of the conference attendees?"

"NO!" Pierre shouted. "He tried to kill me!"

"Why would one of the conference attendees try to kill you, Pierre?"

"Because I saw them."

"Saw who?" the doctor asked.

"The alien ships."

"Now, Pierre, you know there's no such thing as aliens. You've been watching too many science fiction movies."

"No," Pierre replied. "The ship was invisible."

"You saw an invisible ship?"

"No, weapons fire from an invisible ship," Pierre said, his voice becoming annoyed.

"You saw an invisible ship fire on what?"

"On the ship at the folding gate. The... eh... Hrabrost."

"You can't see the folding gate from TCO-72, Pierre," the doctor replied, shaking his head. "And we looked at the camera footage. There was no alien ship."

"No, I did not see it myself. The ship saw it. I was able to reconstruct some of the sensor logs. The explosion came from the *outside* of the ship, but there was nothing on the cameras."

"Pierre," the doctor replied, "couldn't there have been a ship *behind* the Hrabrost that fired on it, then folded away before the explosion settled down?"

Pierre looked at the doctor like he was crazy.

"Wouldn't that make a lot more sense than an alien ship?" the doctor continued. "Wouldn't that be a simpler explanation?"

"No," Pierre replied.

"Why not?"

"Because you cannot fold so close to a folding gate."

"Sure you can, Pierre. It just has to be coordinated."

"There was nothing in the logs."

"Are you sure?" the doctor replied. "Because we checked the logs, and there was a coordinated jump just a half second later."

"Was there a *second* coordinated jump?" Pierre asked.

"I'm not sure. Why?"

"Because the alien ship also destroyed the Aenid," Pierre replied.

"What are you talking about? The Aenid is here at Terran Command Station undergoing repairs."

Pierre shifted uncomfortably in the straitjacket.

"Now are you willing to at least consider the possibility that there might be a simpler explanation?" the doctor asked.

Pierre nodded.

"Good. That's a good start," the doctor said, then walked towards the door.

As the doctor walked, Pierre noticed two things. First, he noticed that the door opened automatically as the doctor approached. Second, he noticed a large bulge in the doctor's back pocket. He now knew how to escape. It was just a matter of choosing *when*.

***

AMANDA waved Laura and Sydney onto the shuttle, then walked over to her father.

"Are you sure you'll be okay?" he asked.

"I'll be fine, Dad."

He smiled at her. "Remember to fasten the buckles on your pressure suit. Complete cabin depressurization is very unpleasant."

"I know, Dad."

"You'll do fine."

With that, Amanda stepped onto the shuttle and closed the door.

"Terran Command Station, this is the shuttle Hermes requesting departure clearance on flyby of Mercury with final destination of Mars gate."

"Reason for using Mars gate?" came the sullen reply.

"Sightseeing," she replied. "I'm taking some friends who have never seen Mars."

There was a brief pause. For a moment, she was concerned that they might deny the request, but after a few moments, her shuttle began its power-up sequence.

"That's affirmative, Hermes," the voice said. "You are cleared for departure on vector oh-two-niner by oh-three-three. Over."

"Copy that, oh-two-niner by oh-three-three, over."

She keyed the takeoff vector into the flight control computer, and it dutifully beeped its understanding. A moment later, she waved at her father through the windows as the ship began its slow ascent through the bay doors.

After a few moments, the ship began accelerating in preparation for a slingshot around Mercury. Amanda disabled the automatic pilot a moment later, pointing the ship well outside a slingshot orbit and reducing speed considerably.

"What are you doing?" Laura asked. "Are you certified to fly this thing manually?"

Amanda smiled. "I've been a certified pilot for almost ten years," she replied. "I'm going to fly us slowly around behind the dark side of Mercury for the rendezvous. It will take more fuel, but it's a lot safer that way."

Before long, their ship was in Mercury's shadow. Amanda checked her pressure suit, then turned to the girls.

"Time to take your pills," Amanda said.

"This is crazy," Laura said. "How do we know we can trust you?"

"Who else are you going to trust?" Amanda replied.

Laura nodded. She had a point.

Laura and Sydney swallowed the two red pills with a glass of water. Within about a minute, they were unconscious and lying by the door.

Amanda re-engaged the autopilot, then attached oxygen masks to both of the girls. They would not stay on during decompression, but they would ensure that the girls' tissues were sufficiently oxygenated for the transfer.

Then, after about three minutes, Amanda lashed herself to the side of the shuttle, pressed the door release button, and watched the girls as they were sucked out the side of the ship. As soon as the ship had fully depressurized, she burned through a wire connected to the door controls with a hand torch, unlashed herself, and ran back to the front of the shuttle.

"Sol orbital control, this is the shuttle Hermes. We have a critical failure. The door to our shuttle just blew open and two passengers were sucked out. The door mechanism appears to have been damaged and we cannot retrieve them. Over."

"Hermes, this is Sol orbital control. You are cleared for emergency landing at Mercurial dark side station. We regret that we cannot get a ship to your location in time to save your passengers."

She could barely keep the amusement off of her face as she saw the flash of the Erebus, designation TCS-627, folding into orbit, just cresting the horizon behind her, its arrival carefully timed to coincide with a five-minute maintenance hold on both the Earth and Mars folding gates.

When she landed, Amanda feigned tears. The base commander assigned her a shuttle to take back to Terran Command Station, and told her that they would send a craft to retrieve the bodies if they did not burn up first. But of course, she knew that there were no bodies to be found.

***

Admiral Jenkins's personal log

November 16, 2390

I have been trying for three days to see Pierre. Doctor Johnson is a very stubborn, obstinate man, and will not allow Pierre to have visitors during his first month of treatment. Although the stories he has been telling the nurses about "aliens" seem a little far-fetched, I am a little concerned that he might not be crazy at all. The evidence against him—the word of his commanding officer—directly contradicts the word of the two women in the shuttle with him.

Unfortunately, those women are now "dead" according to all official records, and must remain so for the time being, leaving me no choice but to keep Pierre locked up for now. If what they told me is true, he is probably safer where he is, anyway.

I also grow concerned that I have not heard from Candy about the women that I helped "disappear". They claim to have proof of a conspiracy that boggles the mind. I guess I have no choice but to wait for her to contact me. Per standard security protocols, I am not privy to their location.

It's going to be a long month.

Chapter Fifteen

One week later (November 23, 2390)

As Laura's eyes flickered open, she saw only a blinding white light. She could hear the murmured whispers of dozens of people lined up in the shadows to either side of her.

Am I dead? she thought. *Is this heaven?*

Slowly, the shadows began to brighten as her peripheral vision began to return. The murmurings turned into the equally uninterpretable chatter of emergency room doctors and nurses, along with all the beeps, chirps, and blinking lights that accompanied such a setting.

Or hell, she thought as she realized she was in a hospital.

Laura sat up suddenly.

"Sydney!?"

Sydney put her hand on Laura's shoulder. "I'm right here. It's okay."

"What happened?"

Sydney put her hand back down.

"It worked.... Mostly."

"What do you mean, mostly?" Laura asked.

"Well... your heart kind of stopped."

"My what!?! For how long!?!"

"Six or seven minutes," Sydney replied. "They had to oxygenate your blood externally and pump it through your body using an artery in your groin."

No wonder my leg hurts, Laura thought.

"You're okay now, though," Sydney continued. "You've been unconscious for ten days. We were getting a little worried, to be honest."

Laura rubbed her head. "Doc," she asked, "you got anything for this hangover?"

Everyone laughed.

That's when Laura looked around. She looked up at the glass ceiling, down at the glass floor, and around at the glass walls, and all around her, she saw a panoramic view of... well... nothing. There were a few stars, but no signs of a ship, a planet's surface, or any other clues as to their location.

"Wait, where are we?" she asked.

"You're in the recovery ball on Triton Station," the doctor replied. "It's an advanced, holographic projection room. We can create a three-dimensional projection on the walls that mimics almost any environment imaginable."

"Why aren't you using it?" Laura asked.

"We are. You don't think you're in the middle of empty space, do you?" the doctor replied, chuckling.

"Of course not. I just figured this was the lighting when the system was turned off. In that case, I have to ask.... Why empty space?"

"We find it eases the shock of extra-atmospheric transits in cases where the newly 'dead' were not fully unconscious during the transit," the doctor replied, mockingly using quote fingers around the word "dead" as he said it.

Laura nodded. "So about that hangover?"

***

PIERRE stared at the man entering the white room. *You put me here,* he thought to himself. *You unholy bastard.*

Fred Ebberstein looked smug—not the sort of smug when you know you've won, but rather that heady, over-the-top sort of smug that supervillains get right before the end when they reveal their entire plan in painfully pedantic detail to the hero, who the supervillain believes cannot escape.

Fred stepped up to the chair where the straitjacketed Pierre was seated.

"I suppose," Pierre said, "that this is where you tell me your evil plan in all its details because I cannot possibly escape?"

Fred snorted.

"Very well. I suppose you have a right to know. First of all, you are right," he replied, "about almost everything. We have a ship that can almost completely disappear using a spatial fold. It's not alien. It is classified. We shot the Hrabrost because it was a security risk. It was... unfortunate... but necessary. If the Colonial Alliance knew of this, our ability to monitor their actions would be greatly reduced."

"And the Aenid?"

Fred looked confused. "The Aenid has been in dry dock for six weeks to repair an engine malfunction."

"But I heard Captain Paulson tell us about the explosion."

Fred shook his head. "I don't know what you heard or thought you heard, but the Aenid was never there."

He's lying.

"If you say so," Pierre replied.

"Well, I should probably let you get some rest," Fred said. With that, he turned and walked away.

***

LAURA walked down the main corridor of Triton Station to the mess hall. To be fair, the words "corridor" and "hall" were something of an overstatement. The top floor of the main section of Triton Station more closely resembled a high-ceilinged airport concourse than a corridor, with glass-walled offices sticking out on both sides.

The mess hall was a glorified food court, with tables, chairs, and some soft seating areas. It stuck out from one side of the corridor about halfway down. On the opposite side of the corridor, a glass-walled tube led out to the landing bay building.

When Laura reached the mess hall, she found Sydney already sitting at a table waiting for her.

"Grab something and join me," Sydney shouted at her from across the room.

As Laura walked past Sydney to the refrigerated cooler and opened the glass doors to grab a soda, it suddenly hit her.

The Aenid. I forgot to tell him about the Aenid.

"Sydney, I have to get a message to Admiral Jenkins."

Sydney sighed. "Food first, talk later."

Laura complied begrudgingly, eschewing the can of soda for a resealable bottle of water and the pasta for a sandwich that she could carry more easily if she had any leftovers. She sat down across from Sydney and rapidly wolfed down the sandwich.

"Happy?"

Sydney giggled.

"You missed a great Thanksgiving dinner yesterday," Sydney said after a bit.

Laura looked down at her watch and shook her head.

"I can't believe I was out that long."

"I put some leftovers in the fridge for you. We can heat them up for dinner tonight."

Laura smiled groggily. "Thanks. I'd like that."

***

Admiral Jameson stepped into Admiral Jenkins's office.

Admiral Jenkins looked up from his lunch and greeted his old friend.

"Phil," Thomas said. "In for the day?"

"The week, actually," Admiral Jameson replied. "I made the fleet admiral mad again, so he ordered me to babysit some retrofit. The Aenid, I think."

Jenkins chuckled. "So how is your daughter, Emily liking Harvard?"

"Yale. And she hates it," Jameson replied, "but she's doing well. And Amanda? Is she up to her usual tricks?"

"She just started a rock climbing class at the gym. She said to tell Emily that she's looking forward to seeing her over the holidays."

Admiral Jameson laughed. "Sounds like her, all right."

"So what's up?"

"Tom," he began, "I think we have a problem."

Thomas frowned. *We have a lot of problems. Which of the thousand problems are you referring to?*

"And that would be?"

"We have a spy in our ranks," Jameson replied. "We just finished poring through a data archive that we recovered from a captured Colonial ship. It contained decrypted copies of encrypted communications sent from this station to various ships in the fleet over the past week."

Admiral Jenkins buried his head in his hands for a moment.

"I assume we've already revoked everyone's public keys?"

"Yes," Jameson replied, "and we're rekeying everyone's comm systems now. Yours is first. I did it myself. I don't trust... anybody else but you right now."

"Skylarov failed?"

"You bet," Jameson replied. "He didn't mention the key word from our last conversation before he went out to the front lines. I even dropped hints. He completely missed them."

"Same with me."

Jameson frowned. "It's like he's a different person."

"Maybe he is," Admiral Jenkins replied, then spun around when the intercom on his desk started beeping at him. He pressed the talk button. "Yes?"

"Sir," Admiral Jenkins's private secretary said through the intercom, "I know you asked me to hold all calls while you spoke with Admiral Jameson, but there's a priority heliotrope message for you. I can't screen it."

"I'll take it," Thomas replied. "Thanks."

Thomas enabled additional electronic countermeasures before turning on the viewscreen.

"Jenkins."

The familiar face of Admiral Sinclair appeared on the screen.

"Hello, Tom."

"Hi, Candy."

"Is your office secure?" she asked.

"Of course," he replied, glancing at Admiral Jameson.

"I have an important message for you from Laura Rodolfo."

"Go ahead," he replied. "But first, is Ralph on vacation this week?"

"No," she replied. "He's saving up his post-retirement time off from being my live-in chef so that he can spend time with you when you retire next week. Oh, and trimming the kudzu around the mailbox."

Jenkins nodded. *It's her.*

"Laura said that Pierre said that there were two ships destroyed. She thinks the other ship was called the Aenid."

"I'll look into it. Was that all?"

She nodded.

"Tell Ralph that he still owes me a round of golf..."
She smiled.
"... at Roswell country club..."
Her smile disappeared as quickly as it appeared.
"...with Skylarov and Ebberstein."
She nodded solemnly and sighed.
"Be well, Tom."
"Be well, Candy."

Chapter Sixteen

Three days later
November 26, 2390

PIERRE sat at a data terminal in the white room and grumbled.

At least they let me out of the straitjacket, he thought.

At first, he amused himself by viewing various news reports from the front line and other nonclassified data that his newly reduced access allowed him to see.

After a few hours, he got bored and decided to test the limits. Sure enough, he found that he had access to basic military information as well—crew manifests, repair orders, that sort of thing. So he decided to go digging for more information about the Aenid.

His first search brought up the crew manifest and basic status information. True to the doctor's word, the Aenid was listed as being under repair in bay 17. Captain Paulson was not listed as the commanding officer.

Then where is Captain Paulson?

He did a quick search to see if there was a Captain Paulson currently on active duty. The search returned no results. A Captain Paulson was, however, listed as a recent

KIA. He opened the record and found a news report about a shuttlecraft accident that killed three people.

I'm betting they were all on the crew of the Aenid, he thought, and after a quick check, he confirmed it.

Wow. Whoever tried to cover this up didn't try very hard.

Still, this was not proof. He needed something more solid. He sat there for what seemed like hours trying to think of a query that might shed some light on the situation before it suddenly came to him.

If the Aenid is undergoing repairs, that means there must be an ***actual ship*** *called the Aenid that is undergoing repairs. Ships don't appear out of thin air, and it takes longer than a few days to build one, so they must have changed the name on the hull of another ship.*

And so, Pierre began searching for painting orders—more specifically, stenciling orders. After a few minutes, he found one, along with an order for replacement exterior metal panels damaged in an accidental fire in bay 17.

Accidental, my ass. Still not enough proof. I need to find the smoking gun.

With that realization, he began searching through all of the old work orders for the ship currently undergoing repairs in bay 17, trying to see if any of them had a name associated with them. Unfortunately, he came up blank... until he cross-referenced the work order numbers against the purchasing database.

In the maintenance database, the work orders were listed as being for the U.S.S. Aenid. In the purchasing database, it correctly listed them as being for the newly constructed U.S.S. Constitution.

Pierre's eyes widened. He slipped off his left shoe (which the doctors had thankfully paid little attention to), pulled the data cartridge from the hidden compartment in its heel, and copied the documents onto it. He replaced the cartridge and put his shoe back on, then began running further searches for information about his boss, Fred Ebberstein. A moment later, the doctor entered the room.

"What are you doing!?!" he shouted.

Pierre grimaced as Doctor Johnson and three goons grabbed him and strapped him down to the table. Pierre took a deep breath, tightened all of his muscles, and pressed his fingertips hard against the table to raise his arms up a bit as they strapped the restraints down around him. Then, the doctors injected him with something.

Merde. That's new. I hadn't planned on that.

Pierre knew that he would have only seconds to make his escape once the doctor and the psychiatric nurses left the room, so he began mentally preparing himself. Sure enough, true to the norm, the doctor left the room to get a camcorder so that he could record the session.

Pierre could already feel the effects of the sodium thiopental as his wrist slipped free from its restraint. He struggled to release the other wrist restraint, then unbuckled the straps holding his legs.

Finally, he took off his left shoe, removed the data cartridge, and put his shoe back on.

He walked over to the door to wait for the doctor so that he could get out. The door opened easily when he approached it from the inside, much to his amazement.

The sick bay was not designed as a prison, he mused. *Wait a minute. Does that mean I could have walked out of here at any time for the last two days?*

His hope was short-lived, however; within moments, he found himself wishing he had a good place to hide when the doctors appeared at one end of the corridor.

He quickly ran away from them to the opposite end of the hall, turned right, ran through a door into a larger hall, turned left, and finally ran through the double doors to his right.

Once through those doors, he found himself inside the Crew's Quarter, a large eating establishment. Were it not for his medical gown, he probably could have gotten lost in the crowd, but alas, it was not to be, so all he could hope to do was to tell everyone what he knew.

"This is mad!" Pierre shouted, feigning insanity. "I demand to be heard. The Alliance is corrupt!"

Suddenly, the elite security forces crashed through the doors behind him.

"They're killing us!" he screamed. "They're killing us! Their own people!"

Then, he saw Amanda Jenkins, and he knew what he had to do. He took the data cartridge and dropped it down the back of her shirt as he passed by her.

As the security team wrestled him to the ground, he continued to try to speak. "You have to believe me! There are traitors in waiting!"

Then, he felt the familiar jab of a stunner in his back, and everything went black.

***

The room slowly returned to its usual din, but Amanda remained quiet.

"Amanda? What's wrong?" Joseph asked after a few moments, his concern clearly showing.

"Nothing important.... No, I think someone just walked over my grave," Amanda replied as she reached behind her back and slipped a data cartridge out from under her shirt.

"What's that?" Joseph asked, eyeing the cartridge in spite of her best attempt at being stealthy about moving it to her shirt pocket.

"I'm not sure," she replied, "but I think it's important."

"Should we leave?" Joseph asked.

"No, we'd better finish our dinner first. We wouldn't want to arouse suspicion."

Joseph nodded.

***

Pierre groggily opened his eyes and found himself restrained to his bed in the white room, this time with no slack to allow him to escape. Worse, the face in front of him was that of the last person he wanted to see.

"I suppose you think you're pretty smart," Fred said. "I guess you think you're a hero. What were you trying to do, tell someone about the Aenid?"

Pierre shrugged.

"You're crazy. Who are they going to believe? Me or some lunatic rambling on about discrepancies in a purchasing database?"

Pierre's eyes opened wider.

"Yeah, you think we weren't monitoring your terminal? We know exactly what information you got."

Pierre looked back at him with disgust. "I'm sure there's more evidence where that came from, you sniveling merdetête."

Fred smacked him across the face with the back of his hand.

"Since nobody is going to believe you anyway," Fred replied, "I might as well tell you the good part."

Pierre turned his head quizzically.

"I'm not Fred Ebberstein. Fred Ebberstein had a little skiing accident during spring break of his senior year in high school. I've been him ever since. His parents wondered why he suddenly stopped making good grades and decided to join the military, but I guess they figured he was just a moody teenager."

Pierre stared at him coldly.

"Yeah. We've been replacing people for years, making our way into the deepest reaches of the Terran Alliance military forces, waiting for a chance to make our move."

"You'll never get away with this!" Pierre shouted before realizing that he was playing right into a cliché.

"But we already have," Fred said as he turned to leave the room.

"I'll tell everyone!" Pierre shouted as Fred reached the now-open doorway.

"And who is going to believe you?"

Moments later, Doctor Johnson entered the room and injected him with something else.

Pierre slipped into unconsciousness again.

***

11:48 that night

Pierre awoke suddenly to the station shaking violently. Within seconds, he heard alarms sounding in the distance, but he could not tell where they were coming from. Then, the screen in front of him sprang to life with a familiar face spread across it.

"This is Amanda Jenkins in C&C to all station personnel," she said. "There has been an explosion in the central nexus near the crew quarters arm. All personnel in levels 27 through 29 in the vicinity of the crew quarters arm or the central nexus are instructed to immediately proceed to lower or higher levels via stairs or access ladders where possible, or to pressure pods if you cannot leave the level."

"All personnel in other levels are instructed to remain where you are," she continued. "Fire suppression teams have been dispatched. We will bring you more information as we get it. C&C out."

The interruptions continued through much of the night before Pierre managed to tune out the noise and go back to sleep in spite of it.

Chapter Seventeen

The next morning

Amanda Jenkins grumbled as 5:00 A.M. rolled around and she realized that her next shift started in four hours. Worse, she could not go to her quarters to sleep. She had promises to keep.

Amanda covertly fingered the shape of the data cartridge in her shirt pocket to make sure it was still there, then groggily stood and walked to the top central lift.

...which isn't in the center at all, she mused.

The upper and lower central lifts, much like the main lifts, were just inside the outermost hull of the station's central nexus (the main tube part of the station). Unlike the main lifts, however, they were just inside the outermost hull at the *top and bottom levels* of the station, which were significantly smaller than the middle levels. Thus, by the time you reached the bottom of the upper central lift or the top of the lower central lift, you were fairly close to the center of the station, hence the name.

She took the upper lift down to level 5 and met Joseph for breakfast. After breakfast, she walked to the outer edge of the central nexus before taking an exterior lift down to the bottom, walking back towards the center, and taking the lower central lift down to her father's office near the bottom of the station.

Her father greeted her at the door.

"Amanda! What's going on? You said it was urgent."

Amanda reached into her pocket, fumbled for a moment, then retrieved the data cartridge.

"This is for you," she said.

"What is it?" Admiral Jenkins asked.

"I don't know. Pierre slipped it to me just before they grabbed him and drugged him."

Thomas Jenkins looked perturbed. He took the cartridge from her, walked over to the secure computer terminal on his desk, and inserted it.

"Come," he said. "You have more clearance than he ever did. Oh, and shut the door."

Amanda did as she was told. She stood behind her father, staring at the screen in silence as he paged through pages of seemingly meaningless information.

"Does this mean anything to you?" Amanda asked.

Her father shook his head. Then, he turned to the next page.

"U.S.S. Constitution?" Amanda asked. "What's that?"

"New ship under construction," he replied. "It's in bay 17."

"Are you sure?" Amanda asked.

"Yes. Why?"

"Because the last page said that the Aenid is in bay 17."

Admiral Jenkins frowned, turned to the previous page, and frowned some more.

"Wouldn't someone notice?" Amanda asked.

"That they were changing the name on the hull?" her father replied. "Probably not. Ships change repair bays every so often, and different crews work on different aspects of the repair. And even if somebody did, it's not like this doesn't happen every so often. A ship gets destroyed, another one takes its name."

"But this one wasn't officially destroyed," Amanda countered.

"I'm willing to bet that the U.S.S. Constitution will be 'destroyed' in an 'accident'," her father replied.

"Either way, you do realize what this means, right?"

The look of fear crossed the admiral's face faster than a skateboarder at a zebra crossing.

"Amanda, you have to promise me something. You didn't hear any of this. You weren't here. When I tell you that I am taking a trip, you will act surprised. Also, I want you to get off base for a while. It's not safe for you here right now."

"Okay," Amanda said, nodding. "Joseph asked me to go on a trip this morning."

"Are you sure you can trust him?" Admiral Jenkins asked.

"Yeah, Dad. He's safe."

"Joseph Kurtz is safe," her father replied, "but are you sure *he* is *Joseph*?"

Amanda walked out of the room in utter confusion.

Chapter Eighteen

Doctor Johnson spun as the door opened.

"Mr. Jenkins," he said, immediately recognizing the man in the doorway, "as I've told you before, Pierre is not allowed to have any visitors."

Admiral Jenkins pulled back his jacket with his left hand to reveal a sidearm.

"This isn't a request."

The doctor's eyes opened wider than Thomas thought humanly possible as he glanced alternately between the weapon and the face of its owner.

"Surely you can't be serious!"

Thomas moved his right hand over to the weapon and began fingering the handle.

"Sir, the man is not sane. He's been going on about aliens and a destroyed ship that isn't really destroyed and people trying to kill him and...."

"Doctor," the admiral interrupted, "This is no longer a medical matter. In fact, it never was."

The doctor nodded curtly, then stepped through the door and into the holding room. He pushed past two attendants and approached Pierre.

"Hi, Pierre," Doctor Johnson said carefully. "Do you know who I am?"

"Of course I know who you are," Pierre replied. "You are doctor Johnson."

The doctor nodded.

"Look, doc," he continued, "I am not crazy."

"Sure. That's what they all say," the doctor replied, chuckling.

"Zey really are out to get us."

"Who are?" the doctor asked.

"Ze aliens," Pierre replied calmly. "Zey are trying to destroy us all."

The doctor sighed and shook his head.

"There's no such thing as aliens, Pierre," he replied. "You're experiencing a paranoid delusion brought on by the stress of losing your job."

"I didn't lose my job. I'm on shore leave."

The doctor sighed. "You were fired for negligence, Pierre."

"No, it's not true," Pierre said, shaking his head as if to clear his thoughts. "I took shore leave because ze aliens were manipulating people. I'm not crazy. Zese drugs, they are making me crazy. I'm not crazy. I'm not, not crazy, not crazy."

"Someone is here to see you," the doctor interrupted. "Do you think you can keep your head together long enough to talk to him?"

Pierre nodded groggily.

"Okay, then," he said gently as he nodded to the attendants.

Admiral Jenkins stepped in.

"Pierre, my good man."

And so, Admiral Jenkins spent most of the remaining hours of the day with Pierre.

***

The next day

DOCTOR Johnson went into the holding room. Pierre sat in his chair.

"Doctor, you have to let me out," he cried. "The aliens... they are replacing people."

"There are no aliens, Pierre. I told you that this morning."

"And they planted the bomb."

"How do you know it was a bomb, Pierre?"

"It had to be. If a ship folded in to fire on us, we would have seen it."

Pierre suddenly became silent.

"Yes," the doctor replied.

Pierre looked at him with a suddenly worried voice.

"Or perhaps we would not have," Pierre muttered.

***

ADMIRAL Jenkins pressed a few controls on his screen, and Admiral Candy Sinclair's face appeared.

"Admiral," Jenkins began.

"Admiral," she replied.

"Is your old fart doing okay?"

Candy smiled. "Planting petunias. And you?"

"Well, my daughter is right here beside me, so I couldn't be better. Listen, I have a favor to ask."

"Go on."

"One of my good friends, Pierre, has been suffering from some severe post-traumatic stress. I'd like to transfer him to your facility for treatment."

Candy frowned and shook her head. "We're in the middle of a crew rotation. We should have a vacant room tomorrow."

"Do you have room for an old fart admiral? I'd like to personally supervise."

She smiled. "Sure. You know there's always room for you here."

She paused, then added, "In two weeks."

Thomas laughed.

"We'll see you in a day or two."

Then the screen went blank.

***

FRED smiled when he saw the death certificates. *Klern must have taken care of the girls,* he thought. *Perhaps rumors of his death were somewhat exaggerated.*

He looked around his office and smiled, then opened up his data pad and put two check marks next to their names.

Then, he saw it.

Coroner's note:

The bodies were never recovered.

Fred knew he had to make sure, so he checked out a shuttle and headed towards the Beta Persei folding gate. He would orbit Mercury until he found the bodies. He had to be certain. The stakes were too high.

***

AMANDA smiled and kissed Joseph on the cheek as they walked together towards his temporary quarters. Amanda's father greeted her at the door.

"Dad!" she shouted.

"I went by your quarters. You weren't there," he replied.

Amanda blushed a deep lavender behind her blue rouge.

"What do you need, Dad?" she asked, mildly annoyed.

Admiral Jenkins just stood and looked at her for a moment, then sighed.

"You know that I'm retiring soon, right?"

She smiled. "Of course."

"When you get back, I won't be here."

She nodded. "I know."

"I also won't be at home."

She looked a bit puzzled.

"An old friend of mine is going to Triton Station for some therapy. I've asked to be transferred there to finish out my last few weeks, and I might stay a little longer. I'll be leaving momentarily. I'll tell you everything when I get back."

"Okay. When will that be?"

Her father frowned.

"I don't know, Amanda. I don't know."

"Is this about Pierre?" she asked.

"I shouldn't say."

Amanda suddenly grew concerned. "There's something you're not telling me."

Her father shook his head slowly.

"Mannie," he replied, "I can't tell you what's going on. It's for your own good."

Now she knew something was wrong. Her father hadn't called her that since....

Since Mom died, she thought, shuddering.

"I wouldn't want to have to six-twenty-seven you," he continued.

Amanda stared at him. She wasn't sure what was going on, but she knew he was in danger. She also had the sinking feeling that there was nothing she could do about it.

"I love you, hon," he said, embracing her.

"I love you, too, Dad," she replied.

"Have fun on your trip. I'll get in touch with you in a few weeks and we'll talk more... somewhere private."

Amanda nodded. She knew the place.

"One more thing," he added. "Trust no one. Not even me."

Amanda looked puzzled. Joseph merely nodded.

With that, Thomas turned and walked to the lift. He took it up two floors to level 5, then walked inwards to the upper lift and took it up to the medical wing on level 3.

Pierre stood in a straitjacket awaiting his arrival. Doctor Johnson stood beside him.

"Doctor," Admiral Jenkins said, "I will take the prisoner now."

"Excuse me?"

"I'm transferring him to the post-traumatic stress ward at Triton Station," Jenkins replied. "You will see to it that the necessary arrangements are made."

The doctor just stood there.

Thomas Jenkins fingered his sidearm again, savoring the terror in the doctor's eyes. *I should have drawn a gun on him two weeks ago,* he mused. *I could have saved a lot of time that way.*

The doctor gave the admiral an icy glare as he took Pierre by the arm and led him back to the lift. By the time they reached the docking ports on the outer ring, Pierre was no longer wearing the straitjacket. Tom didn't particularly care.

A few minutes later, their shuttle left for Triton Station, a small facility so named because of its location—on the surface of the Neptunian moon, Triton. Designed originally as a research facility, over the past three decades, its primary purpose had shifted more towards being a triage hospital for the war wounded and a mental hospital for those suffering post-traumatic stress.

Triton Station's position on the outskirts of the solar system made it safe to use as a military jump destination without the need to coordinate the jumps with the Earth or Mars gates and their constant civilian traffic, yet its relative proximity to Earth and Mars made it possible to transport patients to larger facilities once stabilized.

It is also a common jumping off point for those operating under false credentials, he noted. *It was used both by people going officially undercover and a few... not so officially,* he knew, though he would never admit it. The six-twenty-seven program depended on absolute secrecy. Only two people knew all the details, and he was one. Admiral Candy Sinclair was the other.

And now we'll both be in the same place.

He shrugged off the thought.

No point worrying about it now.

Chapter Nineteen

Two days later

ADMIRAL Sinclair turned as Sydney entered her office.

"Admiral," Sydney said, "you asked me to tell you when Admiral Jenkins and Pierre's ship arrived."

The admiral nodded. "Yes."

"It arrived."

Candy Sinclair snorted in mild amusement, then stood and walked to the door. She continued alongside Sydney down the main corridor and through the glass "tube" to the landing bay.

"How are you enjoying your job as my assistant?" the admiral asked.

"Beats getting blown out an airlock," she replied.

Admiral Sinclair chuckled, then sighed. "I'm working on a more permanent placement for you and Laura, but it's not exactly easy. With Laura's security clearance, we could give her various jobs working around any of our bases, but there's a risk that she would be noticed. Basically, we need a high tech job well outside the reach of the Terran military. Our friends on the Colonial side of the border are looking."

"And me?"

"You are somewhat easier to hide. There's an artists' colony on Proxima Centauri III that seems like a good fit. We're just trying to find something for Laura in the vicinity so that you can be each other's safety nets."

Sydney smiled as the door opened into the shuttle bay. Laura stood just beyond, waiting for them.

When the door to the shuttle opened, Admiral Jenkins stepped out and walked over to Admiral Sinclair.

"Candy!" he shouted, spreading his arms in her direction.

"Thomas!" she exclaimed, returning the embrace. "So good to see you again in person. How's your wife?"

Thomas paused, frowned, then said, "Damn. I knew there was someone I forgot to call before I left. I told Amanda. I suppose she'll get word to Jessica."

Thomas waited a full three seconds to enjoy the look of horror on her face before shooting her a mischievous grin.

Candy breathed a sigh of relief.

"She's doing fine. Just spoke with her yesterday on the way here. She's supposed to come here next week so that you two can go shopping along the main strip of New Paradise on Mars while Ralph and I go fishing in Nebraska. How is Ralph, anyway?"

Candy glared at him.

Thomas bristled.

"Ralph is the same as always. An old, grouchy, windbag."

Thomas laughed.

Pierre stepped out of the shuttle next. Sydney's eyes lit up. Laura's eyes rolled back into her head.

Pierre walked over.

"Would one of you girls show Pierre to his quarters?" Admiral Sinclair asked.

Sydney shoved Laura out of the way and grabbed Pierre by the arm.

Laura rolled her eyes again as Sydney dragged Pierre through the door and into the hall.

"What about me?" Admiral Jenkins asked.

Laura snorted and smiled. "Right this way," she replied, pointing at the door.

"I'm glad you're finally here to help," Laura admitted once the doors shut. "Admiral Sinclair has me going through classified records looking for possible leaks, and it's starting to rot my brain."

Thomas Jenkins quirked a smile. "She always was good at that sort of thing."

"Looking for intel?"

He shook his head as the door to his quarters opened and he stepped inside.

"Rotting people's brains."

Laura chuckled, shook her head, and started back towards her paperwork.

***

2200 hours

Commander Ebberstein settled into orbit around Mercury. He knew that after weeks in space orbiting Mercury, there might be little left to find, so he had to be thorough.

Because it could take weeks to adequately determine whether the girls had actually perished there, he put the ship into a polar orbit, shut off the lights, stepped into the healing chamber, ordered the computer to begin scanning for any interesting debris, and got some much needed sleep.

By the time the computer found what it was looking for, nearly two weeks had passed.

Chapter Twenty

Two weeks later (December 15, 2390)

"WHAT do you mean he's gone?" Commander Ebberstein shouted as he stepped into Doctor Johnson's cramped private office.

Fred considered for a moment whether to sit in one of the two small chairs across the desk from the doctor's chair, but he decided to stand.

The doctor, meanwhile, found himself awkwardly facing his computer on the farthest part of the U-shaped desk, and thus had to spin a full 180 degrees just to see Fred, then swore as he realized he needed to spin another twenty or so degrees to make proper eye contact.

"I mean," Doctor Johnson replied, "that Admiral Jenkins ordered him remanded to his custody over two weeks ago."

"Why wasn't I notified!?!"

The doctor raised his eyebrows. "You didn't ask?"

The commander's eyes narrowed for a moment. Then, he bowed his head for a moment before regaining his composure.

"Where did the admiral take him?" Fred asked.

"Triton Station. Why?"

The commander stormed out of the room so quickly that he dropped a pile of papers. He quickly stooped to pick them up, then left as quickly as he came.

Doctor Johnson immediately stood and walked to the door. This was his hour off, so he felt the need to shut it to avoid any more non-critical interruptions. As he turned to walk back to his desk chair, he frowned. One piece of paper remained on the floor. He immediately recognized its contents by the distinctive header and the overall shape of the text.

It's a death certificate, he noted. Upon closer investigation, he saw that it was double sided and thus was just a copy. He also noted that, oddly enough, the printing on the back was *also* a copy of a death certificate.

He was just about to pocket the paperwork when he saw the name at the top.

Laura Rodolfo, he thought to himself. *Wasn't that the girl who came in with Pierre? And who was the other girl?*

He flipped the page over and saw it.

Sydney Caruthers.... Dear God, what have I done?

***

KLERN disabled the veil once he got into his quarters. No point in being an ensign now. His true form always felt more comfortable somehow.

The viewscreen on his wall suddenly chirped to indicate an incoming call. He quickly reactivated the veil.

So much for comfort, he thought.

But when the screen activated, he knew he had nothing to worry about.

"Fred!" he shouted. "Good to see you!"

"Are you alone?" Fred asked.

"Yes. Are you?"

"Yes," Fred replied.

"Then you can drop the veil," Klern suggested as he dropped his.

Fred shook his head. "See, that's the difference between you and me. You're always veiling yourself as a different person. Never twice the same combatant."

"And you, Merick?"

"I've been Fred for nearly half my life, Klern. This look seems normal to me. I'm actually more comfortable with the veil *on* now."

Klern nodded, pondering the significance of this.

"Anyway, I heard you were back on board," Fred continued. "What's this I hear about you going all space boy on us?"

Klern winced. *Guess it made somebody else's report.*

"The ship picked me up as programmed," Klern replied. "It was uncomfortable, but not life-threatening. I got out of the pod three days ago and found my way back here to check in. You know how it is."

Fred nodded.

Klern made a note to find out who spilled the beans and make sure he had a little accident.

"Well, I was just calling to congratulate you on the job you did with those two annoying women," Fred said.

Klern's eyes widened. "I thought *you* did that!"

Fred seemed taken aback. "I found Sydney's wedding ring in orbit around Mercury. She *is* dead, right?"

"I think so, but...."

"But you're not sure."

Klern sighed. "No, I'm not sure."

Fred cringed.

Klern thought he saw just a hint of worry in his compatriot's eye, but dismissed it as a figment of his overactive imagination.

"Well, we have a bigger problem," Fred replied. "Admiral Jenkins apparently took Pierre out of our good doctor's protective custody. They are on Triton Station."

Klern winced. *Triton Station is one of the most heavily guarded installations in the fleet. You can't even set* ***foot*** *on the base without orders signed in triplicate.*

"I think it's time to invoke our ace in the hole," Fred continued.

"Skylarov."

"Skylarov."

Klern sighed. *I was hoping we could keep him out of this. Involving our admiral always makes things... messy....*

"Okay," he finally agreed. "We bring in Skylarov. You'll leave in an hour."

"Leave? Why can't we just call him?" Fred asked.

"Two reasons," Klern replied. "First, the orders must be on paper, in triplicate, and signed by hand. Admiral Skylarov is on portable command station 3 inspecting the front lines right now, so unless we want to wait for him to return... well...."

"And the second reason?"

"Terran Command Station is about to have a little... 'accident'," Klern replied. "Had I known you were still here, I would have contacted you already."

"Tonight, tonight, the traitors die," Fred sang.

Klern smirked at the Gilbert and Sullivan reference.

"More like mid-January," he replied. "The flight crew is still procuring the explosives, and I'm still looking for places to conceal the navigation beacons to help guide the ship to the right spot. Either way, I wouldn't stick around here too long if I were you. It could be sooner if things go well."

Fred looked disappointed. Klern couldn't bring himself to care. He didn't need anyone's approval, least of all a permie. Halfway to human, they called them. They lived all their lives beyond the veil; sometimes even Klern couldn't tell them from the real thing. Ugh.

"Look, I have my task here," Klern continued, "and as nice as it would have been if I had taken out the girls,

Pierre, and maybe even Admiral Jenkins with it, in the end, it doesn't matter as long as I get paid."

"Spoken like a true merc," Fred replied.

Klern bowed regally. "At your service. Go. Find Skylarov, kill Pierre. It's not my mission anymore."

Fred nodded, and the viewscreen went black.

The conversation over, Klern threw himself on the bed and turned on the news.

> "You're watching TANN, the Terran Alliance News Network, with news updates every hour on the hour," the anchor said. "Terran Alliance forces on the outskirts of the Chataris sector were pushed back today when they lost a key battle near K17551. Terran forces are reportedly massing near Lenora Prime for a counteroffensive. Commercial traffic is advised to use caution when traveling near the front lines."

Klern turned off the viewscreen and went to sleep. *It's Fred's problem now.*

***

Doctor Johnson fumbled with the communications controls on the wall-mounted viewscreen in his office as he opened a visual link to Admiral Jenkins.

"Admiral," he panted, "Fred, evil, killed...."

"Slow down!" Thomas replied. "I can't understand you."

The doctor pulled out a paper bag and began hyperventilating into it. After a moment, he put it down and resumed the conversation.

"I think Fred Ebberstein may have killed two women," he said. "And I just told him where to find you and Pierre. I think he might be trying to kill you, too."

Admiral Jenkins stared at the screen, unsure what to say. The girls weren't dead, of course, but he could not trust the doctor with that information. And if he told the doctor that he knew about Fred, that could raise suspicions that they conferred prior to the girls' death, which might cast suspicion on whether their death was real. And even if it didn't, it would still put him and Pierre at further risk.

So Jenkins told him exactly what was required.

"I saw the security footage," Jenkins said. "Fred did try to kill the girls, but their death was an accident."

"Are you sure?"

Jenkins shrugged. "As sure as I can be."

The doctor nodded.

"Don't worry," Jenkins added. "He can't come here without approval of an admiral, signed in triplicate, and I can't imagine any admiral granting that permission."

The doctor nodded.

At least no admiral I know, he thought grimly.

"Oh, one more thing," the doctor said. "I've seen him hanging around with an ensign I don't recognize. I believe his name tag said..."

The screen went suddenly black.

What's wrong with this thing? the doctor wondered as he tried in vain to reestablish the connection. He smacked the screen a few times with the butt of his hand, but of course this, too, was ineffectual.

So he turned to his computer and began composing an email message. He had just finished typing the greeting when his computer screen turned suddenly red.

As he looked down at his chest, he understood why.

***

FRED walked from his quarters on Terran Command Station to the shuttle bay and took his personal shuttle back to Beta Persei. He knew that there were no folding gates near Triton, so he decided to spend the travel time on the front end by picking up a larger transport ship with a folding drive. Fortunately, he had one at his disposal at Terran Command Outpost 72.

To Beta Persei, it is, then, he thought.

As he sat down at the controls, he keyed the radio.

"Departure control, this is the shuttlecraft Nimrod requesting gate transit to Beta Persei Gate."

He waited for the reply.

"Shuttlecraft... Nimrod," the voice replied, followed by some hushed laughter, "this is departure control. We're a little busy with all traffic held for a Presidential transport. Suggest you divert to Mars gate."

Ugh. Three more hours, he thought.

Fifteen painful hours later, he arrived at TCO-72, then stepped out of his personal shuttle and directly onto the waiting transport ship. Because the station was well beyond the safety margins for the Beta Persei folding gate, he was able to fold as soon as the docking clamps were disengaged and he cleared the artificial gravity well generated by the station.

Despite folding into the designated arrival zone for the Chataris sector, it took eight more hours to reach Lenora Prime. He arrived to find Admiral Skylarov already sound asleep for the night, so he vowed to find him the next morning.

***

KLERN grumbled as he lifted Doctor Johnson's corpse onto a gurney.

Why, Klern wondered, *do I always have to clean up Merick's messes?*

After Klern had gotten the body onto the gurney and finished cleaning up the blood, he pressed a button on his data pad. About ten seconds later, the power failed throughout the deck. In the darkness, Klern rolled the gurney into the leftmost upper lift.

After a minute, the power came back on, and the left lift automatically headed down to its lowest level, a service level below the lowest level that had an actual button.

Klern then stepped out of the lift into the service level, pushing the gurney in front of him. Ahead of him was a single descent module, designed for evacuation during the station's construction. It could plummet into Earth's atmosphere and allow a crew of ten people to escape.

Klern considered launching the body out of the airlock adjacent to it, but thought better of it.

They shouldn't be able to connect it with me even if they find the body, he thought, *but I don't want to take any chances.*

So Klern spurned the airlock and put the body into the descent module instead. After yanking a couple of breakers to disable the parachute system, he programmed it for an uncontrolled descent over the Atlantic Ocean, stepped out of the descent module, closed the airlock doors, and waited for the separation sequence to commence before taking the lift back up to civilization.

Mission accomplished.

***

The next day (December 17, 2390)

Admiral Skylarov's door chimed. He pressed a few buttons on his desk, and the door opened. Fred entered.

"What in blue blazes do you think you're doing here, Fred?" Skylarov asked immediately.

Fred stammered for a moment before answering. "S-s-s-sir, we have a... situation. Pierre has spoken to Admiral Jenkins, and the admiral took him out of our doctor's care."

"WHAT!?!" Skylarov shouted.

"It happened while I was making sure the girls were dead," he replied. "They are. I found a ring floating in space that belonged to that Sydney girl. Badly charred, half melted, but identifiable."

Skylarov stewed for a moment.

"You're lucky you caught me. I'm heading back to Earth tomorrow to fetch a team to regain access to a base on the planet below us. We need to recover some crucial artifacts and records before we lose this ground to the Colonials."

"Why don't you do it yourself?" Fred asked.

"I thought it would be amusing to send Amanda Jenkins to do it. Sentimental reasons, with her brother and all. Should make it easier to explain to her father. Amanda knows too much, so I'm going to make sure she doesn't come back from this mission."

Fred nodded. "We need access to Triton Station to take out Pierre and the admiral."

Skylarov shook his head. "What you ask is... impossible."

"You have the authority to write the orders," Fred insisted.

"It's not that," Skylarov replied. "Weapons are forbidden on Triton Station. The scanners are very accurate. Going there would do you no good unless you intend to strangle him...."

"There must be a better way. Is there... something else I could use that... isn't a weapon?"

Skylarov appeared to think about this for several moments. Then, he slowly drew up the corners of his mouth into a grim smile.

"There is... one thing," Skylarov said finally. "Come back in four weeks."

Fred scratched his head.

"Four weeks?"

"The base on the planet below," Skylarov replied, "is on a time lock of sorts. It was locked up for 25 years. I'll recover the..."

Skylarov's voice trailed off.

"What's wrong?"

Skylarov shook his head.

"I can't think of a way to describe it without ruining the surprise...."

Fred gave him a puzzled look.

"It may take a few weeks, but I'll ship it to you at Triton station," Skylarov said with an air of finality.

Fred nodded and sighed.

"In the meantime," he continued, handing Fred a packet of papers, "here are your orders, signed, in triplicate. Go gather information."

Chapter Twenty-one

Three days later (December 20, 2390)

VLADIMIR Rejndorv was a heavyset man, with a build and appearance that made him look a lot like a stereotypical gangster, all the way down to the cotton-mouthed voice. Only two things shattered this image: his cheery personality (albeit only on the surface) and his poor taste in clothing. Today was no exception; he sat in a T-shirt and sweat pants in his reading room.

Admiral Skylarov approached cautiously.

"Come! Come!" Rejndorv shouted exuberantly.

After a few moments, Skylarov reached the chair across from him.

"Sit, have a seat."

Skylarov did as he was told.

"So what brings you to me on this, the day of my daughter's wedding?"

Skylarov laughed for a moment, then realized he was serious, and gulped.

"I've come to make a proposal," Skylarov told him.

"Oh? What kind of proposal?" Rejndorv replied.

"The kind you like," Skylarov replied, smiling.

Rejndorv stared at him for a moment, then smiled himself.

"How intriguing."

***

"He WHAT!?!" Admiral Jenkins bellowed.

Admiral Sinclair jumped a bit at the harshness of his tone.

"Look, Tom," she replied. "I don't like this any more than you do, but those are Admiral Skylarov's orders, and this Fred guy is in his chain of command."

Admiral Jenkins shook his head. "Call up Fleet Admiral Ramirez and overrule him."

"Tom, you know I can't do that," she replied.

Admiral Sinclair paused for a moment and sighed, then pressed her hands to her face and stretched it outwards in exasperation as she leaned her head back. When her hands finally came to rest, they were in a prayerful position beneath her tilted head. Then, she leaned her head forward and rested her nose on her fingertips before moving her hands back down to the table.

"I can't act without proof," she said finally. "Two witnesses does not constitute proof. Sure, they say it was Fred who tried to kill them, but even they can't be certain, and the security cameras were... mysteriously offline."

"How convenient," Jenkins replied.

"Isn't it, though? Ten years without a malfunction, and the data storage pools chose that day to catch on fire."

Jenkins nodded.

"Anyway," she continued, "Ramirez would never overrule Skylarov. You should know that better than anyone."

Jenkins grumbled. Two years earlier, he'd had a disagreement with Skylarov when he gave the order to send Colonial troops to attack a suspected terrorist safe house on Mars. The evidence was sketchy at best, but Ramirez sided with Skylarov. The safe house turned out to be an orphanage, and thirteen kids died in the fire. And even now, Ramirez said he would do it again if faced with the same evidence.

Since then, Jenkins had learned the art of following the *letter* of his orders. When Ramirez made a bad call that Tom's chain of command was involved in carrying out, Tom invariably found ways to obey the orders without actually obeying the orders. For example, a few weeks ago, the fleet admiral had ordered them to bomb a bunch of unarmed civilians—*a clearly illegal order,* he noted. When the fleet admiral gave the order to drop the bombs, they did—in the middle of empty parking lots, and without arming them first, mind you, but they technically *did* drop the bombs on the village.

Ramirez had docked his pay three times over these acrobatics, but thus far, the admiralty review board had always failed to find sufficient reason for a formal court-martial.

Indeed, Jenkins knew full well who Ramirez would back, much to his chagrin, but knowing that Admiral Sinclair was right didn't make it suck any less.

"So what do we do?" Jenkins asked.

"For now, we do nothing. His orders are to oversee the rehabilitation of Pierre. He will be searched thoroughly for any weapons, and he will not find any here on the base."

Jenkins shook his head. "What about his ship? He could smuggle weapons aboard that way."

Admiral Sinclair just smiled. Admiral Jenkins raised an eyebrow in reply.

"When he gets here tomorrow," Sinclair answered, "I'm going to allow him on base, but I'll tell him that his ship cannot stay. All of our unused docking bays are on reserve to hold a shipment of artifacts in a few weeks. And to think that I was about to refuse Skylarov's request to store them here...."

Admiral Jenkins nodded. "That should buy us a day or two while he flies back to Terran Command Station and finds someone to fly back here and drop him off. Then what?"

"Well, as I said, he'll be *thoroughly* searched."

Jenkins smiled. "Body cavity search?"

Candy nodded. "By Big Bertha."

***

"In principle, this is intriguing," Rejndorv said. "However, there is still the matter of my fee. Five million Euros."

Admiral Skylarov winced.

"Things are complicated right now," Skylarov replied. "Most of our organization's accounts are frozen. As for my personal accounts, Admiral Jenkins is already looking into me, and I'm sure he is watching my finances closely."

Rejndorv frowned. "As much as I enjoy murder and larceny, I'm failing to see what's in it for me."

"Revenge," Skylarov replied.

Rejndorv raised an eyebrow.

"I'm not sure if you remember," he continued, "but the accident that killed your brothers was caused by a certain Donovan Jenkins."

Rejndorv nodded. "And?"

Skylarov stared at him for a few seconds before replying.

"Thomas Donovan Jenkins Jr., to be precise," Skylarov said, "the son of one Admiral Thomas Jenkins, the brother of one Amanda Jenkins."

Rejndorv's eyes widened, then narrowed. "Vendetta."

***

The next morning

ADMIRAL Jenkins caught up with Laura in the middle of her morning jog around the central atrium. Laura turned her head.

"Oh, hey, Mr. J!" she shouted.

"Hey, Laura," he replied, panting. "I guess you've heard about Fred by now."

"That he's coming here, you mean?"

"Yes."

Laura shrugged. "Not anything I can do about it."

Admiral Jenkins nodded. "We have a ship heading for that artist colony," he replied. "We could send you both. You'd be bored out of your mind, but the offer is on the table."

Laura shook her head. "If we run, they'll find us, and we'll just have to run again. This ends. Now."

Admiral Jenkins nodded again. "Well, I don't trust him not to try anything. I know we don't allow weapons on the base, but I just can't help but think...."

"Don't worry about it. Candy has it covered."

Thomas Jenkins scratched his head, shrugged, and broke pace. He wasn't sure what she meant by that. In fact, he couldn't even begin to imagine.

Flying monkeys with orders to throw him out an airlock, he mused, *or maybe just the automated gun turrets they have in each hall—not that there are enough of them to take him out without killing hostages....*

He shrugged and headed back to his temporary office.

***

LIEUTENANT John Phillips turned when Admiral Sinclair stepped into his office. As the chief security officer of Triton Station, it was his job to oversee all aspects of security.

Nothing happened on the station without attracting his attention. That's why the email he had received the night before had been such a shock. It caught him completely off guard.

"Admiral," he said. "Thank you for coming in. I'm more than a little concerned about these latest changes."

Admiral Sinclair nodded. "I know you don't approve of having an armory on the station, but under the circumstances, I think it best to be prepared."

Lieutenant Phillips crooked his head. "Prepared for what?"

The admiral shook her head. "If I knew that," she replied, "I wouldn't be stocking up the armory. Besides, with the attack on Terran Command Station last month, Tom and I feel that we should not have such limited emergency response capabilities."

Lieutenant Phillips crossed his arms over his chest.

"I know," she said. "You don't like it."

He shook his head. "It's not that I don't like having an armory around. It's just that it seems reckless and irresponsible to have live weapons and munitions within easy reach of hundreds of people recovering from post-traumatic stress disorder."

"Relax, John," she replied. "Only five people will have access: me, you, and the three members of your security staff."

He pondered this for a moment.

"Okay," he replied reluctantly. "Where are we going to put it, then?"

Admiral Sinclair smiled. "Everywhere."

"Pardon?"

***

"TRITON Station," Fred said into the radio, "this is the shuttlecraft Lacedaemon *(which he incorrectly pronounced 'lace demon')* requesting permission to land."

"That's affirmative," a young man's voice replied. "You are cleared to land for a three-hour drop-off."

Fred shook his head in confusion. "I'm sorry, but my orders are to remain here indefinitely."

"And your shuttlecraft," the man replied, "has permission to remain for three hours. We're expecting a shipment of artifacts next month by order of Admiral Skylarov, and as a result, we do not have room for any long-term shuttle storage. If you need to stay longer than three hours, we recommend that you fly to Terran Command Station, leave your shuttle in one of their ample docking bays, and have someone fly you back here."

Fred stammered for a moment. "O-o-o-okay."

And with those words, his shuttle departed as quickly as it had arrived.

***

The next day

FRED stepped out onto the flight deck and walked to the computer station. After receiving temporary quarters, he proceeded to them. His viewscreen was beeping at him by the time he walked into the room.

"Fred," Klern bellowed as the screen sprang to life, "why are you back here?"

Fred was momentarily taken aback. *How did he know?*

"They said I could not keep my shuttle there," Fred replied. "Something about a shipment of artifacts that would take much of their shuttle bay space."

"You idiot," Klern replied. "Triton Station has an entire planet's surface to store shuttles on. They sent you back because you were made."

"Impossible!" Fred shouted. "I destroyed all the evidence. They can't possibly know that I was involved in anything."

Klern grimaced as he reached down and pressed a few buttons on a control pad.

"I'm sorry to have to do this," Klern said calmly.

Suddenly, Fred's appearance changed.

"What did you do?" Fred asked, tapping wildly on the controls for his veil, to no avail.

"Enjoy prison," Klern replied, and closed the connection.

Fred asked the viewscreen to switch to the Terran Alliance News Network.

"An anonymous source has reported sightings of the known colonial terrorist Stephen Martini on board Terran Command Station. Martini, whose aliases include such historical figures as Caesar Augustus, Judas Iscariot, and Richard Nixon, is wanted in both the Colonial Alliance and the Terran Alliance for crimes against humanity."

The viewscreen suddenly switched to a stock photo of the man in question. Fred's eyes widened with a sense of familiarity. He turned and looked at a mirror, and though the face in the mirror that looked back at him was older, there was little doubt that he was now the man on the screen.

"Martini is believed to have played a key role in planning the 2360 bombing of the presidential inauguration on Kinji, the 2372 gas attack on the subway system in New San Francisco, and the 2385 suicide bombing that killed foreign dignitaries from Proxima Centauri III during the summit in Madrid."

Fred blinked.

"Martini is believed to be armed and extremely dangerous."

With that, Fred ran. He ran out of his quarters, down the hall, across the Crew's Quarter, and towards the lift.

As he pressed the activation button, the lift doors opened. He stepped quickly into the lift and pressed and held the button for the bottom floor to access the service level below it. According to the ship's schematic, an emergency descent module clung to the station's side on that floor, left over from when the station was still being constructed. He would be much harder to find if he could make it to the surface.

The doors closed, and the lift began falling. It accelerated as it went down. Then, suddenly, the lights went dark, and the car slowed to a halt.

Fred's panic overcame him, and he began climbing the walls. Literally. He pushed the escape hatch open at the top of the car in an effort to climb up into the lift shaft. He managed to get up onto the roof of the car, then sealed the door behind him.

That's when the lights came back on. Suddenly, the car began moving. Like many elevators, in the absence of a floor call, the cars automatically return to opposite ends of the shaft. Unfortunately for Fred, this one was heading *up*.

Fred scrambled in vain trying to open the roof hatch, but being an escape hatch, it was designed to let people out, not to let people back in. And so he watched in horror as the top of the lift shaft grew ever closer.

***

CRUNCH. Laura's breakfast cereal made a noise that could only be described as ethereal. It was as though a single voice cried out in terror and was suddenly silenced.

Sydney sat across from her and smirked.

"You look happy," Laura observed. "What's the sitch?"

Sydney pointed at a guy walking down the hall with a hand trolley loaded up with equipment and grinned ear to ear.

Laura rolled her eyes. “Oh, Sydney....”

Behind them, Admiral Jenkins and Admiral Sinclair sat, eating breakfast.

“Tom,” Admiral Sinclair began, “we have another request for a personnel transfer from Admiral Skylarov.”

“Who is it this time?” he replied.

“Somebody named Ensign Nichols. Scheduled for arrival on Sunday, January 13th.”

“Never heard of ’im,” Tom replied.

“Nor I,” Admiral Sinclair noted, “but I’m nervous about Skylarov sending anyone, particularly given the last person he sent.”

Admiral Jenkins nodded. “Cavity search?”

Admiral Sinclair smiled and shook her head. “A little much, I’m afraid. Not without probable cause, anyway.”

Laura overheard their conversation and spun around.

“What’s he look like?” she asked.

Admiral Sinclair pulled out her data pad and brought up a photo.

Laura shook her head.

Sydney’s eyes widened.

“I’ve seen him. On Terran Command Outpost 72. He left the hall a few hours before we did, and I never saw him again.”

Admiral Sinclair’s brow grew furrowed.

“Was that before or after the attempt on Pierre’s life?” she asked.

Sydney thought about this for several moments.

“I’m not sure. Before, I think.”

Admiral Jenkins turned and looked Sydney right in the eyes with a look that would freeze the surface of the sun.

“In that case,” he replied, “we may have a problem.”

***

"Ensign Nichols," Captain Barber bellowed. "My console is showing some sort of fault in lift tube number three. Could you send someone to check it out?"

"Right away," Klern replied. "I'll put Ralph on it."

Being shift lead has its privileges, Klern thought. He tried to keep the amusement out of his voice when he realized that he was sending the most squeamish engineer on the base to go find Fred.

After about ten minutes of mindless banter and a few scattered landing and departure requests, Ralph's voice cut through the din of command and control.

"C&C, this is Ralph. I'm here," Ralph said over his radio, "and I'm opening the doors now."

Klern bit his lip to stifle the laughter as the sound of Ralph losing his lunch echoed through C&C.

"What do you see?" Captain Barber asked.

"It's... a body," Ralph replied. Then, after a pause, he lost more of his lunch. After what seemed like an eternity, he continued. "Hey, I think I recognize this guy!"

Excellent, Klern thought. *It's a pity Doctor Johnson won't be around to sign off on the death certificate. It's a good thing we were able to find someone to replace him. Ah, the irony.*

Chapter Twenty-two

January 5, 2390

"ADMIRAL on the bridge!" Klern shouted as Admiral Skylarov walked out of the lift onto the command deck of Terran Command Station's C&C. Amanda Jenkins rose to attention. Joseph Kurtz sat in his chair with his leg in a splint; he merely spun his chair around.

"As you were," Skylarov instructed.

Klern watched as an engineering tech plugged a new circuit board into the underside of a console, then cursed loudly as smoke poured out of it within seconds.

"Sir," Klern bellowed.

"Yes, ensign," the admiral said testily.

"We've been having some electrical problems up here today, and, with all due respect to the admiral, this is probably not the safest place for you to be right now."

"With all due respect to the ensign," he replied, "this admiral will go wherever he wants to go."

"Sir, yes sir!" Klern replied, feigning embarrassment.

"Relax, ensign," he said. "I'm about to send some of you on an important mission. Carlos, Sanderson, Jenkins, my ready room at 1500 hours."

Admiral Skylarov continued to talk with the mission team for a few minutes. After they left, Klern and Skylarov were the only people remaining on the bridge, with the next shift not due to arrive for almost fifteen minutes.

"So, Mikhail," Klern said after disabling the internal security system to ensure that they could converse privately, "how are things going?"

Admiral Skylarov chuckled. "They're great, Klern. Have all the materials arrived?"

Klern shook his head. "The detonators just got here this morning. The beacons are in place, and the ship is basically ready. The explosives are ready to plant, but without the detonators, it wouldn't be a very big bang."

"So day-by-day slip, then?"

Klern nodded. "They're installing the detonators and planting the explosives today and tomorrow, while most of the staff is planetside for the weekend. The big bang is scheduled for Monday night, assuming no delays."

Skylarov nodded. "Very good."

Klern nodded. "So I'll head to Mars on Monday afternoon, then lie low until I leave for Triton Station on Saturday or so. And you?"

"I'm scheduled to leave again for the front lines tomorrow," Skylarov replied. "Don't worry about me. I'll be long gone before you have your little party."

Klern chuckled. "Well, I'm not sure about the party, but there will definitely be fireworks and a barbecue."

***

ADMIRAL Jenkins smiled when his daughter's face appeared on his viewscreen.

"Amanda! Nice to see you!"

Amanda smiled. "Good to see you, too, Dad."

"What brings you to call so late in the evening?"

Amanda paused. *Is it late?* She checked her watch. *1900 hours and change. Damn. I'm late for dinner with Joseph. Better hurry.*

"I didn't realize it was quite so late."

"Dinner with Joseph?" her father asked knowingly.

Amanda nodded. "Anyway, I thought you should know that Skylarov is sending us on a mission to Lenora Prime."

Her father's eyes widened. "They're not unsealing the base? Tell me they're not unsealing the base."

Amanda nodded. "Why? What should I know? What's down there?"

"Promise me you won't go down to the planet. Stay on the ship. Make up any excuse."

Amanda could see the terror in his eyes. *Something is very wrong.*

"What's down there, Dad?" she asked again, more insistently this time.

He told her.

***

PIERRE stepped warily into Admiral Sinclair's office.

"You asked to see me, Admiral?"

"Yes, Lieutenant," she replied. "Please be seated."

Pierre sat down across the desk from her, then folded his hands across his lap.

"I'm sure by now you've noticed some unusual maintenance work being done around the station," Admiral Sinclair said.

"You mean the secret weapons caches you've been installing all over the station?"

She froze.

"It's not like it isn't obvious. Maintenance teams working at night, shipments that don't appear on any shipping manifests, sections of the station locked down with high security clearance...."

"Wow," she replied. "So pretty much everyone knows?"

He shook his head. "I have trouble sleeping, so I take walks in the wee hours of the morning."

Admiral Sinclair nodded.

"Well, the reason for it is..."

"Fred," he said, interrupting.

"Yes."

"He's not the one you have to worry about," Pierre replied. "He's the devil we know. There was another assassin who had the ability to mimic my face and subvert our security. If history tells us anything, it is that when you see one termite, there are others hiding in the woodwork."

Admiral Sinclair nodded.

"Speaking of termites," she replied, "we have reason to believe that there are several other high-ranking personnel who have been compromised."

"Why are you telling me this?" Pierre asked.

Admiral Sinclair stood and walked to the door, closed it, and walked calmly back to her seat.

"In case you haven't noticed," she said finally, "most of the military personnel on base are... to put it bluntly, in dire straits emotionally and mentally. The remainder of the personnel are almost all civilian except for a six-man security force, plus myself and Admiral Jenkins. Needless to say, we're all a little on edge, and when one of the security team saw you snooping around last night... well, they grew concerned. I needed to know what you knew."

Pierre nodded.

"More importantly," she continued, "I need your word that this goes no further than this room. Even the maintenance crews don't know what's going on yet. There are only two people who know what's happening. You make three."

"Admiral Jenkins?"

The admiral shook her head. "He's supposed to be retired already. He has enough to worry about. I don't want to burden him with this. Things are going to get ugly around here, and I'm hoping he'll be off relaxing on some nice beach planet by then."

Pierre nodded. "Fair enough, but if things get ugly...."

Admiral Sinclair grimaced. "You can tell him if I don't tell him first. I've already granted you both full access to all of the weapons cabinets."

She smiled, raised her eyebrows, and added, "Just in case."

Chapter Twenty-three

Monday afternoon (January 7, 2391)

KLERN boarded his shuttle a few hours late. The charges were set.

He pressed a few buttons and left the shuttle bay without contacting departure control.

No reason to tip anyone off.

Three minutes later, he reached a safe distance and enabled the folding comm link. A few seconds later, Vladimir Rejndorv appeared on the screen.

"We're ready," Klern said, simply.

"As are we," Rejndorv replied.

Klern paused for a moment to make sure he was far enough from the station. He was.

"You have a go," Klern said.

Rejndorv nodded and closed the link. A few button presses later, a carefully written computer virus took over the Earth and Mars gates and disabled them both for five minutes, then spread to the newly installed defense satellites to ensure that there were no surprises.

Ten seconds later, an unmanned ship folded a few thousand feet from the station, traveling at about 1,000 miles per hour—a mere crawl as interstellar ships go, but still plenty fast enough to get the job done.

Klern had to shield his eyes from the flash of light as Terran Command Station exploded in a giant fireball. The secondary nuclear explosion when the reactor core went supercritical was an added bonus.

Klern smiled.

All in a day's work, he thought as he keyed in a course for Mars.

***

ADMIRAL Jenkins and Admiral Sinclair stared in awe at the images before them on TANN.

> "You're watching TANN, the Terran Alliance News Network, with news updates every hour on the hour," the anchorwoman said. "Shock and horror were the words of the day as a stolen Colonial ship reportedly flown by terrorists crashed into and destroyed Terran Command Station."
>
> The onscreen image changed to show the ship heading towards the station, as seen from a security camera on the outer ring. A few seconds later, it cut away to footage from a nearby ship or satellite that showed the Colonial ship crashing first into the outer ring, smashing through it on its way to the central nexus, then exploding in a giant fireball after colliding with the central nexus itself.

Moments later, various parts of the station began to explode onscreen. A few seconds after that, a giant flash washed out the image sensor on the camera as the nuclear reactor exploded. When the image returned from white, there was nothing left but debris.

"Some portions of the station did remain relatively intact, however," the anchor continued. "Part of the outer ring was knocked free from the station in the initial explosion and escaped the reactor explosion that destroyed the rest of the station. No word yet on whether there were any survivors."

"We'll keep you up-to-date minute by minute as the situation unfolds," she continued, then paused for a moment to let the prompter catch up.

"In Mars news...."

Admiral Jenkins continued to stare for almost a minute after Admiral Sinclair shut off the viewscreen. His moment of silence was interrupted when Laura ran in.

"Did you..." Laura shouted excitedly, then stopped short.

Admiral Jenkins turned towards her, then looked over at Admiral Sinclair.

"Did Amanda..."

Admiral Sinclair rolled her chair over to her computer terminal and brought up the flight logs. She nodded. "Amanda left the station a few hours before the explosion."

Admiral Jenkins relaxed visibly.

"And Fred?" Laura asked.

Admiral Sinclair shook her head. "He just... disappeared. The station has no record of him being there. At all."

Laura shivered.

***

KLERN's shuttle settled onto the surface of Mars. He flashed his orders from Skylarov at the landing pad security team, and they waved him through without question (though, he noted, the security detail was somewhat superfluous anyway, given the fifty-million-plus square miles of unused land on which a shuttle could land).

After walking past the Connely Center, he made his way to the nearest hotel and booked a room. No sooner had he walked in than the viewscreen signalled an incoming message.

Klern activated the viewscreen, and Skylarov appeared.

"Klern," Skylarov said, "I have some information for you about the... well... package."

Klern nodded. "You told Fred you would deliver something that could be used as a weapon, but you wouldn't tell him what."

Skylarov laughed. "And ruin the surprise? I just wish I could see the look on your face when you open the box."

Klern shivered.

"Just three things to tell you," he said, then looked at Klern with a concerned expression. "Are you taking notes?"

Klern fumbled with the hotel desk drawer and pulled out a complimentary notepad.

"I am now," Klern replied. "Go ahead."

"Three things. One, open the small box—number 3158026—first."

Klern scratched down the number and a note to that effect, then looked at Skylarov with a puzzled look on his face.

"Two," Skylarov continued, "it will be there in about a week or so. Try to lie low until then."

"And three?" Klern asked.

"Three. If you don't turn on the device inside that box before you open box number 3158027, you'd better not be standing in front of it when the box opens."

Klern gulped.

"Bring food," Skylarov continued. "A whole lot of it."

***

Four days later (Jan. 11, 2391)

"I demand to see my father!" Amanda shouted.

The secretary in front of his office is such a pain in the ass, she thought.

"I'm sorry, miss, but as I told you before, Admiral Jenkins is in a very important meeting," the secretary replied.

"Well I think he'll be very interested to find out that *I'M DEAD*!" Amanda shouted, pointing to a data tablet showing an electronic death certificate dated the day before.

"Well, now, this *is* interesting," the secretary said. "I thought you smelled funny."

"Stupid bitch," Amanda muttered.

"What was that," she snapped.

"I said it was a computer glitch," Amanda answered.

"Yes, I suppose it was," the woman answered.

Amanda jumped as the door behind her swung open. Her father emerged, accompanied by two men she had never seen before.

"Ah, Amanda, my little hell-raiser," he said cheerily. "How are you today?"

"Funny you should ask," she answered, handing him the pad.

Her father shivered.

"I'm sorry you had to find out like this," he told her. "I'll explain everything later... some place more private... but not right now. For now, you and the rest of your crew no longer exist."

At that moment, Amanda noticed that the room was quite warm. She found it strange that he would shiver—very strange, indeed.

"Join me for dinner?" he asked. "We have a lot to talk about."

Amanda nodded.

A moment later, Laura walked in. Suddenly, the secretary vanished into nothingness. Amanda did a double take.

"T-minus two days and counting," Laura said to Admiral Jenkins. Laura then noticed that they were not alone, and added, "Oh, hi, Amanda."

Amanda just stared and pointed at the empty chair.

Laura laughed at her for a moment. "It's a hologram with a basic AI. Primitive, rude... you know, the sort of secretary that keeps everyone out until I can get back from my bathroom break."

Amanda chuckled awkwardly and nodded as though this made some sort of sense.

"Who were those guys in your office?" Amanda asked.

"The man on the left," he replied, "was Lieutenant Phillips, the station's chief of security."

"And the other guy?"

"Admiral Jameson?" her father replied incredulously, his concern palpable. "You remember him."

Amanda was equally shocked. "That's Jameson? I didn't even recognize him."

"Well, to be fair, you haven't seen him since you were eight," her father replied.

"Nine," she countered. "And he had hair then."

Everyone chuckled.

"We've been getting ready for an expected arrival," her father told her. "It's going to be a little rough around here pretty soon. I'll tell you everything later. 1800 hours at the Hot Spot?"

Amanda nodded. "See you there."

Once Amanda was safely out of earshot, Admiral Jenkins addressed Laura.

"You know the people who were tailing you?"

Laura nodded.

"How would you like to return the favor?"

Laura's eyes widened.

"We just got word that a person of interest just checked into a hotel on Mars," he continued. "I'd like to send you and an old friend of mine to perform some surveillance."

"Why me?"

"Sydney doesn't have the stomach for spy stuff, Pierre is officially not on active duty, Candy would break a hip, and there's no one else I trust."

"Except your friend."

He nodded. "I think."

***

THE air was motionless in the evac station. An eerie stillness swept over Vladimir Rejndorv and his companion, shrouded in black.

"So how long have they been down there?" Rejndorv asked in a coarse whisper.

"Thirty-one hours," came the shadowy figure's reply.

"Is everything ready?" Rejndorv asked.

Thirty more troops, all dressed in black, appeared in the distant shadows for a moment, then were gone.

"Completely. Tomorrow, we will send in the... 'rescue' party," Admiral Skylarov replied as he stepped forward into the light.

Rejndorv nodded.

"Just so we're clear," Rejndorv noted, "I'll be going in first. Tessa should recognize me."

Skylarov frowned.

"We'll be disabling the security system," Skylarov replied. "It shouldn't matter what Tessa does. She won't be able to cause us harm."

"Still," Rejndorv replied, "she *can't* hurt me. And if anyone sees you...."

Skylarov nodded. "Fair enough."

No one said anything for a few moments. Rejndorv took the opportunity to review the plans. When he got to page three, he became troubled.

"Question," Rejndorv said. "What, precisely, do you intend to do once we have captured the mechlizard?"

Skylarov simply shook his head in silence.

***

The neon lights flickered on and off rhythmically over the Hot Spot on Triton Station. A mere five minutes into the conversation, Amanda was already getting tired of the place, but she knew she had to persevere. She knew her father wouldn't have pulled a six-twenty-seven without good reason. According to the official mission logs, when Joseph's shuttle crash-landed on Lenora Prime, Amanda had attempted a rescue mission and had burned up while entering the atmosphere after a similar malfunction in her mini-shuttle.

"There's a lot more going on in the Terran Alliance than you're probably aware of," her father continued. "Several key bases have been taken by rebel forces, and all signs point to traitors in our midst—conspirators willing to aid the enemy."

"What does this have to do with me?" Amanda asked.

"We suspect that Admiral Skylarov may be one of those traitors," he told her.

"And so you faked my death so that I could... study Skylarov safely?" she asked.

"No. I faked your death to get you out of harm's way," he answered. "I want you to go back home to Earth and stay with your stepmother and your sister. Don't come back out here until I get home."

"I can't do that, Dad," Amanda informed him matter-of-factly. "I have friends trapped on Lenora Prime in a secret base that *we* helped create. In twenty-eight years, they will have long since starved to death. I have to get them out. There's only one more window after tomorrow before the doors close again... for the rest of their lives."

"Amanda, you know I can't let you do that," he replied. "That area is controlled by our enemies now. It isn't safe. And besides, they can probably find their way out much more easily than you can find a way in."

"Dammit, Father!" she shouted. "I have to try!"

"It's not your decision," he said testily.

"It *is* my decision. I'm *going* to Lenora Prime," she told him. "The decision is made."

"Amanda! Don't do this," he pleaded. "You'll be jeopardizing your career... your life...."

Amanda stood, as if to leave. "Like you ever cared about that," she scolded.

"If you go to Lenora Prime, I may not be able to protect you," he warned.

By this time, Amanda was halfway across the room. She angrily marched towards the door, pausing only for a moment to snap back a reply. "What are you going to do? Court-martial me? I'm dead, remember?"

"Amanda!" her father shouted.

The bar grew suddenly silent. Thomas Jenkins stared her down as he calmly walked outside after her.

"Dammit, Amanda!" he shouted. "You just don't get it, do you?"

What aren't you telling me? she wondered as she turned to face him. "What's going on?"

"Follow me," he replied, leading her towards a narrow underground tunnel that connected back to the main building.

He paused for a moment as though deciding whether it was wise to continue. Finally, he pulled her into the service tunnel and shut the door behind them. Even after he was sure that they were alone, he still spoke in a hushed tone.

"Skylarov and Fred... I'm pretty sure they're... not human."

Amanda stared at him, unsure of what to say next—unsure that there was anything *to* say after such a comment.

"Pierre's would-be assassin on TCO-72 wasn't. I studied the security camera footage from when the cameras showed Pierre shutting off the gravity generators. At the same time, another camera showed him on the other side of the ship. That footage was conveniently erased, but I was able to reconstruct enough of it to see the time stamps and a few still frames."

"Are you serious?" Amanda replied, trying hard to resist laughing.

The look on his face told her everything. Amanda's smile quickly faded.

"I saw Pierre go into a room and a different man—the assassin—come out."

"So what, Dad?" Amanda asked. "People go into and out of rooms all the time."

"It was a bathroom. Single occupancy."

Amanda shivered.

Neither Amanda nor her father spoke for what seemed like an eternity. Amanda couldn't be sure, but she thought she saw fear in his eyes. She had not seen that for many years....

Since my brother....

She could not bring herself to finish the thought. *No, he's not dead. I know it. I don't know how, I don't know where, I don't know....*

When.

"Go," her father said finally. "Help your friends. And again, trust no one, *especially* the other admirals. Jameson and Sinclair are okay for now, but who knows how long that will last. And if you hear from me again... know that you'll always be my little buttercup."

Huh?

Oh....

Chapter Twenty-four

The next day (January 12th, 2391)

Admiral Jenkins sat in his office early that morning, watching the security cameras from the shuttle bay.

The bay was deserted when Amanda stepped out onto the hangar deck. Her father watched her check her watch. It was 0300 hours, so the crew was in the middle of a shift change. No one would notice her departure, but Admiral Jenkins had disabled the feeds from the security cameras temporarily just to make sure.

"You watching the great escape?" Admiral Sinclair asked.

In his concentration, he hadn't even noticed her entrance.

"Yeah, Candy," he replied.

She appeared to think about that for a moment.

"I take it you're not going to stop her."

"No," he replied.

They sat in silence for another moment before anyone spoke.

"I know she's disobeying orders, but... I'm kind of proud of her," Admiral Jenkins admitted.

He watched Amanda run across the tarmac, up the ladder, and into the cockpit of the fold fighter Heel of Achilles before turning off the screen.

***

As Amanda took the fighter out, she began to wonder if her departure was too easy.

So happy was she while she reveled in her accomplishments that she failed to notice one small detail—a small red light under the console.

Blinking.

***

Laura frowned when she looked around the hotel room. It was your usual hotel room—nothing fancy, but not awful, either—certainly a step up from her accommodations on Triton Station, but nothing to write home about.

On the other bed sat James Moore, Admiral Jenkins's old friend from the Earth Central Intelligence Agency (ECIA). A tall man with a balding scalp, he looked very much like your average Joe. That's what made him so good at these things; he could blend in with a crowd of nuns if he had to.

Among the pieces of kit James brought with him were a camera with a high power zoom lens, a laser microphone, a thermal imaging camera, and a handgun.

Laura pulled out the laser microphone and aimed it stealthily at the window across the atrium. She heard mostly the usual things at first—the Terran Alliance News Network blaring, someone putting ice into a glass and pouring some sort of drink, and a guy yelling back at the TV.

Then, she heard the familiar chirp of an incoming call. She looked around for the source briefly before realizing that it was not in her room, but rather coming through the receiver.

The conversation that followed was hushed, so Laura could only occasionally make out what was being said.

"Everything is on track. I'll go check out as soon as I finish packing my things, and I'll be there around noon tomorrow," the man said.

She aimed the camera at the window, but saw nothing—it was predawn, so she wasn't really expecting much anyway, and the man across the way had pulled his curtains shut, making visibility impossible. On a hunch, however, she decided to try the thermal imaging camera.

"No, I'm not going to kill him tomorrow. It would raise too much suspicion," the man said.

"Get it done as soon as you can," another voice said—*possibly from the viewscreen,* Laura suspected. "Jenkins is too big a security risk. I want him gone."

Laura gulped.

"Wednesday," the first man said.

As soon as she said this, Laura heard the familiar chirp of a closing connection. A moment later, she finally saw the man walk close enough to the curtain to get a good image using thermal imaging.

Initially, everything seemed normal. The man walked past the curtains, then apparently curled up for a nap. That's when she saw something that seemed completely incongruous.

He has a tail?

***

ON Lenora Prime, the Great Doors of Irazus opened—an inch at first, then a foot, then three feet.

"Everyone!" Rejndorv shouted. "Let's move!"

Vladimir Rejndorv walked through the doors. Thirty troops followed him carrying weapons that ranged from automatic weapons to heavy artillery. The last few troops moved slowly through the door, lugging a large portable missile launcher.

"Hurry, you fools!" Rejndorv shouted. "The doors are about to close!"

Just then, one of the four hand straps snapped under the weapon's weight, landing the missile launcher firmly on the foot of one of the four soldiers who were carrying it.

"You IDIOTS!" Rejndorv screamed. "That launcher is LIVE!"

The doors started moving in an instant, and Rejndorv's eyes became suddenly alert. "Down!" he ordered.

A moment later, the cave's entryway was filled with a blinding light as 200 kg of black powder exploded in a giant fireball.

When the dust settled, Rejndorv was unscathed. He stood slowly, dragging two other soldiers up with him. They seemed slightly dazed, but otherwise unhurt.

"Comrades," Rejndorv sputtered, "the time has come for us to act. The crystal is somewhere in these caves. Don't come back until you've found it. Go!"

One by one, the still-conscious troops fanned out through the cave system in search of the Ackerman Crystal. Rejndorv, however, did not. His target was somewhat different.

My orders are to capture a mechlizard alive and bring it back to Skylarov. Insane, but possible.

So Rejndorv walked for what seemed like an eternity until he reached one particular wall. Then, he stepped through the hologram and into a metallic corridor. After a few hundred more yards, he reached a security door and encountered the AI that protected the base.

"Hello, Mr. Rejndorv," the AI said in greeting.

"Hello, Tessa," he replied. "I need to get into the lab."

The door opened a few seconds later. After a brief stop at a base computer terminal, he left the entry room and headed into the main hall—a giant hall that spiralled down into the depths of the mountain. He walked through sections one through six.

Rejndorv could tell that someone was following him by the slight echoes of footfalls in the shadows, but he dared not reveal that knowledge. *Better to scare him away*, he thought.

Rejndorv walked over to a keypad and typed a message to Tessa.

Tobias is following me. Lose him.

On the display screen, Tessa printed the words "eat this" as a chicken sandwich appeared in the food slot. Rejndorv grabbed the food. Then, the screen changed to say, "Calling Tobias. Walk to the door."

Rejndorv did as he was told. Then, while Tobias was distracted by his desperate attempt at silencing his communicator, a holographic wall appeared about a foot in front of Rejndorv.

This could get interesting, Rejndorv thought.

From this side of the wall, it was partially transparent, though he knew it was almost certainly opaque from the other side. He sat and watched a projected version of himself get attacked and killed by a projected mechlizard as Tobias looked on.

Tobias gulped and staggered back out the way he came.

As soon as the door closed, Rejndorv pressed a few more buttons, and Tessa disabled the projections, starting with holo-Vlad and the mech, followed by the wall. He then continued through the door and into section eight.

***

Early the next morning

WHEN he reached the entrance to section nine, he stopped and retrieved a device from his knapsack.

The screen on the hand scanner showed three blips.

Three mechlizards? In hydroponics? Well, Rejndorv thought, *I can't go around it, so I guess I'll just have to subdue all three.*

***

KLERN hauled his bags into the glass elevator and headed down through the atrium to the lobby level. As the doors were about to close, a strangely familiar-looking woman pushed her way in.

"Where you heading?" Laura asked after a few moments of awkward silence.

"Neptune," he replied. "You?"

"Downtown for a burger."

The elevator arrived on the ground floor, and Klern walked to the front desk.

"Hello, Mr. Nichols," the desk worker said as he approached. "I hope your stay was a pleasant one."

Laura walked past him and out the door, where James sat in a limo waiting for her arrival.

As she stepped inside the limo, she began a video call to Triton Station.

"Hi, Laura," Admiral Jenkins said as his face appeared on the screen.

"The eagle has left the nest," she replied.

"Understood. Come back here as soon as you can."

***

Vladimir Rejndorv made sure his particle rifle was armed and ready. Then, he pulled out two plasma grenades. His timing had to be perfect. With his memory of the hydroponics bay, he estimated that one mechlizard was in the tomato area, one in the cabbage garden, and one in a storage cabinet off to the side. He knew he could take out the one in the storage cabinet with a plasma grenade before any of them noticed him. The others would be tricky.

The last thing he pulled from his bag was a proximity mine and a pistol with three tranquilizer darts. He armed the proximity mine with a ten second delay. As soon as it was armed, he opened the door and tossed grenades at the mechlizard in the storage cabinet and at the mechlizard in the cabbage garden. Then, he ran. A few seconds later, they went off.

Rejndorv looked at his screen and saw three dots.

Shit.

He dropped to his knees and pointed his particle rifle at the door. A few seconds later, one mechlizard wandered up. The whine of the proximity mine activating made his ears scream in pain. Then, that mechlizard was no more... along with a large chunk of the wall nearby.

He relaxed for only a moment; as he stared at the rubble, four mechlizard eyes stared back at him from the darkness beyond.

Shit.

Rejndorv ran.

The door to section eight opened in front of him and he ran through. As it shut, he turned and aimed his particle rifle just in time to see a mechlizard flying through the air at him. He fired six shots before the mechlizard landed in a heap on top of him, knocking him to the ground.

He quickly threw the carcass to the side, then emptied another ten rounds into it just to make sure.

On the scanner, he saw only one dot inside section nine. Then, the dot disappeared.

What the....

Then the dot reappeared, this time in the room he was in.

Double shit.

Rejndorv had no sooner raised the tranquilizer pistol than the mechlizard came crashing through the drop ceiling in front of him. He took careful aim and fired. The first shot went wild. He fired again as the mechlizard slowly stalked its prey. Another miss. He closed his eyes and fired his final shot. It, too, missed by a mile.

***

KLERN landed cautiously on the Neptunian moon Triton, dropping his shuttle a few hundred meters away from the station.

Dozens of other ships littered the surface nearby, taking advantage of Triton as a temporary base of operation until the shipyard at Brooks Station around Mars could be retrofitted with sufficient usable office space, housing, and food facilities to take the place of Terran Command Station. In the midst of this barely bounded chaos, Klern was able to easily land and EVA across the surface to Triton Station without drawing undue attention.

***

REJNDORV crawled slowly away from the creature as it crawled slowly towards him. He watched in horror as the mechlizard licked its lips in anticipation. Then, it happened.

The door behind it opened.

"Tessa?" Rejndorv asked.

The android adjunct to the base computer did not even acknowledge him as she jumped on top of the lizard. Holding it up in front of her with one hand, she grabbed the dart with the other and stabbed the creature with it.

"Wow!" Rejndorv said. "Why couldn't you have done that when they got free thirty-odd years ago?"

Tessa looked at him incredulously. "It's hard enough to grab *one* of these things. *You* try doing that with fifty or a hundred."

Rejndorv smiled. *Same old Tessa.*

"So what are you doing with the mechlizard?" she asked.

Rejndorv frowned. *Same old Tessa.*

"I can't tell you," he replied. "It's classified."

Tessa nodded.

"Look, Tessa," Rejndorv said, "I have some new orders for you."

"Do they involve the people who came to this base?"

Rejndorv shook his head. "They are... unimportant. I need to know where the Ackerman crystal is."

She paused for a moment before replying, "It's probably where you left it."

Rejndorv nodded. *Section 13.*

"In that case," he replied, "go back to Joseph Kurtz's team. Tell them nothing."

With that, Tessa left. As soon as she was out of sight, Rejndorv lifted the beast and headed for the nuclear storage vault.

***

THE airlock door creaked open as Klern stepped into the lower maintenance level of Triton Station. He walked down one corridor looking for any sort of elevator or computer station, but there weren't any, so he turned around and walked a different direction with equally poor luck.

After a few minutes, a man walked up to him.

"Lost?" he asked.

Klern looked at his attire and realized he was a civilian.

"Yeah. I got turned around. Which way to the mess hall?"

The man stared at him. "Boy, you really must be lost. You're five floors down...."

Klern chuckled.

"Head down that hall," he said, pointing, "then turn right at that blue sign, left at the first hall, and the lifts are about halfway down on the right."

"Thanks," Klern replied.

Klern followed the man's instructions and found the lift. Then, he headed up to the fifth floor. Once he had located a computer terminal, he requested to be assigned quarters, then headed to them.

***

REJNDORV relaxed as he placed the beast on the escape pad and programmed it to send the creature to Proxima Centauri III, where a shuttle was waiting to transport it to its final destination, wherever that was.

Still, something bothered him. It almost seemed too easy.

That's when it hit him.

The mechlizard's razor-sharp talons flew faster than lightning as it ripped into his chest. Through the open door behind him, Vladimir Rejndorv could just make out someone looking at him—Tobias perhaps. He tried to scream for help, but he found himself unable to breathe, the mechlizard's claws already penetrating his chest. And as quickly as it had opened, the door closed again. He was alone... with the beast.

Suddenly, from out of nowhere, something appeared. *No, not something*, he thought. *Someone.*

"Help! Over here!" he wheezed.

A moment later, the lizard was motionless—frozen in place.

"Coward," the man said. "Why should I help you?"

"Donovan?"

"Die. Die like you would have let me die—a slow, painful death—a coward's death."

And as quickly as he appeared, Donovan Jenkins shimmered and vanished.

Displaced.

In spite of his terror, Rejndorv took the brief moment of stillness as an opportunity. He threw the mechlizard at the pad and jumped at the button.

> *Emergency escape portal system. Press this button only in the event of an emergency.*

Upon pressing it, the mechlizard shimmered and vanished.

It's somebody else's problem now, he thought as he collapsed to the floor.

Chapter Twenty-five

Later that night (January 13th, 2391)

Technically, this isn't legal, Amanda thought as she used a small planet's gravity well to slingshot her to about twice the speed allowable within an inhabited system. *What the hell.... It's not like the Lenorans are going to complain.*

She only hoped that the approaching ships' captains didn't think of doing something similar. The last thing she needed was a horde of rogue Colonial troops landing while she was trying to break into the underground base.

"ETA is three hours, fifteen minutes," the computer intoned.

"Ugh," she grunted.

That's when the ship shook violently around her as a volley of particle weapons fire struck it, fired by a ghostly ship that appeared out of nowhere, as if by magic, about a hundred feet off her port bow.

A cloaked ship that can't be detected from such a short distance? Is that even possible? Amanda swung the ship hard to starboard. The ship made a metallic scream as shearing forces tried to rip it apart.

The ghost ship fired again, this time clipping one of her engines. Her ship lurched and whined in response. Suddenly, one of the lateral stabilizers flew off, and the resulting explosion momentarily sent the ship into a spin.

"Lateral stabilizers nonfunctional," the computer intoned.

Well, I guess I won't be landing anywhere with an atmosphere, she thought.

Without warning, the ghost ship began to shimmer. As it faded into nothingness, Amanda fired a smart missile. A huge fireball rocked the ship in response, and Amanda could do nothing but hang on for dear life.

Amanda desperately scanned the surrounding area looking for cover. Without serious repairs, she wouldn't be going anywhere. After a few moments, she spotted a small cave in an asteroid a few hundred meters away.

Well, it's cover, I suppose.

The light from outside the ship grew slowly dimmer as the ship slid gracefully into the cave. Though it was little more than a crevice, its deep shadows could hide much. She would need to turn on the lights soon....

But are some things better left hidden? With that final thought, her world went black except for the dim glow of the radar images on her heads-up display.

Amanda pressed a few buttons, and the exterior illumination slowly flickered to life, weakly, as though tired from general disuse. *Strange,* she thought. *If this is a cave, shouldn't there be stalactites or something?* And then she saw them—blast marks. *This isn't a cave; it's a mine, or at least it used to be. But for what?* She wasn't sure, but she knew she didn't want to stick around long enough to find out.

"Computer, passive sensors only," she ordered. *We don't want to be that easy to find. Now where can I find a spare stabilizer?*

Amanda fell hard against a console as the ship rocked violently. *Dammit! I thought that engine manifold was intact.* "Computer, shut the engines down."

The bridge shook again.

That's no fuel leak, she thought. *Someone is shooting at this asteroid.*

"Warning: missile detected," the computer intoned.

A moment later, Amanda felt the ship slam against the mine walls. *Direct hit, port side. How did they DO that? The missile didn't just find us by blind luck, that's for sure.*

"Computer, are we emitting any signals?" she asked.

"Affirmative."

"Can you localize it?"

"Affirmative. The signal is emanating from the main control console."

Another missile slammed against the ship. *The console? Wait a second.... What's this box underneath? Red light... blinking.... SHIT!*

A few moments and a screwdriver later, Amanda had removed the tracking device. She smashed it with a rock she brought with her.

The next missile crashed harmlessly into a mine wall a few feet ahead of the ship. *Now for the counterstrike,* Amanda thought. "Computer, launch a class four probe."

The ship shook slightly as the roughly one meter by one meter cylinder launched out of a torpedo tube, its kickstart motor pushing it far enough away from the ship to allow it to fire its control thrusters safely.

Amanda watched nervously as the probe made its way around the corner. Then, telemetry data began to fill the screen beneath her fingers. *We've got them now.*

"Computer, set two missiles to get tracking data from the probe. Targets are oh-two-one mark four by oh-three-four mark nine and oh-two-one mark five by oh-three-four mark five," she ordered.

"Target locked," it replied.

Amanda keyed in the launch code and pressed the big red button beside the keypad. "Firing."

Nearby, two Terran Command ships exploded....

"Computer, status report!" she shouted.

"Navigation systems offline. Steering thrusters heavily damaged. Folding drive offline. Primary engines damaged beyond repair. Weapons targeting offline."

Damn. "Were the targets destroyed?" she asked.

"Affirmative," the computer intoned.

Well, at least that's something, she thought, *but I'm stuck. Maybe I can scavenge some metal for raw materials outside.*

"Computer, is exterior illumination working?" she asked.

"Affirmative."

"Flood the place."

"Command not understood. Please restate."

"Engage maximum exterior illumination."

"Illumination engaged."

As she looked out the front windows, her jaw dropped. Before her stood a small shuttle, barely big enough for two people. *It will do,* she thought. *It will do.*

Amanda quickly donned a pressure suit, then stepped out of the fold fighter to the deck below, activating her magnetic footwear as she landed. Once on solid ground, she walked across to the shuttle, opened it, and stepped inside.

The shuttle controls were sticky, like a small child had recently eaten there. *Or a mechlizard,* she thought. Amanda shivered.

She looked down at her watch again and sighed. *0200 hours. How can it be tomorrow already?*

She checked the shuttle's clock.

Sure enough. It's January 14th. My father's birthday. Happy birthday, Dad.

After a brief conversation with the fold fighter's core AI, she powered up the shuttle. It coughed and lurched its way through space, its engines barely managing a few hundred kph.

If only I had fixed the folding drive, Amanda thought.

"Computer," she asked, "estimated time to Lenora Prime?"

"Seventy-six hours, fifteen minutes, twelve seconds," it replied in a droning male monotone.

Great. Just great, she thought. *Even the computer is bored. Either that or I got the one ship in the fleet whose computer sounds more depressed than I am.*

Amanda thought for a moment that she should pass the time watching the news. As the viewscreen crackled to life, a terrified news reporter could be seen leaning against the window of what looked like a Terran Alliance modular space station.

> "...looks like some sort of explosion.... Oh, my.... Dear God.... It's burning.... The *entire* planet is literally burning! Oh, God! Oh, God! Oh, God! The humanity!"

I can't take any more news like this, she thought as she shut the monitor off. *Things are bad enough already.*

In a last ditch effort to pass the time, Amanda turned on some music, closed her eyes, leaned back, and fell asleep.

***

Admiral Skylarov awoke to the chirping of his viewscreen.

"What!?!" he shouted.

The viewscreen activated and a woman's face appeared.

"Svetlana."

"Hello, Mikhail," the woman replied. "We have a problem. Amanda escaped."

"She WHAT!?!" he shouted.

"She took out two of our heavy cruisers and then took off in some sort of shuttlecraft," Svetlana replied. "We don't know where she is."

"We know where she's heading," Skylarov countered. "She'll be here soon enough. Concentrate your search between her last known coordinates and Lenora Prime. It can't be that hard."

"Yes, sir," Svetlana Rusakova replied. "And when we find her?"

"Same plan as before," Skylarov replied. "Make it look real."

She nodded.

Chapter Twenty-six

The next day (January 15, 2391)

ADMIRAL Jenkins sat in his office chair, waiting for word of his daughter.

She should have checked in by now, he thought. *Something is wrong.*

"Admiral Jenkins?" a young man asked from behind him.

He turned, looked up, and saw an unfamiliar man in his twenties. His dark skin and chiseled features immediately caught Tom's attention.

"Hi. I'm Mat... uh... Lieutenant Junior Grade Mat Reinhold," he said.

Will has a son? I remember when his daughter was born, but....

"I believe you knew my Uncle William," he added.

Whew. Thank God. For a minute, I thought Will's daughter had gotten an operation....

"I come bringing news... of your daughter."

"What's the news?" the admiral asked.

From the uncomfortable pause and the blank look in the child's eyes, he knew the news could not be good.

"I'm afraid her ship was found crash-landed on the surface of an asteroid," Mat replied. "The ship showed signs of explosive decompression. She would have fallen unconscious instantly. She probably felt... very little pain as she was sucked through the hull breach."

Amanda....

"If there's anything I can do, sir, just let me know."

Admiral Jenkins nodded.

***

The next day (January 16, 2391)

"ADMIRAL," Laura said through the intercom.

"Yes?" Admiral Jenkins replied.

"There's an incoming message for you," Laura said. "It's encrypted and marked high priority."

"Patch it through," he replied.

Amanda's face appeared on the viewscreen. While he watched, a man in a ski mask struck her across the face.

> "You bastards!" Amanda shouted.
>
> "Shut up, bitch," the man replied, and slapped her again.
>
> Amanda shook her head, then spat in his face. As he wiped the mixture of saliva and blood from his eyes, he glared at her with hatred.
>
> "We have your daughter," the man said. "You will meet our demands in 72 hours or she dies."

With that, the screen went black.

"Computer, get me Rick Glasgow," he commanded.

A few seconds passed, and a man's face appeared on the viewscreen.

"Rick, I need help," Admiral Jenkins said.

After one look at Tom's face, Rick's expression changed to one of concern.

"What can I do?" he asked.

"It's Amanda," Admiral Jenkins replied. "She's been kidnapped. Can you be in conference room A in an hour?"

"It's done," Rick replied.

"And bring Joseph Kurtz with you."

Rick nodded and closed the connection.

***

"THEY what!?!" Admiral Skylarov bellowed.

Even on the other end of the video link, the young lieutenant's eyes grew fearful.

"Sir," he replied, "apparently, Miss Rusakova has decided she can make more money by holding the admiral's daughter for random."

"I wanted her gone. Out of the way. Permanently. She is a liability," Skylarov fumed.

The young lieutenant just stood there, staring.

Skylarov sighed. "No matter. In a few short days, they won't be a problem anymore."

"I'm sorry?" the lieutenant replied.

"The front lines are moving towards the Tularis system," Skylarov explained. "We will simply have to make certain that Amanda Jenkins is buried by a molten pool of rock, and Miss Rusakova along with her."

"But what if Admiral Jenkins orders a rescue mission?" the lieutenant asked.

Skylarov stared at him as though he had just asked the dumbest question in the world. After a few moments, he realized, much to his disappointment, that the lieutenant still wasn't getting it.

"Then volunteer to join?" Skylarov offered before closing the channel with his fist.

After a moment of seething, he made another call.

"Svetlana," Admiral Skylarov said pleasantly.

"Mikhail," she replied.

"Do I not pay you well?" he asked.

Her eyes grew suddenly wide. "Of... of course, sir," she replied.

"Then why do you feel the need to betray me?" he asked.

He paused for a moment to let that sink in, then continued, saying, "That was rhetorical."

The woman's face grew cold with anger, but the nervous twitch of her left eye betrayed her inner fear.

"So you thought you could make a few extra bucks by playing us against each other," Skylarov said. "I admire that."

Svetlana Rusakova squirmed visibly.

"Of course, you know," he warned, "that the good admiral will try to mount a rescue attempt."

"We can handle it," Svetlana replied.

"Oh can you?" Skylarov asked. "Then I suppose you can handle the three weeks of orbital bombardment that I intend to unleash if Amanda Jenkins is still breathing when they arrive?"

The woman's eyes narrowed to a slit.

"See that she is taken care of," he ordered. "Now."

"Fuck you," she spat as she closed the channel.

No, he thought. *It is you who is fucked.*

***

KLERN stepped into the lift as Mat Reinhold entered from the other side.

"Yakhol," Klern said.

"Klern," Mat replied.

"What's the latest word?" Klern asked.

"Everything is going according to plan," Mat replied. "The hardware is ready for you."

"Excellent. And what are we going to do about those humans who decided to turn our perfect murder into a damned kidnapping?"

Mat shook his head. "I just heard about it a few minutes ago. I'm sure Admiral Jenkins will arrange a rescue mission, and when he does, I'll ask to be assigned to it."

Klern nodded.

A moment later, the lift reached his floor, and Klern stepped out.

***

LAURA and Sydney walked down the main concourse towards the mess hall.

"So what happened out there?" Sydney asked.

Laura shook her head. "It... wasn't human."

Sydney's eyes widened.

"I couldn't see anything out of the ordinary with my eyes," Laura said, "but when I used the thermal imaging camera, I could see a tail."

Sydney stopped walking. "Are you serious? Actual aliens?"

Laura nodded.

"I thought they were just... you know, the other kind of aliens," Sydney replied. "Illegal aliens."

Laura stifled a laugh.

Sydney pouted. "What?"

***

ADMIRAL Jenkins had just propped up his feet on the conference table to get comfortable when the door chimed.

Timing is everything, he thought as he put his feet back down.

"Come in."

The doors opened, and Rick Glasgow entered.

"Hey, Rick," Jenkins said.

"Hey, Tom," Captain Glasgow replied.

Jenkins chuckled. "Rick, I know this is a laid back station, and I know I've known you since you were born, but so help me, if you call me Tom in front of Joseph...."

Rick laughed.

About that time, the door chimed again.

"Come in," they both said in unison as Admiral Jenkins began pouring a stiff drink.

"Ah, Mr. Kurtz," Admiral Jenkins said.

"Yes, sir," Joseph answered.

"Lieutenant, this is Captain Rick Glasgow," Jenkins said, pointing. "Rick, this is Lieutenant Joseph Kurtz."

"A pleasure," Rick said.

"Likewise, I hope," Joseph replied.

Jenkins scoffed. "I called you in here because we just received communication from Amanda's captors."

"Any idea where it came from?" Joseph asked.

"Our best guess is somewhere in the vicinity of the Tularis System," Rick answered.

Joseph looks puzzled, Jenkins thought. *Guess he hasn't spent much time in the colonies.*

"The Tularis System?" Joseph asked.

"One of the rebel colonial systems near the border with T.E.R.R.A. Population 350 million," Rick replied. "Our sources seem to think she's being held in a base deep in the Felton Mountains."

"What's the plan?" Joseph asked.

Finally, Jenkins thought. *My turn.*

"I'm putting you in command of the rescue, Joseph," Jenkins answered. "I don't trust my judgment anymore, and Rick has a more pressing assignment."

"Well, how about fifty troops with guerrilla training," Joseph suggested. "We spatial fold a chunk out of the middle of the base and fold us in its place, then we come out fighting."

"Too risky," the admiral answered. "Too risky at so many levels. We were thinking more along the lines of an all-out assault on the base by a hundred troops to provide a distraction, with an elite team of twenty entering through a vent shaft or something."

"Works for me," Joseph told him.

"Rick and the rest of Terran Command Intelligence are going to be working around the clock to locate her more precisely," Admiral Jenkins replied. "We'll have a final planning meeting to work out the last few details at 0800 hours tomorrow morning. You'll lead the troops into battle at 1200 hours."

"I'll see you then, then," Joseph replied.

"One more thing," Jenkins added. "Just so we're clear, I want my daughter out safe, but it's also important to send a message that the Terran Alliance will not kowtow to terrorists taking our personnel hostage. Officially, your first priority is to ensure that the people responsible are *all* captured or killed. No exceptions."

Joseph nodded.

Jenkins could tell that Joseph didn't like the order any more than he did, but that was just the way it had to be.

As long as we're combatting a known terrorist threat, he thought cynically, *we can get just about anything past the brass. Anything less, and Admiral Skylarov will call up Fleet Admiral Ramirez and overrule me, and that would be the end of the rescue mission.*

No, he thought. *This one has to be by the books, as much as I wish I could burn them.*

***

Later that afternoon

MAT Reinhold stepped into Admiral Sinclair's office.

"Admiral, requesting permission to be a member of the rescue party," he said.

Admiral Sinclair crooked her head. "For Amanda Jenkins?"

"Yes, sir," he replied. "She's a friend of the family, and my uncle would have wanted me there."

"Ask Lieutenant Kurtz. It's his train wreck."

Mat sighed. *Delegated to a Lieutenant. How far the mighty have fallen.*

"Understood," he replied, then spun on his heel and walked out of the office.

***

JOSEPH sat alone at a table in the mess hall, staring at leaked floor plans that Terran Intelligence believed *might* be for the right building. He paused for a moment to pick up a bite of orange chicken with his chopsticks, then swore when a drip fell on the printout. After he wiped it clean, he laughed when he realized it had landed on the mess hall.

Suddenly, a young man jogged up to him from a nearby lift.

"Lieutenant Kurtz?" the young man asked.

"Yes?" Joseph replied.

"I'm Lieutenant Junior Grade Mat Reinhold. Amanda was... is... was a friend of my uncle before he died. I would like to request permission to lead a team on the rescue mission."

Joseph nodded. "Done. We need someone else with leadership experience to head the second squad. We're meeting at 0800 hours for a final briefing on our way out the door."

"Conference room?"

"Uh," Joseph stammered, "is there a conference room big enough to hold a couple hundred people?"

"No," Mat replied.

"Didn't think so. We'll assemble on the flight deck at 0800 hours."

Mat nodded.

"Dismissed," Joseph added.

I always wanted to say that, he thought as the way-too-eager young lieutenant scurried away.

***

KLERN's ears perked up as the viewscreen signalled an incoming message.

"Yo," Mat said as soon as his face appeared.

"Status?" Klern asked brusquely.

"I'm on the mission," Mat replied. "You have a go for your part. Time to clean up the mess that Merick left behind."

***

ADMIRAL Jenkins was sitting in his office helping Laura pore through intelligence notes from field operatives when Joseph entered.

"Admiral," Joseph asked, "do you have any new information about the number of troops we'll be facing? That part of the report is a little thin."

The admiral shook his head. "No, but we did find a more complete wiring diagram from the county planning office."

"When will evil overlords learn to build unapproved, nonconforming structures?" Laura quipped.

Joseph chuckled. "And you are?"

"Forgive me for being rude," the Admiral replied. "Joseph, this is Laura. Laura, Joseph."

"Nice to meet you," Laura said as she shook his hand. "I've seen you around... with Amanda back on Terran Command Station."

Joseph nodded. "Likewise."

"Laura," the admiral interrupted, "Joseph is a trusted friend of the family. If you ever need anything and I'm not around to help, he's your man."

Laura nodded as she handed Joseph the wiring diagram on an optical storage crystal.

"Is there anything else?" Joseph asked.

"Not for now," Admiral Jenkins replied. "Check with Admiral Sinclair before you leave, though, just in case she turns up something useful."

"Understood," Joseph said. "It was nice meeting you, Laura."

"Nice meeting you as well. When you see Amanda, tell her I said 'thanks'."

***

PIERRE stared at the data pad. Over the past few hours, he had located twelve of the weapons storage cabinets and lockers. Most of them eluded him, though. Either the locations on the map were wrong, they were hidden particularly well, or those cabinets had not been installed yet. He suspected the latter.

His last stop was the shuttle bay. As he walked into the buffer zone, three people he didn't recognize were walking out.

"That's the last of them," one man said.

The last of what? Pierre wondered.

As he stepped through the second door (from the buffer zone into the shuttle bay itself), he found himself staring at hundreds and hundreds of wooden boxes and crates filling most of the bay. Each box had markings that Pierre could not identify, along with various common markings like "This Side Up" and "Fragile Artifacts. Do not drop."

The frontmost crates still had bills of lading attached, so Pierre decided to take a look.

Contents:

Prototype robot pet Qty: 1

How curious, Pierre thought. *The artifacts from Lenora are toys?*

A few moments later, he heard a sound coming from the box.

Nah. Couldn't be, he thought.

A few seconds passed without any further sound, so Pierre walked to where the weapons cache was supposed to be. As with many of the others, there were no weapons—not even an empty cabinet.

One last cache to check, he thought as he climbed the ladder to the control booth overhead.

As he stepped into the control booth, he was greeted by the head of security.

"Hey, Pierre," John said. "What are you up to?"

Pierre smirked. "I'm scoping out weapons caches."

"It's under the loose deck plate over in the corner there," John replied, pointing to one corner of the shuttle bay.

"Under the boxes?" Pierre asked.

John nodded. "There's also one in here."

"Really?" Pierre replied. "It's not on the list."

A moment later, the doors to the shuttle bay opened and a man walked in.

"It's here," John replied. "Trust me."

Pierre and John watched through the two-way mirrored window as a man matching the description of Ensign Nichols walked over to the pile of boxes.

Pierre stared at him. *What's he doing?*

The man opened up a small wooden box and pulled out some sort of device. He then put on a pressure suit and walked out through the airlock.

Pierre continued to watch him on the monitors adorning the console in the control booth.

The man walked to a shuttle outside, then tossed the empty wooden box inside. When he returned, he was carrying a large ham and was wearing a different face.

My face, Pierre realized as the man took off his pressure suit.

The man then proceeded to climb on top of the box Pierre had examined previously.

"What the?" John asked rhetorically.

Next, he produced a small key from his pocket and unlocked the padlock that held the latch mechanism on the crate. He then released the latch, and the end of the box fell away, revealing a metallic creature about the size of a large dog.

Finally, the man who looked like Pierre tossed the large ham into the middle of the shuttle bay floor.

Pierre watched in horror as the creature took a flying leap, landed on the ham, and devoured it in seconds. Pierre then turned to John.

"Get the guns."

***

ADMIRAL Jenkins stepped out of his office at 1700 hours just as he would on any other day. As he neared the corner, he heard a strange sound—scratching, squawking—click, clack, click, clack, clickety-clack. It got louder. Click, Clack,

Click. Louder and louder it grew, and louder still, until it seemed to be right on top of him. As he peered around the corner, a small rodent scurried across the hall. He jumped for a moment, then relaxed slightly.

But as he stepped into his quarters, he saw utter chaos. Papers were strewn about carelessly, and equipment had been tossed around like toys. His favorite aquarium was cracked—*probably by the chair leaning against it,* he mused—and the water was slowly leaking through the gap.

"Who is responsible for this!?!" he bellowed.

CLICK!

...and then he turned and saw it in the flickering fluorescent light... and at last, he understood.

The rifle barrel flashed twice. Then, as quickly as it had begun, it was over, and all was silent.

Pierre stood hovering over two bodies. The first was... indescribable. It looked a bit like a large lizard, but with robotic appendages. Next to him was...

Pierre? And what's that in his hand?

"There is no time to explain," Pierre said quickly, his accent even thicker than usual.

Admiral Jenkins relaxed a little when John walked up behind the two Pierres a moment later.

"That's not Pierre," John added, pointing at the body.

Thomas stood, jaw agape, for about five seconds before he hauled the other Pierre's body into his quarters. Pierre and John followed suit with the mechlizard, then shut the door.

"You remember those aliens?" Pierre asked. He then reached down to corpse-Pierre's chest, slipped his hand into its shirt, and pressed on something. Suddenly, corpse-Pierre became something very different.

"But... how?" Jenkins asked, staring at the rifle.

Pierre just smiled.

"Candy?"

"Candy."

A few seconds later, Admiral Sinclair opened the door and jogged in from the corridor.

"Speak of the devil," John said.

"Did I miss anything?"

Jenkins just stared at her. Instead of her usual uniform, she was clad in body armor, with assault rifles draped from both shoulders, pointed forwards, ready to rock and roll.

"Oh, yeah," she added, tossing Jenkins an assault rifle. "Don't say I never gave you anything."

"I thought..." he began.

"Weapons aren't allowed on base?" she replied, laughing. "Yeah, like that makes any sense. Do you really think that I'd leave this place defenseless if somebody did manage to sneak one in?"

Jenkins shook his head in disbelief.

"Oh, there are weapons, all right," she continued. "I'm just pretty particular about who has access to them. Welcome to the club, boys."

Jenkins nodded, bent over, picked up the veil, and slipped it into his pocket.

"Could come in handy," he said.

***

Wendy Carlson, Triton Station's only medical examiner, stepped into Admiral Jenkins's quarters. By the time she arrived, the scene was staged. The alien's corpse lay on the floor, surrounded by a pool of blood. The two admirals had long since cleaned up any evidence that indicated that the body had been moved.

With a little help from the geeks in Terran Command Research, they had also managed to add a new face into the veil. It helped that the veil was actually *designed* to download new scans from the Terran Command personnel database.

She stood looking down on the body of Admiral Jenkins, killed by a bullet to the head from behind. Admiral Jenkins was pronounced dead on arrival. The autopsy that followed was mercifully brief—none, in fact, by order of Admiral Sinclair.

***

The sky over Lenora Prime shimmered a greenish blue as the sun rose over the mountains.

Admiral Skylarov frowned as he stared at the three-dimensional holographic projection showing a composite of radar and other sensor data from the front lines. Suddenly, his attention was drawn to the viewscreen across the room as it chirped to indicate an urgent incoming message.

"Viewscreen on," the admiral intoned.

The screen displayed a text message.

> *Attention S,*
>
> *Terran forces preparing invasion of Tularis Prime by order of Admiral Jenkins.*
>
> *Admiral Jenkins found dead. Bullet wound to head.*
>
> *Awaiting orders.*
>
> *—M*

Skylarov sent back a reply.

> *Bombs drop on Tularis colonies tonight. Attempting to cancel rescue mission. If*

mission proceeds, Amanda Jenkins will be casualty of war. Make certain.

—S

After sending the encrypted message, Skylarov still had one more call to make.

"Computer, connect me to Admiral Jameson."

The computer dutifully complied, and Admiral Jameson's face came on the screen a few moments later.

"Admiral Jameson," Skylarov said.

"Admiral Skylarov," Jameson replied.

Admiral Skylarov quickly finished typing a message on his terminal.

"Could you deliver a message to Lieutenant Kurtz for me?" Skylarov asked. "Things are rocky between Kurtz and me, so I really don't want to be there when he gets this message."

"Sure. I'll pass it on," Admiral Jameson replied.

Admiral Skylarov attached the text message, then closed the connection. On his screen, the message read:

To: *Lieutenant Kurtz*

From: *Admiral Skylarov*

Subject: *Mission Change*

The mission to Tularis Prime is hereby canceled, effective immediately. Your orders are rescinded.

***

ADMIRAL Jenkins and Admiral Sinclair watched the investigation unfold from the safety of Admiral Sinclair's office.

"How are we going to dispose of the body?" Admiral Sinclair asked.

"We can't do that yet," Admiral Jenkins replied. "We have to get the ensign declared dead, too."

Admiral Sinclair scratched her head.

"Why? You could pose as the ensign and gather information."

"Too risky," Jenkins replied. "There are probably protocols, scheduled check-ins, that sort of thing. We'd be flying blind. No, better to tap Skylarov's communications and learn about their organization that way."

"So how do we dispose of the body?" Sinclair asked. "Won't it be a little obvious if the medical examiner finds two bodies, both shot in the head from behind?"

Admiral Jenkins smiled. "I have a plan."

Suddenly Admiral Sinclair's viewscreen chimed. Admiral Jenkins stepped off camera before Admiral Sinclair activated it.

"Sinclair."

"Candy, my dear," Admiral Jameson began.

"Brent, darling," Admiral Sinclair replied. "To what do I owe the pleasure?"

"It's business this time. I'm about to have to pass on an order that I know is illegitimate and may cost one of our officers her life."

"So don't pass it on," she replied, then looked down at the message on her screen and grunted disapprovingly.

"But I have to," he said. "I think Admiral Jenkins probably refused, and now he's buried in a hollowed out torpedo casing in orbit around some sun."

Admiral Jenkins stepped into the picture about that time. *Might as well trust Jameson. Nobody else could be that debonair.*

"Well, you could always do what I would do," Candy replied, barely stifling a laugh at the expression on Admiral Jameson's face at seeing a ghost.

"Which is?" Jameson asked.

"Create plausible deniability," she replied, "then make sure that Joseph knows it's a fake."

"So you're saying I should find someone to deliver the message who Joseph outranks?" Jameson suggested.

"It's a start," she replied. "And add something to the message that will make him question its authenticity as much as you do."

"Like what?"

"Give him an absolutely absurd order that can't possibly be right," Admiral Sinclair suggested. "Are there any admirals on vacation?"

"Admiral Johnson," Jameson replied. "He's out on medical leave until next month, but I think everyone thinks he's on vacation."

"Order him to report to Johnson's office," Sinclair said. "Tomorrow."

Admiral Jameson laughed. "That just might do it. Oh, and good to see that rumors of your demise are greatly exaggerated, Tom."

Jenkins smiled and closed the channel. A few moments later, Admiral Sinclair received a blind carbon copy of the altered message. It read:

> *To: Lieutenant Kurtz*
>
> *From: Admiral Skylarov*
>
> *Subject: Mission Change*
>
> *The mission to Tularis Prime is hereby canceled, effective immediately. Your orders are rescinded.*
>
> *From: Admiral Jameson*
>
> *Subject: Addendum*

You are requested to appear in the office of Rear Admiral Johnson at 0200 hours for reassignment.

We apologize for the inconvenience.

Classic, Admiral Jenkins thought. *Absolutely classic.*

***

By the time Wendy got back to her office, she already had a text message about another death on the station.

This is getting old rather quickly, she thought as she skimmed the message on her screen.

ATTENTION:

The man who fatally shot Admiral Jenkins was killed by automated defense system fire trying to leave the station. The charred corpse can be retrieved on the surface at the attached coordinates.

Note that several corridors are temporarily closed for a security drill. Access to the outside of the station is not possible until 2100 hours.

Wendy groaned. *Argh. Another one. It looks like it's going to be a long night.*

***

Admiral Sinclair hailed Lieutenant Phillips on the radio.

"Phillips here," he replied.

"Lieutenant," Jenkins said, "We need something from you."

"Admiral, Admiral, what can I do for the two of you?"

Admiral Sinclair brought up a map of the base.

"Your security forces are doing exercises from now until 2100 hours," she said.

"Sir?" he asked incredulously. "We have no exercises on the schedule."

Admiral Sinclair smiled.

"Admiral Jenkins was just declared dead," she replied, "and we need to have Ensign Nichols declared dead as well. To do that, we need a way to get from here to the Admiral's quarters, from there to the nearest convenient airlock, and back here. We will also need the automated defenses to... destroy some evidence on the planet's surface outside the station."

"But sir," he replied, "the exterior lighting will make you visible to every ship out on the surface. There are thousands of ships outside the nearest airlock. You'd need to go out the airlock on the opposite end of the station, and even then, someone might spot you."

"Power outage drill, base-wide?" Jenkins suggested.

"That might do it," Lieutenant Phillips replied. "We'll get right on it."

"No," Admiral Sinclair insisted. "Just you. No one else must know. As far as everyone else is concerned, Admiral Jenkins was killed an hour ago."

Admiral Jenkins cut in. "Uh, as far as your security team is concerned, you are securing sections of the station as part of a drill. You will track our movement from the control room, and your security personnel will block access to the corridors based on your orders."

The lieutenant was momentarily nonplussed. When he had recovered his voice, he was incredulous.

"Sirs, securing a corridor is easy. Securing safe passage to the opposite end of the base...."

Admiral Sinclair pressed a few buttons on her console.

"Attention all personnel," she said. "We have a security emergency on our hands. All personnel are instructed to immediately return to your quarters. The base is on full lockdown until you receive further instructions. This is not a drill."

The alert sirens began to blare almost immediately.

"All security personnel, report to security control," Lieutenant Phillips ordered. "This is not a drill."

"Happy?" she asked.

"Ecstatic."

Admiral Sinclair closed the channel. After waiting a few minutes for the corridors to clear completely, they made their way to Admiral Jenkins's quarters.

Admiral Jenkins and Admiral Sinclair hauled the body onto a gurney and reset the veil to its previous image—that of Ensign Nichols.

By the time they finished, security teams had already sealed off the necessary corridors that would allow them to haul the body to the airlock at the opposite end of the base.

They hauled the gurney down the corridor to the lift, then took the lift down three levels to the maintenance tunnels. After a few twists and turns, they reached the airlock doors, stepped inside, and donned pressure suits. Then, they waited for the power to fail.

Once the exterior illumination went dark, they manually opened the airlock, then slowly and carefully made their way out onto the surface using night vision goggles to find their way. They placed the dead man's shoes on the surface periodically to create footprints. Then, they dropped the body face down and removed the veil. After stepping back twenty feet, Admiral Jenkins hailed Lieutenant Phillips again.

"John, fire when ready," Admiral Jenkins ordered.

A flurry of hot weapons fire bathed the corpse, burning it almost beyond recognition. Admiral Jenkins only hoped that the blinding light did not give away their presence.

Once the security chief stopped firing, they returned to the body and activated the veil. The once gruesome image of a cooked alien was replaced by an equally gruesome image of a cooked human.

With skill rivaling that of expert assassins, they brushed away all footprints leading up to the body except for the prints belonging to the alien, then stepped inside the station, stripped off the pressure suits, returned to Admiral Sinclair's office by the previously secured route, and waited.

***

Joseph stared at the data tablet for a moment. "I need to speak to Admiral Jenkins," Joseph said.

"Mistah Kurtz, he dead," the ensign replied.

Joseph bristled at the literary reference. "Dead?"

"Snipah bullet ta the hade. Horrible rilly."

Joseph paused. *The mission is canceled, and the one person who could reinstate it is dead. And isn't Johnson still on vacation? Something is terribly wrong.*

"Where did you get this?" Joseph demanded.

"Admiral Jameson, suh," he replied.

Joseph knew what he had to do.

"Smash it."

"Suh?" the ensign asked.

"Smash it, then flush it down the toilet. If anyone asks, I never got this message."

"Yessuh."

"And we didn't have this conversation."

"Yessuh."

As the ensign scurried away, Joseph surveyed the crowd. The second ground assault team still hadn't arrived.

Maybe they got the message, too, Joseph thought. *Oh well. No point worrying about it now.*

***

"I hate pressure suits," Wendy Carlson thought out loud as she stepped out of the airlock onto the surface of Triton.

"What was that?" Lieutenant Phillips asked over the radio.

"Nothing," she replied.

As she walked up to the body, Admiral Sinclair came up behind her.

"I wouldn't get too close," Candy said as she bent over.

Wendy stood back up.

"Why not?"

"Turn around," Admiral Sinclair replied.

Wendy turned to face her and jumped a little when she realized she wasn't alone.

"We have reason to believe," Sinclair explained, "that he may have been compromised by a parasitic organism that causes severe damage to the brain and central nervous system, and that this may be the reason he went nuts."

Wendy nodded.

"We still need you to verify his identity," she continued, "but after that, we're going to scorch the body to cinders just to make sure."

Wendy nodded again, took a few photos, kicked the body to roll him over so that she could see his face, took a few more photos, and nodded.

"It's him," she declared. "I'll write up the death certificate."

The admiral nodded.

Wendy began walking back to the station. Admiral Sinclair stood by the body and waited for her to disappear into the airlock before reaching down, disabling the veil, and picking it up.

Admiral Sinclair took about thirty steps back. When she had reached the requisite distance, she gave the order.

"Mr. Phillips, light it up," she ordered.

With those words, her chief of security ensured that there would be no evidence of the alien remaining.

***

"THIRTY seconds to fold," the computer chimed.

Why didn't Skylarov cancel the mission? Mat wondered.

"Fifteen seconds...."

Or maybe he did.

"Ten... Nine... Eight... Seven... Six... Five..."

Mat grimaced.

"Four... Three... Two... One...."

The world seemed to shimmer around them as the spacial folding drive deposited them in the air above the mountain.

Suddenly, the ship shook.

"We just took a direct hit," Jennifer shouted.

"Chutes on!" Joseph ordered.

A moment later, the entire crew stood ready to jump.

"Next hit, we blow this thing," Joseph told them. "Computer, on my mark, dump smoke for ten seconds, then engage auto-destruct with zero-length countdown."

"Affirmative," the computer whined.

Another impact rocked the ship.

"Computer, open jump doors," Joseph shouted.

The doors quickly slid open.

"Everybody, go, go, go!" he ordered. "Computer, dump smoke, and destruct in ten."

Mat heard the computer chirp its acknowledgment as he stepped through the jump doors. Seconds later, the searing heat of the exploding ship at his back told him that one way or another, he would likely not live to see tomorrow. He could only hope to die a hero, or at least to die undiscovered.

"Chutes, everyone, on my mark," Joseph ordered. "Three... Two... One... MARK!"

The rustle of six parachutes suddenly deploying filled the comm channel for a moment.

A few brief seconds later, they were on the ground with their parachutes disconnected.

So it has come to this.

Chapter Twenty-seven

The next morning.

LAURA stumbled into Admiral Sinclair's office at 0500 hours.

"What's the emergency?" she asked. "The damn machine just woke me up and said there was an emergency."

Admiral Sinclair frowned. "Admiral Jenkins is six-twenty-sevened."

Laura gulped. "How do you six-twenty-seven someone from the hub of six-twenty-sevens? That's like arranging protective custody for someone already in protective custody."

"That's the emergency," Sinclair replied. "I've already dispatched Sydney under an assumed identity to collect his wife on Earth and explain the situation—hopefully before she gets the death certificate."

"And me?"

"I have a more important job for you. Admiral Jenkins will be disguised as a diplomat from Kinji visiting this station en route to Earth. You will be her escort."

"Excuse me. Her?"

***

Admiral Jenkins enabled the veil, and emerged Lynna Franklin, Kinji ambassador—a rather remarkably detailed cover identity created with the assistance of Admiral Sinclair's friends at Mikarta Central Intelligence.

"I hate you all," he said as he looked at the elderly woman that greeted him in the mirror, while Laura laughed maniacally for what seemed like ten minutes.

"Do I get one?" Laura asked.

Admiral Sinclair shook her head. "We only have one. You'll have to be altered the old-fashioned way."

Laura gulped. "You're going to rearrange my face?"

Admiral Sinclair chuckled. "Latex, my dear. Latex."

Laura sighed visibly.

"Your trip to Earth is a cover," the admiral continued. "Officially, you're meeting with the prime minister of Earth. Unofficially, you will be escorted from the palace to a secure underground facility where a team of scientists is standing by to study that thing."

The admiral pointed at her compatriot's chest and the veil that lay hidden beneath it.

Laura nodded.

"If you'll follow me down to the medical floor," she added, "Dr. Carlson will show you how to put on your latex face mask."

Laura followed her down two floors and watched in amazement as Dr. Carlson scanned her face with a holographic imager, selected the desired appearance, and instructed the computer to generate a latex mask.

After a few minutes, Dr. Carlson took the finished mask from the automold and placed it on Laura's face. After Wendy applied a few strips of masking latex around the borders, Laura looked like a new woman. Literally.

"I look like I'm having a food allergy," she protested.

"Oh, yes," Admiral Sinclair replied. "You'll have to wear the fat suit, too."

Laura groaned. In spite of her protestations, however, by 0700 hours, they were on a shuttle heading towards Earth.

***

MAT Reinhold's head was spinning.

First, we had to parachute from an exploding ship, and now, one of Svetlana's idiots is shooting at us? What's next, elephants in footie pajamas jumping on trampolines?

As he rounded the corner, he found himself standing in a hallway looking on as Amanda lay strapped to a chair.

We weren't supposed to get this far, he thought. *They were supposed to kill her before we reached her. Those idiots can't get anything right.*

Mat begrudgingly tried to pick up Amanda to haul her out of the room.

"I can walk, thanks," she said as she shoved him away.

Well, if they don't shoot her between here and the exit, he thought, *at least I'll have the pleasure of seeing Joseph's face when I kill her. Small comfort, but what can you do?*

As they rounded the final bend before the doors to the evac area, pulse weapons fire burned the corridor walls ahead of them. Amanda ducked as one shot grazed the shoulder of her clothing. She grabbed her shoulder in pain, then remembered what her captors had done to her left hand, and grabbed it in pain instead.

One of the other soldiers (*Casey,* Mat thought) jumped to protect Amanda, firing three shots as he did so. One member of Svetlana's security force collapsed in front of them, but five more remained. Just then, a bullet missed Mat's head by inches.

Damn it, Svetlana! Tell your troops to shoot at ***her****, not me!*

The soldiers rushed at their position. Mat froze. Then, one of the soldiers suddenly burst into flames, and the troops made a quick 180. Mat could just make out Joseph in the distance picking them off one by one.

After the last of Svetlana's troops went down, Amanda ran to Joseph.

Mat took careful aim and fired. He watched with glee as Amanda collapsed into Joseph's arms. Mat's ecstasy was so complete that he barely even felt the pain as a half dozen Terran Command troops filled him full of holes.

I die content.

***

ADMIRAL Jenkins stepped out of the shuttle onto the Block Island landing platform, south of Providence. Laura followed close behind him. Greeting them on the platform were several members of the Swiss Guard, all wearing fuzzy hats.

One of the guardsmen approached.

"Laura," the girl said. "Laura, it's me. Sydney."

Laura could not contain her laughter.

"It's not funny," Sydney chided. "You get to wear a fake face, and I have to wear a chicken on my head."

"I'm sorry, it's just... you... a guard?"

Sydney had Laura on the ground and in a choke hold faster than you could say "Ouch." When she lifted her back to her feet and let go a few seconds later, Laura stumbled for several seconds before fully catching her breath.

"Wow," Laura said.

"Yeah, they taught me a few moves this morning," Sydney replied. "I won't take a bullet for the Prime Minister of Earth any time soon, but I'm learning."

"I have to admit, no one will ever recognize you," Lynna Franklin née (né?) Admiral Thomas Jenkins said, laughing.

"Who is that?" Sydney asked.

"Amanda's dad," Laura replied.

Sydney snorted. “Okay,” she said, snorting a few more times. “You win.”

Thomas Jenkins folded his (her?) arms and pouted.

“Come on,” Sydney said. “Follow me.”

Sydney led them through the main hallway, whereupon they turned down a small corridor and stepped into a service elevator. They took it to the bottom floor. Then, Sydney inserted a key, and the metal panel below the elevator controls slid aside, revealing a second set of buttons.

Sydney pressed subbasement forty-two, then turned the key back. The doors closed, the metal plate slid back over the extra buttons, and the lift continued its descent.

“For security reasons,” she explained, “you can only access the additional floors from the bottom floor. You’ll notice that the agent at the desk was studying us intently. If he had decided you didn’t belong, the lift would not be moving now.”

Laura nodded. “Creepy weird security.”

“The people who built this place were nuts,” Sydney explained, as though that needed further clarification.

When they finally arrived at subbasement forty-two, the doors opened, and they stepped out into a foyer with a number of halls branching off from it. The sign at the left end of the room said:

> WARNING: Ever-changing maze ahead. Do not proceed without proper authorization and equipment.

Sydney forged ahead. Soon after they entered, they found themselves surrounded by an odd hydroponics area with living walls made of vegetables. She expertly navigated the maze of twisty little cabbages, all alike. Eventually, they stepped out into a large, open control room with huge screens lining every wall and dozens of consoles sticking up from the floor.

"Welcome to the nerve center," Sydney announced proudly.

"How did you..." Laura asked, her voice trailing off.

"There's a speaker in the hat," Sydney replied, chuckling.

A few moments later, Admiral Jenkins disabled the veil, the geeks began to arrive, and Sydney headed back to the lift.

"You look familiar," one morbidly obese man said to Laura.

Laura shook her head.

Oh, crap, she thought, mildly amused. *He's the guy who asked me to play AD&D at AlgolCon.*

Chapter Twenty-eight

The next day:

Admiral Skylarov watched in horror as Joseph Kurtz and a team of Colonial Alliance medical forces carried Amanda Jenkins out of the medical transport to the temporary hospital on Sirius IV.

He could barely keep from spitting as he complimented them on their success.

"Congratulations," Admiral Skylarov offered. "You did it."

"Yes, but at what cost, Admiral?" Joseph asked. "At what cost?"

Skylarov walked away in stony silence. He immediately boarded the nearest transport, folded into the folding zone outside the Chataris sector, and sped off towards the fleet at Lenora Prime, where troops loyal to him stood waiting.

***

Admiral Jenkins grumbled as he awoke in a bunkhouse in the capitol complex. The lumpy bed made his bed on Triton Station seem positively comfortable by comparison.

After taking a couple of minutes to get his bearings, he stood, walked into the capitol building proper, and into the lift. Sydney was already waiting to take him to the right floor. This time, she was carrying a sniper rifle.

Admiral Jenkins wasn't sure whether to be impressed or terrified.

Terrified, he thought. *Definitely terrified.*

When they reached the control center, an older gentleman named Paul approached him and delivered a brief message.

> Mrs. Jenkins,
>
> Your daughter is safe in a medical ward on Sirius IV. Skylarov just left. Will stay by her side until she wakes up.
>
> —Joseph.

"Thank you," Jenkins said as he disabled his veil once again.

The man merely nodded and went on his way.

***

Skylarov stepped out onto the command deck of the Aenid. Troops saluted him, but he ignored them and made his way to Fleet Admiral Ramirez, who was sitting in the captain's chair.

"We need to talk," he said calmly.

Admiral Ramirez nodded, then followed him off the bridge and into an adjacent conference room.

"This isn't working," Skylarov said. "We have failed to capture Earth's Ackerman crystal. We have failed to stop those who know our secret. We have failed to do much of anything, really, while our enemies have picked us off one by one. There are only a few of us left."

"What do you propose?" Ramirez asked.

"We have to strike at the heart of Earth's government," Skylarov replied. "That will draw out the other admirals, and when they countermand your orders, their troops will mutiny."

Ramirez appeared to think about this for a moment.

"Of course you know that you're insane," Ramirez eventually replied.

Skylarov nodded.

"Make it happen."

***

"WHAT have you learned so far?" Admiral Jenkins asked the scientists studying the veil.

The scientists shook their heads. "We really don't know much more than we started out knowing. It projects a holographic field that behaves like nothing we've ever seen."

"Can you at least detect the emissions?" Jenkins asked.

The scientist shook his head.

Jenkins sighed.

***

ADMIRAL Sinclair sat at her desk drinking a cup of tea when her chief of security ran in, panting.

"Admiral," Lieutenant Phillips gasped.

"What is it, John?"

The lieutenant took a few seconds to catch his breath before speaking.

"We just decoded an encrypted message from Admiral Skylarov," he replied. "I thought I should tell you quickly."

"And you couldn't just call me?"

"Not secure enough," he replied. "We've already had two spies on board."

She conceded the point. It had been a rather insane week already. *Glad it's Friday,* she thought, nodding her head.

"What's the message?"

"It says that they are planning an attack on Earth," he replied. "Tomorrow."

She gasped.

If we beef up Earth's defenses, they will know we can tap their communications, but if we do nothing, they will attack Earth. That's just not a target we can afford to lose.

"I already know what you're thinking," he added. "You're wondering if we'd be tipping our hand to send troops to Earth ahead of time."

She nodded.

"It's worse than that," he continued. "I think they wanted us to decrypt that message. It was sent using an encryption key that Skylarov accidentally leaked about a month ago. It was revoked... well, about a month ago."

"You think it could be a trap," Sinclair said matter-of-factly.

Lieutenant Phillips nodded. "It's likely, sir."

"Leave me," she replied. "I need some time to think."

***

SYDNEY smiled as she took Laura on a tour around various parts of the capitol complex.

"And that," Sydney said, pointing to a seemingly solid section of marble wall above them on the circular balcony that encircled the rotunda on the second floor, "is the emergency exit staircase. If you know how to open it, the stairs beyond it lead to a tunnel that takes you out to the coastline."

"How many ways out of this place are there?" Laura asked.

"Only five," Sydney replied. "There's the landing pad inside the capitol grounds, the main front entrance, the rear entrance used by service vehicles and delivery vehicles, and this emergency exit."

"You said five," Laura corrected. "That was only four."

Sydney smiled. "The fifth is an underwater submarine bay. You were about five hundred feet from it when you landed yesterday."

Laura shook her head. "You're right. The people who designed this *were* nuts."

Sydney continued the tour.

"Upstairs, you'll find the main doors to the upper parliament chambers. Whenever both houses meet jointly, they use those chambers. Except for speakers, the able-bodied members of parliament generally enter by walking up these steps," she said, pointing at the two giant, curved staircases that encircled the rotunda, "and through those doors."

"Speakers have to go through those doors," she said, pointing at another set of doors on the lower floor. "Then, they follow the halls below the parliament floor to a narrow staircase that leads up to the back of the hall."

"And for people who can't make it up the stairs?" Laura asked.

"There's a staff elevator in the west wing," she replied, pointing down a long corridor. "There's a handicapped entrance right beside it. There's also an outdoor ramp that leads to the back of the hall."

Laura nodded.

Suddenly, Sydney turned her head to the side for a moment and closed her eyes. When she turned back, she addressed Laura again.

"Laura, there's an urgent message for you from Admiral Sinclair," Sydney said. "You can take it in the office there on the right."

"Thank you," Laura replied, then disappeared into the office.

***

ADMIRAL Sinclair relaxed a bit when she saw Laura's altered face on the viewscreen.

"Laura!" she exclaimed. "Good to see you. How's Sydney?"

Laura burst into laughter. After a few seconds, she regained her composure. "Sorry," she replied. "Funny hat."

The admiral smiled.

"I need a favor from someone who knows her way around the Terran Command provisioning system," Admiral Sinclair said. "Is this line secure?"

Laura nodded.

"Skylarov is moving to attack Earth tomorrow," she continued. "We're going to protect Earth at all costs, but there's no way I'll be able to shut down the civilian shipping lanes without tipping our hand. I need a folding gate delivered quietly to somewhere in the Kuiper belt."

"Pardon?" Laura replied. "Can't your ships fold themselves?"

"Sure, we can do coordinated folds so that we don't interfere with the Earth gate's operation," Sinclair explained, "but that won't get enough ships in there quickly enough. Even at maximum speed, Earth is a long way from Triton Station. We'd be sitting ducks."

"So you're going to use GlobeGate."

Sinclair nodded. "We're going to redirect all civilian traffic automatically to MarsGate. There are enough troops loyal to me in the gate command and control center that we should be able to send out a gate restriction bulletin. That will free up GlobeGate for military purposes. By doing so, we can move the entire fleet in a little under two hours."

Laura was impressed.

"But we need that gate," Sinclair replied. "And get one of the old first-generation models. No need to put a new gate in harm's way."

Laura began writing up a provisioning request to deliver a second folding gate to Sirius IV under the guise of replacing one of the oldest gates still in active operation. That was the easy part.

"Computer, get me Joseph Kurtz," she asked.

"Joseph here," he replied almost immediately.

Laura could tell from his face that he hadn't gotten much sleep. Amanda lay motionless in a hospital bed next to him, still unconscious.

"Joseph, I hate to put this on you," she began, "but Skylarov is up to something."

Joseph nodded. "I got that impression from Jameson."

"He doesn't know the half of it," she replied. "We're delivering a folding gate into orbit around Sirius IV in about two hours. I need you to pick up the existing Sirius gate and deliver it to the Kuiper belt, near the farthest reaches of our solar system. And keep this quiet...."

Joseph shook his head. "I can't leave Amanda."

"Her dad's in trouble," Laura countered.

"Her dad is alive?"

Laura nodded. "Not for long, though, if we can't get almost the entire Terran fleet into Earth's orbit by tomorrow."

"Jen!" Joseph shouted. "I need you!"

Jennifer ran in. "What's the emergency?" she asked.

"Amanda's father is in trouble," he replied. "I don't have time to explain. I need you to take a fold fighter, pick up the old folding gate that's in orbit above us, and deliver it to the Kuiper belt—preferably close to Neptune."

Jen nodded. "Will do. Anything for Amanda."

Joseph smiled as she walked over to Marc and his little sister.

"Could you babysit for us?" she asked, smiling.

Joseph chuckled. “Sure. Come ’ere, kid.”

***

LAURA grabbed a railing when the ground shook suddenly.

“What’s going on?” she asked.

Sydney listened to her hat for a moment, then grabbed Laura and ran as hard as she could for the service elevator. They took the elevator to the bottom.

When they reached the posted bottom, Sydney inserted her key and took them further down to the underground command center.

“Sydney?” she asked again. “What’s happening?”

“The capitol complex,” Sydney replied, “is under attack from space, and the orbital bombardment is just the beginning. We have word that Terran Alliance troop ships containing hundreds of troops are descending from orbit towards the capitol complex as we speak.”

Laura gulped.

“We’re going back to the command center,” she continued.

“What about Earth’s prime minister?” Laura asked.

“If he isn’t here as expected,” Sydney replied, “then they will know that he must be somewhere else. Unless you want the secret subbasements to be discovered, we must allow the prime minister to be captured.”

“How very... strategic of you.”

“Wasn’t my call,” Sydney told her. “I’m just doing what the hat tells me to do.”

Laura smirked.

***

ADMIRAL Jenkins appeared on Admiral Sinclair’s viewscreen.

"Admiral Sinclair," Admiral Jenkins said in a panicked voice.

"Yes, Tom," she replied.

"The capitol building is under attack," Jenkins told her. "They're bombing the surrounding grounds from space, and there's a troop ship landing in the courtyard. We expect the upper levels to be overrun fairly quickly, with all hands killed or captured."

Admiral Sinclair nodded. "What do we do?"

"We need those ships here ASAP," he replied. "Let Jameson lead them. I need you to take a fleet of fold fighters and drop them into the ocean."

"Pardon?"

Admiral Jenkins smiled. "There's an underwater submarine bay attached to this base. You should be able to get your fold fighters in easily. Fill up every nook and cranny with troops, including the bomb bays, and drop into the ocean on a ballistic trajectory. Reverse thrust when you hit the water. It won't be a fun landing, but it should be survivable."

Should be, she thought. *Always the optimist.*

"We have to take the palace from the inside," Jenkins explained. "There's no feasible way to take it from the outside. At best, troops attacking from the outside will create a useful distraction. At worst, it will be a slaughter."

Admiral Sinclair nodded. "Let's hope for the best, then. I'm sending troops on the surface, too."

Admiral Jenkins nodded.

Suddenly, Admiral Jameson's face appeared on their screens.

"I heard you were planning a coup without me," Jameson joked.

"It's looking like that, Phil," Admiral Sinclair replied. "You'll be leading the main attack force from space. I'll be crash landing a bunch of fold fighters into an underwater shuttle bay or some such insanity."

Admiral Jameson chuckled. "You always did have a flair for the dramatic, Tom."

"I'll send you all the base schematics you'll need and all the coordinates as soon as I get them," Jenkins replied. "Beyond that, we'll just wait for the cavalry to arrive and we'll start the attack when you get here."

Admirals Sinclair and Jameson both nodded.

"Jenkins out," Admiral Jenkins replied, closing the connection.

With that, Admiral Sinclair began making calls. Half of the captains in the fleet refused to have any part of the mission even after she showed them the evidence; the other half were skeptical.

She knew that halfway across the known universe, Admiral Jameson was making similar calls. Between the two of them, she felt sure that they would get through to enough of the captains to make a difference.

Admiral Jameson was scheduled to arrive within the hour to lead the attack. She almost envied him. His role was basically doing what he had been trained to do. Her role, however, was anything but.

I'll be plunging under the force of gravity into an ocean, then flying a space fighter under a thousand feet of ocean water and bringing it to rest in an underwater landing bay, she thought. *Jenkins must have lost his mind.*

Chapter Twenty-nine

The next morning.

ADMIRAL Jenkins awoke to the beeping of a viewscreen in the command bunker. A moment later, Jennifer's face appeared on the screen.

"Jennifer, what a surprise," he exclaimed.

"Admiral, I just dropped off a folding gate near Triton Station with a fold fighter," she replied. "The rest of the fleet is converging there for deployment through Globe-Gate in about ten minutes. If all goes as planned, I'll be leading the second wave of fold fighters behind Admiral Sinclair."

He nodded. "We'll leave the door open for you."

Jennifer smiled.

"And when we're done, my orders are to escort you to Sirius IV," she continued.

The admiral nodded. "As it should be, love. As it should be. Was that all?"

"No, Admiral Sinclair asked me to tell you that a rolling stone gathers moss just fine."

He nodded at the code. "Tell her that my peonies outclass her petunias any day, and that her husband still owes me a round of golf at Roswell country club. With Skylarov and Ramirez."

Jennifer's eyes widened as she nodded. "Ramirez?"

Jenkins nodded.

"Fleet Admiral Ramirez?" she asked again.

Again, Jenkins nodded.

"I'll pass it along," she replied, her voice wavering. "Oh, and one more thing."

"Yes?"

"She said that she was going to sell her Les Paul, and she knew you revered it, so she wanted to know if you wanted to take it for a ride then, before she sold it."

Admiral Jenkins was momentarily puzzled, then he understood.

"Tell her hardly a man alive remembers that guitar, but I'd love to play it a bit in the tower of the Old North Church."

She nodded. "Triton Station out."

Jennifer reached up to close the channel, and the viewscreen went black.

Good. Now I can sleep, he thought.

Ten seconds later, the first of another round of explosions shook the bunker.

So much for that.

***

Later that evening.

ADMIRAL Sinclair stood on a dais erected on the flight deck just below the observation windows that overlooked it from the main corridor. Around her, thousands of Terran Command officers and troops stood awaiting their final orders. Outside, she knew, tens of thousands more stood and sat watching her speech on viewscreens in conference rooms and mess halls on hundreds of ships on the surface and in orbit overhead.

"Honored Terran soldiers," she began, "to borrow a famous quote, 'Today is a day that will define tomorrow.' Truly, no truer words were ever spoken. When President Mikaela Cartwright spoke those words more than two hundred and fifty years ago, our planet was in the midst of a great war—a war that nearly cost humanity its very existence. We stand here today because of the countless brave men and women who gave their lives that day to defeat the Southern Front and take back the nuclear arms that fell into their hands."

Admiral Sinclair paused for a moment to let that sink in (and to let the translators catch up; she felt particularly sorry for the sign language translator, who was signing furiously at a pace that could only be described as "warp speed").

"President Cartwright went on to say," Admiral Sinclair continued, "that there is no greater threat to humanity than humanity. She spoke of the Southern Front not as traitors or terrorists or madmen, but as people—as those led astray by the leaders that they trusted. Many credit that speech as the pivotal moment in the war, not because it spurred the troops, not because it inspired patriotism, but because it won the hearts and minds of the public and dried up the terrorists' supply of new recruits."

"Today, we once again stand on the precipice between heaven and hell, between peace and all-out civil war. Yesterday, our planet was attacked by the very forces sworn to protect us, and for what reason? To protect a secret that matters more to our so-called leaders than the lives of our own people."

"But the people we fight this day are not the enemy; they are our own people, led astray by our true enemy. Today's battle will be the hardest you will ever endure—not because of the battle, not because of the risk of imminent death, but because you will be fighting those who claim allegiance to Terran Command, led by those who would subversively plot to destroy it. Today, we will meet the enemy; today, we will meet ourselves."

"And so, I send you out today, knowing that many of you will not return. Know that I will stand with you, I will fight with you, and if necessary, I will die with you, for this is a battle that we must not lose. The fate of Earth, of the Terran Alliance, and indeed of all of humanity rests with you in this, our greatest battle. We must fight, and we must win. Onward, and Godspeed."

***

ADMIRAL Jenkins sat in the control center and watched the giant screens as they cycled through feeds from various security cameras in the building. Remarkably, the invading forces did not disable them. In fact, on camera 73, he could see two of their troops sitting in the somewhat more public version of the control room (on the ground floor) watching the security camera feeds themselves.

Rule #1 of infiltrating a facility: destroy communications. They forgot rule #1, he thought. *Good thing I remembered.*

"Sydney, could you be a dear and ask the hat how to turn off the security camera feed to the upstairs?" he asked.

Sydney chuckled.

"No way," she replied a moment later.

"No you won't ask?"

"No, it can't be done," she replied, then paused for a moment and inclined her head.

"So there's nothing we can do?" Jenkins asked.

Sydney glared at him and made a flapping gesture towards him with her hand to indicate that he should be silent.

"Hmm?" he asked.

She continued the gesture, and a few seconds later, shut her eyes. When she opened them again, she turned her head back to the admiral.

"But we can cut the power," she said.

Admiral Jenkins perked up. "How?"

"This bunker has an internal backup generator," she replied, "but the upstairs doesn't. We just have to shut down the power grid."

Jenkins nodded. "So how do we do this?"

Sydney shook her head. "Uh, I don't think you quite understand. This island's power system was designed to withstand a direct nuclear attack without even using the emergency generators. It draws power from a dozen different cities using dozens of undersea cables. And those troops are no doubt protecting the cutoffs on both ends."

He looked at her uncomprehendingly.

"If we want to cut power to the island," she explained, "we have to *shut down* the power grid."

"Uh huh."

"For all of the Eastern seaboard."

Jenkins blinked. Twice.

"Make the call," he replied.

Sydney nodded and pressed a few keys on the control panel in front of her.

"When?" she asked.

"When what?"

"When should they shut down the grid?"

"When Paul Revere rides," he muttered.

"Huh?" Sydney asked.

"Uh..." he stammered. "Midnight. That's when Admiral Sinclair said she'd meet us."

"When did she say that?" Sydney asked, puzzled.

"You remember that call from Jen?" he replied. "She passed on the message. I don't play guitar. I wouldn't know a Les Paul from a Telecaster. She said she knew I 'revered' it and asked if I wanted to take it for a 'ride'. It was a code. The midnight ride of Paul Revere. I quoted a couple lines from it to indicate my understanding. They ride at midnight."

"And you're telling us this now?" Sydney asked incredulously.

He shrugged. "I didn't think it was all that important. We'll go in when our backup arrives, whether that's midnight or next month."

"Well, it looks like the city that never sleeps is about to get some relief from its insomnia," she replied as she passed along his instructions.

Admiral Jenkins nodded.

Chapter Thirty

The next day (January 20, 2391)

THE fateful hour arrived, and Admiral Sinclair boarded her fold fighter.

"I'll lead the first attack wave," she said as she addressed the troops. "If it's a trap, I want it to be me out there. They're probably gonna be waiting for us, so wait for my signal, then fold in with your guns hot."

As her ship took off, she called for folding clearance.

"Triton gate," Sinclair asked, "this is Admiral Sinclair aboard fold fighter Tango-Sierra-three-niner requesting clearance to fold."

"Admiral Sinclair," a girl's whispered voice replied, "this is Adele Ginsburg in folding control. Hold, please. Beta team, folding you to Mars now. Okay, Admiral Sinclair, you are clear to fold."

Now, Adele folding softly for another, says to me: Thou must die, she thought, shivering. *Never send to know for whom Adele folds. She folds for thee.*

Admiral Sinclair keyed in the folding sequence, shimmered, and reappeared in orbit around Earth just outside GlobeGate. As she reached for the weapons controls, twelve satellites simultaneously targeted her position. The beam weapons sliced through the hull like knives through butter, and the hissing told her that the ship was open to space.

As the fireball enveloped her, she closed her eyes and waited for the end.

***

"SHIT!" Admiral Jameson shouted as he watched the tactical display. "They were waiting for us. They got Candy."

"What do we do?" Jen asked.

"Did you get telemetry and active sensor data?" Joseph asked from his place of honor on the viewscreen.

"Yeah, why?" Jen asked in reply.

"I could program cruise missiles with vectors based on the last known locations of those satellites," Joseph suggested. "Maybe you can punch through."

"Don't bother, Kurtz," Jameson replied, shaking his head. "We don't need to."

Jen stared at him. Joseph merely sat at Amanda's bedside in silence.

"Admiral Sinclair's mission was a success," he replied. "They think we're going to send ships through the gate."

"We're not?" Jen asked.

"Well, if Admiral Sinclair's ship had gotten through, that was plan A," Jameson explained, "but we didn't hold out much hope for that. No, Sinclair's primary mission was to distract them long enough for the beta team to fold the Mars gate out of the solar system. That's one of the rare advantages of being near superior conjunction; Mars is nowhere near Earth right now, so there was no need to coordinate the fold with GlobeGate."

Joseph's jaw dropped. "You're going to blow up GlobeGate."

Jameson nodded. "It's the only way, son."

Jen just stared at the admiral a bit harder.

"It's obvious now that I think about it," Joseph explained. "Our folding ships can safely fold near each other, but not in proximity to a folding gate. Those use older technology, so it's not safe to fold within a few AU of an active folding gate. The ship would be torn apart. That's why GlobeGate is synchronized with the Mars gate so that they can't fold at the same time."

"If GlobeGate were unguarded," Jen commented, "we would end up with lots of delays when folding because of Mars gate activity, but we'd get there. Okay, I get that. But it's not, so you're just going to blow it up?"

"By taking the Mars gate out of the picture, the only thing preventing unsynchronized folds is GlobeGate, and by getting rid of it, we can fold the whole fleet into orbit in minutes."

"Why can't we just move the Mars gate out and shut down GlobeGate?" Jen asked incredulously.

"We're not in control of GlobeGate. Sure, we could divert all legitimate traffic with a gate restrictions bulletin," Joseph replied, "but as long as the enemy is in physical control of the gate, they could maliciously enable it at any time, causing the catastrophic failure of any ships in transit. They could take out all of our ships without ever firing a shot. It's really the only logical..."

"But won't blowing up GlobeGate knock the planet out of orbit?" Jen interrupted. "Isn't that why terrorists kept trying to blow up Mars gate back in the 50s?"

"Mars gate, sure," Joseph replied, "because it's in orbit around the planet. GlobeGate is in a solar orbit at Earth's L4 Lagrange point. It's nowhere near Earth, unless you're talking about distance on astronomical scales."

Jen nodded. "Okay. So how do we blow up the gate?" she asked, looking at Admiral Jameson for clarification. "A bomb or missile would just get shot apart by the defense satellites before it finished folding. It would never get closer than tens of kilometers from the gate itself."

Admiral Jameson smiled knowingly. "To be honest, the physics is a bit beyond me, but the eggheads say it will work, so..." he replied, then stopped himself. "Anyway, I'm guessing that Joseph has it figured out by now, so I'll let him explain it."

Joseph shook his head. "The easiest way to blow up GlobeGate is to send a fold fighter through and have it fold while folding."

Jen looked at the viewscreen with a "what the heck are you talking about" look.

Joseph rubbed his temples for a moment before continuing. "I don't know how much theoretical physics you've taken, but... if you remember the history of folding theory at all, it was originally hypothesized that it would take infinite energy to fold without a pair of gates because the entanglement caused by the fold itself was not taken into account in the math. Well, a fold within a fold breaks that entanglement rather completely, so suddenly, the power draw becomes infinite."

"But the power source isn't infinite," Jen protested. "Won't the gate just shut down?"

"GlobeGate," Joseph replied, "was built in the day when these things routinely had to fold colossal ships—back before single-ended folding technology existed. It is quite literally powered by the sun itself, drawing superheated plasma through a microfold. The size of the fold is dependent upon the amount of energy being drained on the output."

Jen nodded blankly.

"So the power source may not be infinite," he continued, "but it can provide way more heat than the gate can withstand. A few decades back, someone folded just a little too soon and caused a lot of smoke. There was a three year moratorium on folding drive testing after that incident.

Even in the most conservative models, a properly timed fold will draw enough power to fry the gate. In the most paranoid models, the whole thing will go off with the force of several dozen fusion reactors."

Jen raised her eyebrows. "Why hasn't anyone exploited this?" Jen asked. "Terrorists have been trying to blow up Mars gate for years—decades, even. Do you mean to tell me that all they needed was a fold fighter?"

"There are safeties on the newer gates to prevent this very scenario. The gate would simply shut down, leaving the ship in two pieces. That's why they picked the gate from Sirius IV," Joseph replied. "There are only a handful of first-generation gates still out there—GlobeGate, Sirius IV, Tau Ceti, maybe a couple of fringe gates around Polaris.... Basically, they almost never call each other. When they do, the gate system bounces you to a newer gate as a go-between."

"So you're going to reprogram it to not do that?" she asked.

"Not me," he replied. "Someone will have to physically swap out the control boards aboard our folding gate itself. I'm guessing Admiral Jameson has obtained some old military surplus boards from before the accident at Pollux V?"

The admiral nodded. "And multiple backups, just in case."

"And once that's done?" Jen asked.

"If you dial directly and fold within a fold?" Kurtz asked rhetorically. "Instant fireworks—on both ends, I might add. How far is your gate from the fleet, again?"

"About 10,000 km," Jameson replied.

"You're gonna want to have the Sirius gate towed a lot farther out than that. Heck, Mars gate orbits almost twice that high. I'd say take it to at least ten or twenty *million* kilometers."

Jameson nodded. "We'll take care of it," he replied, and began keying in a message on the nearest data pad.

"Why do I have a feeling this is gonna get ugly?" Joseph asked.

Suddenly, a light blinking on the console told them that they were receiving a fleetwide priority mauve broadcast.

Jen shook her head. "Too late."

***

ADMIRAL Jenkins sat in the bunker below the capitol complex and watched as midnight came and went. He knew what that meant.

Plan B, he thought, sighing. *Guess Candy won't be joining us for that round of golf.*

The lights went out suddenly, then came back on.

"We're now operating on emergency power," Sydney announced. "The power grid for the entire Eastern seaboard is down. They'd better get here soon. We can't maintain this state for very long."

Bloody hell, he thought. *It's going to be that kind of day.*

That's when a blinking light on the console told him that he was receiving a fleetwide priority mauve broadcast.

Admiral Jenkins enabled the viewscreen, only to see the face of Fleet Admiral Ramirez.

"Attention, all Terran Command personnel," he began. "This is Fleet Admiral Ramirez. You are hereby ordered to stand down, effective immediately. Any and all orders from Admirals Jenkins, Jameson, and Sinclair are hereby rescinded. They are no longer your commanding officers. If you follow their orders, you will all be courts-martialled and executed for high treason against the Terran Alliance."

Admiral Jenkins cut off the message, then issued a similar broadcast message to the troops.

"As you are probably all aware by now, Admiral Skylarov and Fleet Admiral Ramirez have been compromised by hostile forces as evidenced by Fleet Admiral Ramirez's recent illegal order to attack the capitol complex on Earth to subvert our government's control over Earth's defense satellites and violate the proper chain of command."

"Troops allied with Skylarov and Ramirez have already taken physical control of many of those satellites and have used them to assassinate Admiral Sinclair. Clearly, this action represents a fundamental abrogation of their duty as leaders in our military. Further, their capture of the prime minister of the Terran Alliance constitutes an act of treason and an illegal coup, an action punishable by death under the Uniform Code of Military Justice."

"If you follow their orders, it will be considered an act of sedition under the UCMJ, and as this is a time of imminent threat, anyone caught doing so may be summarily executed *without* court-martial. Admiral Jenkins out."

***

"ADMIRAL Jameson?" a young cadet asked.

Admiral Jameson nodded. "What is it, son?"

"We have confirmation," the pimply faced boy replied. "The Triton folding gate is at ten million kilometers. We should be well outside the blast radius. The tech team has just completed the upgrade, and they are folding back... now."

"Excellent," Jameson replied. "Let me know when the fold fighter is ready."

"Already there, sir," he replied. "A computer-controlled fold fighter is standing by at the gate and awaiting your orders."

"Let's do this, then," he replied. "Upload the program to the shuttle."

The cadet pressed a few buttons on his data pad, waited for a green indicator, then nodded. "It's done, sir."

"Fold the ship," Jameson ordered, "and may God help us all."

The sudden flash of light looked like a star going supernova in the distance as the newly installed Triton gate exploded in a giant fireball.

"Sir, we're getting word from the beta squad," the cadet reported. "There was a large explosion near Earth's L4 Lagrange point. GlobeGate is down for the count. All satellites and monitoring systems at the L4 point should have been vaporized as well, judging from the reported blast intensity."

Joseph frowned as he watched the events unfold on his viewscreen. *This is truly the end of an era,* he thought.

"Okay, then," Jameson replied. "Looks like this is turning out to be my lucky day. First wave, you have a go."

And with those words, the fleet begin folding en masse out of orbit around Triton and into orbit around Earth.

***

The lights in the submarine bay flickered slowly to life as twelve fold fighters surfaced. Within seconds, the security system switched its attention to that area, and the viewscreen in the control room began showing the sub bay from various angles.

Admiral Jenkins watched as about fifty unfamiliar faces emerged from the fighters and began swimming across the pool of water in the gaping hole in the floor. When they reached the side of the pool, they climbed up onto the five-foot-wide platform that surrounded it, then walked to the door. Each one carried a sea bag laden with gear. Based on the soldiers' altered gait, he suspected that the bags were heavy.

As they approached the doors to the various decompression chambers that surrounded the platform, their platoon leader smiled at the security camera.

"Admiral Jenkins," the man said in a thick English accent, "I'm Captain Schoeffield, Terran command infantry. Admiral Jameson sends his regards. Sorry we're late, but finally the Regulars are coming out."

Admiral Jenkins smirked at the oblique reference and unlocked the doors to the decompression chambers.

The British are coming, he mused.

A few minutes later, the troops emerged from the hyperbaric chambers into a large storage area. Admiral Jenkins stood there waiting for them.

"Admiral?" the young captain asked.

Admiral Jenkins nodded.

"What are your orders?"

***

"Lieutenant Sanderson," Admiral Jameson barked, "report."

Jennifer sat bolt upright. She hadn't even heard him enter C&C.

"Admiral," she replied, "the first wave has finished folding. There's still no word from Admiral Jenkins. I'm monitoring comms traffic from the battle in space, but I'm not getting much."

"I need to know where we stand," he replied. "Do we even have telemetry data from the ships on our side?"

Joseph shook his head from his position of power on the viewscreen. "The background noise is too high from all the explosions. Nothing is getting through except the occasional data burst from a folding tracker, and even that is surprisingly sporadic. It's like trying to whisper in a crowded gymnasium."

Admiral Jameson nodded his understanding.

Jen suddenly tilted her head to one side. "Sir, we just got a data burst with some logs and an active sensor sweep. We're evenly matched—about two hundred ships apiece. It's going to be a long, ugly fight. Captain Glasgow is maneuvering his forces to drag the fighting away from Earth, but it's slow going."

"Understood," he replied. "Keep me informed. If you haven't heard from Jenkins, we'll send the second wave in two hours."

***

Admiral Jenkins and Captain Schoeffield stared at a map on the control center's main viewscreen.

"Here's the plan. We're here," Admiral Jenkins said, pointing. "The green dot on level 3 is the prime minister. Exits are here, here, and here. Based on the security cameras, we estimate that there are about thirty-five enemy troops scattered at strategic locations throughout the capitol complex. There are three men guarding the prime minister from inside the room, plus two at the door, and several more in various hallways leading up to the room."

"Still not hearing the plan," Captain Schoeffield replied testily.

"There are a series of maintenance corridors throughout the complex in short levels between floors," Jenkins replied. "We'll have to crouch, but we can move freely in those levels. Once in there, we can lower someone down through an air vent to take out the three guards with a sniper rifle, then pull the prime minister up through the hole."

"Won't those maintenance corridors be guarded?"

"Doubtful. The only access is through a ladder here," Jenkins said, pointing at a small closet-sized room in the same place on every floor, just a few meters from the main elevator. "They would have no reason to know about those floors, much less guard them."

"The elevator is guarded," Captain Schoeffield replied, "so I'm guessing this won't be a sneak attack by any means."

Admiral Jenkins shook his head. "The elevator is guarded on the *first floor*. Normally, you have to stop there when transitioning between normal lift mode and the secure mode leading to the underground levels, but we can keep the doors closed with a fireman's key."

"And you'll get one where?"

Laura pulled a multi-tool out of her pocket and showed him the screwdriver.

"Next question."

"Houston, we have a problem," Sydney said, interrupting. "The deep space relay network is down."

"Damn," Jenkins replied. "So there's no way to send a message to Admiral Johnson to let him know that you arrived."

Captain Schoeffield nodded. "He'll assume that we didn't make it, and will send reinforcements in a couple of hours. Probably Sanderson."

"As much as I'd love to have her here to take the first shot, this can't wait," Jenkins replied. "They could move him at any moment, and we might lose the opportunity to pull him out. We'll have to send someone back down for Jennifer and company once we've reached the maintenance level."

Admiral Jenkins thought he heard Captain Schoeffield swearing under his breath, but he ignored it.

"I'll go back," Sydney replied. "I'm not going to be of much use to you in your little invasion. Plus, I have the hat."

Jenkins chuckled just thinking about the hat, while Schoeffield just stared at them quizzically.

"How will we get back?" Schoeffield asked.

Jenkins grimaced. He had a point.

"You don't," Sydney replied. "When the reinforcements arrive, I'll bring them to you at the maze entrance."

"And if they don't arrive?" Schoeffield asked.

"Then you'd better haul everything you need with you the first time," Sydney replied. "It's really the only way."

***

CAPTAIN Rick Glasgow stood aboard the bridge of the battle cruiser Augustus. Its sleek, comfortable, modern interior belied its deadly purpose.

All around him, the battle raged. Twelve battle cruisers from Skylarov's forces were pitted against the nine Terran cruisers he commanded, but the bulk of the fighting was not being waged by the cruisers. Instead, each cruiser had more than fifty fold fighters deployed in close-range combat. Those front-line soldiers were taking the brunt of the weapons fire, both from each other and from the cruisers.

For the moment, they were at a convenient stalemate, save for one nagging problem. One of Skylarov's cruisers had taken a position directly above the capitol complex. Rick knew that if the second wave of Triton fold fighters folded in to reinforce Admiral Jenkins and his troops on the ground, they would be obliterated in short order.

We need a plan, he thought, *and fast.*

Then, out of the corner of his eye, he spotted it—a Terran defense satellite in orbit around the planet.

"Tom," he shouted. "Send another data burst, and tell Admiral Jameson that I need help from Joseph Kurtz. We need to crack into a defense satellite."

***

Remind me to have the person who designed this place committed, Jenkins thought as he and Captain Schoeffield followed Sydney through the ridiculous maze that limited access to the underground command center.

"How much further" Captain Schoeffield asked.

Admiral Jenkins laughed. "Hard to say. These tunnels are just about indistinguishable. Sydney?"

Sydney paused for a moment to listen to the hat.

"Four more turns," she replied.

They continued to follow her down four more corridors until they emerged into the foyer outside the elevators.

"You're on your own, guys," Sydney said as she slipped into a different passageway that led somewhat less circuitously to the submarine bay.

As she departed, Admiral Jenkins couldn't help but chuckle a little as he watched her engage in a seemingly one-sided conversation with the hat.

He quickly pressed the call button on the elevator and waited. Suddenly, Sydney dashed back into the room.

"I forgot to do something," she explained as she walked over to the desk in the basement lobby. "Normally, we have somebody stationed in the main lobby to manually release the elevator for subbasement duty. This prevents people from accidentally bringing unauthorized personnel down when they call the elevator. Since there's nobody stationed up there, I have to override it from here."

She sat down at the console. "Perfect. Empty," she said as she requested that the elevator doors close. After staring at the security camera and confirming that the elevator was empty, she released it to service their floor.

"Your problem now," she said as the elevator arrived. Then, she dashed back out the way she came.

Admiral Jenkins just shook his head.

"A strange girl," Captain Schoeffield remarked. "I can never figure out what she's thinking."

"That's okay," Jenkins remarked. "Neither can she."

Laura glared at them, then stepped into the elevator. Admiral Jenkins started to follow, but she motioned him off.

"It's going to be a few minutes," she said as she disassembled the main panel.

Suddenly, a beeping noise from the podium across the room caught her attention.

"Admiral," Laura shouted, "could you get that?"

Admiral Jenkins walked over and grumbled.

"It's telling me that somebody tripped the tamper sensor and it is asking me if I want to disable access," Jenkins said.

"Tell it no," Laura replied as she clipped two jumper leads to the back of the firefighter operation switch and then crudely taped the panel back into place with gaffer's tape, letting the wires hang out from behind the panel.

"Come on in," she said.

About half of the fifty soldiers packed themselves into the elevator. Once they were in, Laura connected the two leads together, enabling firefighter operation mode. Then, she pressed and held the "Door Close" button. After a few seconds, the door closed. She then pressed the "Call Cancel" button to reset all of the floor lights before pressing the first floor button on the panel.

Once they reached the first floor, Laura turned off the secure area key and pressed the button for the fifth floor.

"When you want to get back in," Laura said, "knock the Russian Dance from the Nutcracker suite."

She demonstrated it briefly. A few moments later, they arrived on the fifth floor, and she pressed and held the door open button.

Captain Schoeffield stepped forward, peeked carefully around the corner, then signalled for them to move forward. As soon as they were clear, Laura reversed the process and headed back to the staging area below.

***

Sydney was standing in the submarine bay waiting for the second wave when her hat signalled an incoming message.

"Yes?" she asked.

"This is Lieutenant Joseph Kurtz to Admiral Jenkins. We need your assistance with an urgent matter. Over."

"Lieutenant Kurtz," Sydney replied. "Admiral Jenkins is not available at the moment. Can I be of assistance?"

There was a long pause. She couldn't be certain if he was thinking about it or if the signal was just going a long way.

"Maybe," the voice in her hat replied. "I'm going to give you a series of instructions. We need someone to carry them out from the satellite operations center."

"There's a tunnel to there from here," Sydney replied as she started jogging back to the control room, "but I'd imagine the SOC will be guarded."

There's that long pause again, she noted. *I guess they're relaying the messages using a ship in space.*

"That's affirmative. Do not proceed until you have a strike team backing you."

"Mmm-hmm," she replied. "What are your instructions for when we get there?"

"Do you have paper and a pencil?" Joseph's voice asked after a few seconds.

She reached the control room, opened the door, and sat down at the main control desk.

"I do now," she replied.

"I need you to point the defense satellites at these coordinates," Joseph's voice said.

Sydney copied down the coordinates that Joseph gave her, then read them back to him.

"I'll update you with final coordinates if they change enough to require it," he continued. "The ship you're looking for is the Aenid."

"Aenid. Check," Sydney replied.

“We need that ship taken out,” Joseph said. “The second wave can’t land until it’s gone.”

“Understood.”

“Kurtz out.”

***

As Admiral Skylarov entered the bridge of the Aenid, Fleet Admiral Ramirez stood mid-deck, watching the battle unfold as a series of blinking dots on the viewscreen.

“What’s the holdup?” Ramirez asked before turning around. “Oh, it’s you. Sorry, I though it was that idiot engineer. He’s supposed to be getting me a voice link to the planet.”

Skylarov snorted.

Suddenly, the comm system chirped. Ramirez picked up the wired phone just in case it was someone important.

“Fleet Admiral R-R-Ramirez,” the voice at the other end stuttered, “I h-have some b-bad news.”

The admiral rolled his eyes. “Ensign?”

“We can’t raise the planet,” the engineer replied. “C-c-communications are jammed.”

The admiral hung up.

The engineer walked in through the lift door a moment later.

“Sir?” he asked.

Admiral Ramirez spun. “What is it now?”

“That’s not all the bad news, sir,” the engineer replied. “We’ve been reviewing radar data from before the attack. It seems that several fold fighters made it past our defense satellites and dropped underwater just off the coast of Rhode Island. They have yet to resurface.”

“Skylarov?” Fleet Admiral Ramirez asked, smiling. “How would you like to lead a landing party?”

Skylarov began slamming his head repeatedly into the nearest wall.

***

Admiral Jenkins huddled along with twenty-five troops in the five-foot-tall maintenance crawlspace above the third floor. About three minutes later, Sydney arrived with the second group of troops.

"What's going on?" Admiral Jenkins asked. "I thought you were going to wait for the second wave."

Sydney shook her head. "If you can't seize control of the satellite control station on the other side of the island, there's not going to be a second wave."

Admiral Jenkins sighed.

It's going to be that kind of day, he thought.

"What do we have to do?"

Sydney laid out the plan, describing the layout of the island and the tunnel system below it, and giving information about the number of guards and approximate distance.

Admiral Jenkins pointed at Captain Schoeffield. "Captain, take ten men and follow Sydney. Her instructions are your orders."

"But sir, she's a civilian! Surely you can't be serious...."

Admiral Jenkins cut him off. "Of course I'm serious."

"And stop calling him Shirley," Sydney added after a beat, grinning.

Admiral Jenkins rested his face in the palm of his hand.

I really hope this isn't a mistake.

With that thought, Sydney led part of the second strike team back up the maintenance ladder towards the fifth floor.

Admiral Jenkins motioned for the remaining troops to follow him, and they slowly made their way across the low-ceilinged maintenance floor until they were above the central conference room where the prime minister was being held.

When they reached the approximate location, he motioned for the troops to hold, then slowly lowered a fiber optic camera through one of the metal grates along the main horizontal duct, then through it into the vertical duct that led down to the ceiling below.

They watched on the screen as the camera snaked its way through the duct. The first thing they saw was the top of a series of stalls, with a woman walking in.

"Ladies' room," Jenkins said. "Next vent."

As he retracted the camera, one of the younger soldiers protested. "Hey! I was watching that." Everyone chuckled.

Admiral Jenkins lowered the fiber optic camera through the next vent and saw the conference room.

"That's more like it," he said. As they swung the camera around, though, his heart sank. "Damn it. Sydney said there were only two guards. There are four."

"Is there another vent?" one soldier asked.

Jenkins thought for a moment. "Good idea, son."

He walked to the next vent and found that it, too, led to the conference room.

I like these odds better, he thought as he motioned for a couple of soldiers to join him.

"Secure a winch to that steel beam there," Jenkins said, pointing upwards, "and get a sniper ready to lower down. You, over there, do the same thing."

After about three minutes, the teams had lowered two men down into the vent shafts.

"Don't do anything until I give the word," Jenkins said. "We can't take this whole facility with only forty men. If they try to move him, we'll go in anyway. If the prime minister's life is put in immediate danger, we'll go in anyway. Otherwise, we wait for Sanderson and the second wave."

Chapter Thirty-one

Admiral Skylarov's shuttle plummeted through the atmosphere like a rock in a pond. At about ten thousand feet, the ship pulled almost 5 Gs momentarily to level off for landing. Skylarov swore in his native Ya'ana'i tongue.

When the shuttle finally came to rest on the landing pad, a hundred Terran Command troops greeted him. Upon seeing him, they lowered their weapons.

"Admiral Skylarov," their commander said, saluting. "We await your orders."

"Take me to the prime minister," he replied, "and give me your sidearm."

The soldier did as he was told.

Skylarov shot him.

Suddenly, the entire company drew their weapons. Skylarov smiled.

"What have I told you?" he asked. "The enemy looks like us. Trust no one."

The soldiers exchanged puzzled glances, then lowered their weapons cautiously.

"That's better," he muttered as he walked towards the main entrance doors.

***

"ADMIRAL on the bridge!" a young cadet shouted as Admiral Jameson entered Triton Station's C&C.

Everyone stood except for Jen. She remained transfixed by the communications console.

"As you were," Jameson replied.

"Sanderson," Jameson barked, "what's the good news?"

"I'm not sure," Jen replied. "I'm still waiting for it."

The room erupted into an awkward chuckle.

"Get me James Moore at the ECIA," Jameson said after the laughter had died down to a dull roar.

A few moments later, Mr. Moore's bald visage adorned the screen.

"Jim," Jameson said. "Glad we could reach you. It looks like we might not make it to the party tonight."

"Understood," Mr. Moore replied. "We'll get the party started without you. If you're there, you'll be welcomed."

Jameson nodded. "Triton out."

***

SYDNEY and Captain Schoeffield climbed up the emergency ladder and into a small concrete tunnel. They then walked about thirty feet and stepped through a solid steel door into the bottom of a lift shaft.

"Just eight more floors," Sydney said as the other troops appeared one at a time through the narrow opening.

"Are you freaking kidding me?" Schoeffield asked incredulously. "What's keeping the lift from knocking us to the floor below?"

Sydney reached over to a panel and pulled a red handle. "Power is out. Next question?"

Captain Schoeffield shook his head.

"How can we take the floor when we have to approach one at a time?" he asked.

"We're not," Sydney replied as she began climbing the ladder. "We'll climb up the ladder, squeeze past the lift car, drop into the top, then pry open the door."

"You are so totally out of your mind," Schoeffield said as he began climbing the ladder behind her.

After climbing up four floors, they reached the lift.

"Crap," Sydney said. "It's only on five. The control center is on seven."

"Options?" Schoeffield asked.

"Break in on six," Sydney replied. "Stage everyone on top of the lift."

"Or?"

Sydney blinked for a moment before the voices in her hat suggested an alternative.

"Break the panel off the wall, short out the firefighter operations switch so you can control the lift manually, then send me back down to turn the power on and wait for the power grid to come back online."

Schoeffield nodded. "I like that plan better. Get me two shooters up top. We're opening the hatch."

With that, Sydney and a couple of soldiers stepped aside onto a small metal landing at the fourth floor to let Captain Schoeffield and his sharpshooters go past.

***

ECIA deputy director James Moore stood in the situation room at the headquarters of the Earth Central Intelligence Agency.

"Sir," a young intern shouted, "call from Secret Service Director Fitzpatrick."

He reached down and picked up the phone.

"Jim," Director Fitzpatrick said.

"Liam," Mr. Moore replied.

"You asked me to check in after an hour," Director Fitzpatrick said, "so I'm checking in."

Mr. Moore smiled. "Three hundred ECIA field agents are moving from Bangor down to the staging area in Rhode Island with an ETA of thirty minutes."

"We'll be expecting them," Director Fitzpatrick replied.

"Excellent. Report back when they arrive."

***

CAPTAIN Schoeffield stepped out onto the small metal landing opposite the lift doors at the sixth floor. From there, he could basically step off the landing onto the top of the lift car. Two of his sharpshooters stood beside them.

Sydney followed them as far as the landing, but stayed there as he and the sharpshooters stepped out onto the roof of the lift car.

As captain Schoeffield twisted the latches atop the car, the sudden sound of gunfire ripping its way through the top of the car made him stop and jump rather rapidly backwards onto the metal landing.

"Other options?" he asked.

Sydney shook her head.

"Okay, then," he replied. "This is a military operation at this point. We're going to go in hot, and it's going to get ugly. Sydney, go down to the bottom floor, go through the metal door, and *seal it behind you*. After you seal the metal door, go back to the ladder and climb a few dozen rungs. If we need any further help, we'll send someone down for you. Otherwise, don't come up under any circumstances. I can't be responsible for your safety if you do. If we aren't back in one hour, we're dead. Go back to pick up Admiral Jenkins and his team."

Sydney nodded, then hurried back down the ladder.

"Okay, everyone," Captain Schoeffield whispered. "We know that the fifth floor is occupied, and they're waiting for us to drop through the top of that elevator. We're not going to. I want as many people as will fit standing on this platform. Everyone else, be ready to go. I'm going to sneak across and try to pry open the doors on the sixth floor. When the last person is out, we toss a plasma grenade at the lift cables and run like hell."

The troops nodded their understanding. The soldier at the top of the ladder then passed the orders on to the person below, and so on down the line.

A few seconds later, Captain Schoeffield dropped to all fours and began crawling stealthily across the top of the lift car. When he reached the other side, he grabbed the door and pulled on it. The door opened automatically a moment later, and he dropped to the ground.

Two soldiers were waiting for them at the entrance to the elevator shaft, but Schoeffield's sharpshooters were ready and picked them off handily.

"Let's go!" he whispered at the top of his lungs.

The soldiers quickly ran across the top of lift car. Their footsteps were punctuated by the sound of gunfire from the car below, but the blind shots did not connect with their targets.

As the last soldier stepped out, Captain Schoeffield pulled the pin on a plasma grenade, tossed it gently to the middle of the car, and ducked around the corner. A few short seconds later, the explosion shook the building and a tongue of flame shot out of the open elevator shaft door beside him.

As soon as the explosion subsided, he stepped towards the lift doors. He arrived just in time to see the burning car crash into the bottom of the lift shaft in a puff of sparks. The entire scene was brightly lit by the sun shining down from where the shaft's roof used to be—*a side effect of such a large explosion in a nearly sealed tube,* Captain Schoeffield mused.

"Stairs! Quickly!" he shouted. "They won't just wait for us to pick them off one by one."

The sound of machine gun fire from behind them confirmed this.

***

"Sir, we have movement," the soldier announced from across the room.

Admiral Jenkins spun and walked over to where the soldier stood. The pair then watched the screen as Admiral Skylarov entered the room below them with a pistol drawn.

> "You!" the prime minister spat.
>
> Admiral Skylarov responded by hitting him across the face with the back of his hand and the butt of the dead soldier's pistol.
>
> "You will speak when spoken to," Skylarov said.
>
> The prime minister went silent.
>
> "Now, as I was saying," Skylarov continued, "you are going to send a message to someone for us."

Admiral Jenkins turned the camera and zoomed it in to get a clearer view of the screen.

> **From:** *Prime Minister Hardy*
>
> **To:** *Jennifer Sanderson*

Re: *Ackerman Crystal*

You are hereby ordered to turn over the Ackerman crystal you stole from the research lab on Lenora Prime to Admiral Skylarov. Failure to do so will constitute treason and will result in your summary execution.

Franklin Hardy

Prime Minister of Earth

While they pondered this message, Admiral Jenkins zoomed the camera out to show the whole room.

"The Ackerman crystal was destroyed," the prime minister replied, terrified. "I've read the logs."

Skylarov shook his head. "That's just what they want you to believe. Send the message."

The prime minister did as he was told.

"Goodbye," Skylarov said, raising the pistol to the prime minister's head.

Chapter Thirty-two

"ARNOLD! Franks! Cover fire!" Captain Schoeffield shouted.

Two of the troops took positions against the walls to lay down cover fire as Captain Schoeffield and the other troops ran towards the nearest stairway. When they reached the stairs, one soldier stood on each side of the door while Captain Schoeffield grabbed two stun grenades from the pack of the soldier in front of him.

"Ready," he whispered. "On three. One... two..."

The doors suddenly flew open. Captain Schoeffield tossed the grenades into the stairs anyway as three enemy soldiers ran right past him into the hall. The sharpshooters behind him picked off the enemy handily, but not before they got off several shots and took down two of his men.

Eight to go, he thought cynically as he threw the doors open again and nodded for the nearest two soldiers to go through.

"Clear!" the soldier shouted from the other side.

Captain Schoeffield then motioned for the remaining troops to follow him. By this time, a lucky shot from behind had taken out one more soldier.

Damn. Make that seven.

He led them up a floor, then motioned for two more men to stand beside the doors as he prepared the stun grenades.

"On three. One... two... three," he whispered.

Upon that count, they threw open the doors, and he tossed two more stun grenades into the empty hallway.

Damn, he thought as they slammed the doors shut. *What a waste of perfectly good grenades.*

A moment later, they went off with a pop.

And now they know we're here, he thought as he pulled the doors open again.

Within seconds, troops began rushing the floor from the staircase at the opposite end of the hall. The soldiers in front of the doors quickly dropped to the ground and began picking them off one-by-one.

"Paulson, Banks," he shouted over the din of automatic weapons fire, "drop down a level, go to the other end of that hall, and toss four plasma grenades at the stairs."

"Yes, sir," the two men shouted in unison before taking off down the stairs.

An agonizing five minutes and twelve enemy soldiers later, another explosion rocked the building.

"Attaboys," Schoeffield whispered at no one in particular.

When they had finished clearing the floor, Captain Schoeffield motioned for them to enter the hall. They walked to the control room, but found the steel doors locked.

"Detcord," he shouted to one of the soldiers.

The soldier rapidly pulled a piece of PETN cord out of his bag and shoved it between the door and its frame, then attached a blasting cap at the corner, hooked a lead to the blasting cap, and rapidly unrolled about twenty feet of wire.

"Stand clear!" Schoeffield shouted.

Everyone ducked as the soldier pressed the button. About a second later, the door shifted several inches away from its frame and fell harmlessly to the ground.

The grenade team returned about that time, and they all cautiously entered the room, only to find a team of frightened civilian personnel meekly peering out over the tops of consoles.

"Come out," Captain Schoeffield said.

"Who do you report to?" one of the scientists asked meekly.

"Admiral Thomas Jenkins," Schoeffield replied.

"Oh, thank God," the scientist whispered.

***

"TAKE him out!" Admiral Jenkins shouted.

A moment later, four soldiers lowered the pair of sharpshooters rapidly into the air vents, and about a second later, the contents of Admiral Skylarov's head were scattered on the wall.

The enemy troops began firing at random, not knowing where the shots came from. Within just a few seconds, the enemy soldiers were all dead, the prime minister was hiding under his desk, and one of the sharpshooters was trying to kick the vent cover off.

"Drop McHenry!" Jenkins said.

One pair of soldiers lowered down their sharpshooter.

"Mr. Prime Minister!" the soldier shouted. "Admiral Jenkins sends his regards. Come with me! Hurry!"

The prime minister ran over to him.

After the soldier grabbed the prime minister, he shouted, "Pull!" and the soldiers overhead did so.

When he reached the top, the prime minister banged his head on the ceiling.

"Careful!" the soldier shouted.

A few moments later, they successfully slipped the prime minister up through the vent and into the crawlspace above.

"Get back down there and rip the veil off his chest," Jenkins ordered the soldier below, "and move quickly. I have reason to believe that Skylarov isn't the only one pulling strings around here."

The soldiers lowered the sharpshooter back down to the floor.

***

"WHAT do you need us to do?" the scientist asked as the soldiers approached.

"We need you to target a ship," Schoeffield replied. "The Aenid."

"We can't target much of anything," the scientist replied. "The space battle is blanketing all of our active sensors with so much interference that we can't get a solid lock. It's like trying to make out the color of someone's tie when you're on Earth and he's in a low orbit around the sun...."

Schoeffield sighed. "We have their last known coordinates. Will that help?"

"Depends on the coordinates," the scientist replied.

Schoeffield handed him a sheet of paper with the coordinates.

The scientist's eyes widened. "That's right above us," he exclaimed as he ran over to the nearest console. "We can probably spot them visually with imaging satellites."

Within a couple of minutes, the scientist proudly scratched down an updated set of coordinates a few hundred meters from the original location.

"That's our boy," he said.

"Fire when ready," Schoeffield said.

"I don't have authorization to do..." the scientist started to say as Schoeffield walked over to the console, picked him up by his shirt, and deposited him a couple of feet away.

"Here's your authorization," Schoeffield said, then keyed in an authorization code he had received from Admiral Jameson several days earlier. A few seconds later, the image on his screen was replaced by a series of blinding flashes followed by an empty star field littered with debris.

***

"Your team has arrived, and the SS stands ready to move," Director Fitzpatrick said. "We need to know what we're dealing with, though, and we'd prefer to wait to move in until the prime minister has been secured."

"Understood, Director. We are in regular communication with Terran Command military forces inside the facility. I will update you when something happens."

Director Fitzpatrick chuckled. "By that, you mean you'll tell me what you're doing blowing the tops off buildings clear on the other side of the capitol complex."

Deputy Director Moore blinked.

"I'm not sure what you're talking about," he replied.

"The defense satellite control center?" Director Fitzpatrick asked. "Our guys *are* responsible for that, right?"

"Well, maybe," Director Moore replied. "To be honest, I'm not sure."

"And the ship that exploded a few minutes ago?"

Director Moore sighed. "I have no idea."

"Contact me when you know something," Director Fitzpatrick said, then hung up.

"What an asshole," Director Moore muttered.

Chapter Thirty-three

FLEET Admiral Ramirez swore as he jumped into an escape pod.

It's a damn good thing I was watching the satellites, he thought. *Too bad there wasn't time to wait for anyone else. Eh. No great loss. They were all useless anyway.*

A half second later, the escape pod was plunging rapidly into Earth's atmosphere. He watched as the ship he had occupied just moments before exploded into a giant fireball. No other escape pods followed him.

Ramirez sighed. *It's probably better this way.*

By the time the pod's drogue chute deployed, however, he knew things had gone terribly wrong. Below him, he could see pulse rifle and tracer bullet fire flying from the island. Troops inside various buildings were firing at a substantive invasion force attacking from the water.

Ramirez winced as several bullets grazed the hull, but he kept his attention focused on carefully steering the escape pod towards the landing pad at the center of the capitol complex.

Within about two minutes, the pod touched down, and troops quickly surrounded it.

"Now, for the entertainment portion of this evening," he muttered.

***

SYDNEY huddled on the ladder. She had barely managed to keep her grip when the explosion shook the base a few minutes before, followed a few seconds later by a dull thud. She could only imagine what had happened.

After a few minutes, she heard the groaning of the metal hatch to the lift shaft as it opened. She began descending the ladder rapidly as the footsteps grew closer, louder.

"Sydney!" Captain Schoeffield shouted.

Sydney relaxed. Then, she remembered where she was and quickly tensed up her muscles again to avoid falling several stories to the nearest landing.

"Here!" she replied.

Above her, Schoeffield's soldiers (and a half dozen people in lab coats) were already beginning their descent, so she resumed hers.

After an agonizing few minutes, they reached the bottom of the first ladder, then the second, then eventually the fifth. After a few more ladders, they reached subbasement forty-two and followed Sydney back through the underground tunnels to the area underneath the main building.

When they arrived, they found Laura standing in the elevator awaiting their return.

"Stay here," Captain Schoeffield told the scientists. "Someone will pick you up."

They nodded.

Laura took Sydney and Captain Schoeffield's team up the lift to the largely unoccupied fifth floor. After they stepped out, Laura closed the door and waited.

***

THE troops saluted Admiral Ramirez as he stepped out of the escape pod.

"What's your status, Lieutenant?" he shouted as they rushed him rapidly into the nearest building—*the capitol building itself,* he noted.

"We're taking heavy fire," the lieutenant replied. "Probably ECIA and SS. We have lost contact with the team that is holding the prime minister, and we had an incursion from inside the building that houses defense satellite control. They managed to remotely shut down the satellites that were previously under our control, and the defense satellite control computers here in the complex are completely fried. They won't even boot."

Admiral Ramirez cursed under his breath in Spanish.

"Did Admiral Skylarov get the prime minister to send the message?" he asked.

The lieutenant shook his head. "I have no idea."

"Then you are useless," Ramirez replied, shooting the lieutenant in the leg. He then turned to the next soldier. "Bring me someone who knows something."

***

SYDNEY and Captain Schoeffield's team ran down the hall and into the "ladder closet", as Admiral Jenkins had dubbed it, then climbed down a floor and a half before stepping into the maintenance crawlspace.

Admiral Jenkins and his troops were waiting for them with the prime minister. The prime minister jumped behind Admiral Jenkins as though he expected gunfire at any moment. The Admiral politely ignored him.

"So you couldn't wait for us?" Captain Schoeffield joked.

"Skylarov was about to shoot him," Admiral Jenkins replied, pointing at the cowering man behind him. "We had to take him out. Ugly mess, really."

Schoeffield harrumphed. "What's your status, then?"

"Skylarov is down, along with about four of his soldiers." Jenkins replied. "We have his veil, and we've disposed of the alien body over in the corner."

Sydney looked over at the corner of the maintenance floor and cringed.

"Now I understand where the descriptions of the Roswell greys came from," she said, "but taller... and with tails."

Jenkins nodded. "And your status?"

"We lost three men," Schoeffield replied, "but we managed to take out the Aenid and lock out the defense satellites. If everything goes according to schedule, the second wave should follow behind us in about twenty minutes."

Admiral Jenkins nodded. "Sydney, I need you to contact Admiral Jameson and relay our status."

Sydney nodded. "When the second wave gets here, I'll let you know by radio."

Admiral Jenkins shook his head. "First rule of infiltration: no radios. We're fine as long as there's a floor full of concrete between us and anybody else, but as soon as we drop down a floor, our radios are going off. No pulse rifles, either—just mechanicals."

"I don't understand," Captain Schoeffield interrupted.

"Any receiver is also a transmitter, albeit a weak one," Jenkins replied. "If they have the right gear, the enemy can track us with them. Same goes for the pulse rifles. I can spot those on a broadband receiver from a quarter mile."

Captain Schoeffield went pale.

"What?" Jenkins asked.

"You should have told us that *before* we surfaced and took the control room," Schoeffield replied.

Admiral Jenkins also went pale.

"Sydney," Jenkins said. "Go. Quickly. There might not be much time."

Sydney rushed over to the ladder.

"Go with her," Jenkins said to the prime minister.

As the pair disappeared, Admiral Jenkins picked up the veil.

"From here," he said, "things get weird."

With that, Admiral Jenkins enabled the veil and became, for all intents and purposes, Admiral Mikhail Skylarov.

***

LAURA jumped when she heard someone knocking on the door, but after a few moments, she realized that it was a crude approximation of the correct knock, and opened the door.

"Sydney," Laura said. "Going down?"

Sydney nodded.

When they reached the bottom, Sydney stepped out.

"Should I wait for you here?" Laura asked.

Sydney shook her head. "Go back up and wait. If I need the elevator, I'll recall it from down here."

Laura nodded, closed the door, returned to the fifth floor, and waited for the magic knock.

After a few minutes, she got bored and began writing a novel on her data pad.

***

WHEN Fleet Admiral Ramirez reached the security command room in the east wing, he glanced quickly at the walls full of darkened display panels dully glowing amber in the reflected emergency lighting from overhead.

"No power," Ramirez muttered. "Do we have radio communication?"

"Da," a soldier replied from behind him.

Ramirez turned. "And who are you?"

"Commander Nikola Koychev," he replied. "I am commanding officer second after Skylarov."

Ramirez nodded. "Have you secured the control center for Earth's defense satellites?"

Commander Koychev looked at him in confusion.

"On the fifth floor of the Polinsky building," Ramirez offered.

"We find room, sir. No one there," he replied.

"Then look again," Ramirez ordered, pointing at the door.

"Yes, sir," Koychev replied.

"Be alert," Ramirez added. "Someone shot us down using those satellites. We're obviously under siege from within."

"Impossible," Koychev replied incredulously. "Polinsky building in middle of complex. No one else here in other parts of complex is. Da?"

Ramirez smiled. "That's what they want you to believe. Go. Search. Find."

***

"ADMIRAL Jameson?" Jen asked.

Admiral Jameson spun. "Sanderson?"

"There's a video call coming in from Earth," Jen said. "High priority."

Admiral Jameson nodded. "Put it on screen."

Sydney Caruthers appeared on the viewscreen.

"Miss Caruthers," Admiral Jameson greeted her. "I trust you have news?"

Sydney nodded. "The Aenid is down, the defense satellite system is locked out, and the prime minister is with me. Admiral Jenkins is preparing to move in and needs backup."

"Sanderson, have the second wave standing on the flight deck in ten minutes," Jameson ordered.

"Oh, one more thing," Sydney interrupted.

"Yes?"

"Skylarov is dead. Long live Skylarov," she said.

"Jenkins?"

Sydney nodded.

"Head to the submarine bay and wait for the second wave to arrive," Jameson replied. "Triton out."

***

COMMANDER Koychev and his forty-man strike force reached the Polinsky building in record time. As he entered, the stench of burning rubber poured out of the building. His first stop was the security office, where two young Lieutenants stood waiting.

"What happened here?" Koychev demanded.

The lieutenants shook their heads.

"We don't know," one soldier replied. "Someone reported hearing sounds from the top of the elevator, and then a minute later, the elevator exploded and crashed into the bottom of the lift."

"Has anyone come into or out of building?" Koychev asked.

"No, sir," the boy replied. "We have troops near every exit. If anyone came in or out, we would know about it."

"Search the building," Koychev ordered.

"We already did," the boy interrupted. "Every room. There is nobody here."

Koychev paused.

"Then other way out must be. You," Koychev shouted, pointing at one of the ensigns, "pry open lift doors."

The ensign pulled open the heavy doors with the help of two other soldiers. The burned-out elevator shaft that lay beyond reeked of death.

"There," Koychev said, pointing at a metal door in the side of the shaft approximately one floor below them. "That is on front side of building. Cannot lead into building. How do I get to basement?"

The ensign pulled out a building map and pointed at a stairway that led to that level.

Koychev led his team quickly down the stairs and through the basement. After a few moments of groping around in near darkness, they found the steel door that led into the bottom of the lift shaft.

Koychev and his team stepped through the charred remains of the lift car and walked to the other side of the shaft, where Koychev opened the metal hatch. Then, Koychev led his team through it and down the ladder beyond to the forty-second subbasement level.

***

Sydney flipped through the security cameras until she found Admiral Jenkins and his team on the fifth floor.

"Clear," one soldier said as he kicked a door closed.

"Fifth floor secure," Jenkins said. "Moving down."

Sydney watched them clear the fourth floor, then turned to walk towards the submarine bay. Suddenly, the motion detectors sounded an alarm, drawing her attention back to the screen.

On the viewscreen, she saw the foyer for subbasement 42. She watched as a team of unfamiliar soldiers made their way into the elevator shaft.

What the....

Then, the view changed to the submarine bay, where a small fleet of fold fighters began to surface one by one.

Sydney jogged in that direction.

***

Commander Koychev stood in the dimly lit room with a team of forty men. It was an odd room with a pedestal, an elevator, and a dozen hallways leading in various directions. Two in particular caught his attention.

> WARNING: Ever-changing maze ahead. Do not proceed without proper authorization and equipment.

How very strange, he thought. *No matter. They took prime minister, da. Entered main building through this elevator, they must have. If they can, so can we.*

Koychev pulled open the doors and smiled when he saw a ladder on the far side of the lift shaft that led down to the bottom of the shaft, just a few feet below them.

"Follow me," he shouted.

One by one, the soldiers dropped to the bottom of the lift, walked over to the emergency ladder, and began their ascent.

***

"Third floor secure," Jenkins said. "Let's head down to two. Stay sharp."

As they reached the second floor, the gunfire began immediately. He could see at least three doors in the hall with assault rifles sticking out, and possibly more.

After they ducked behind the doorframe, one soldier carefully reached around the corner and pulled the door closed.

Every few seconds, one of the sharpshooters attempted to take a shot, but each time, his rifle was struck by plasma rifle fire, resulting in a nasty jolt that made him jump back.

"Stun grenades," Jenkins shouted.

Three soldiers grabbed stun grenades out of their packs and tossed them one at a time down the hallway. Each time, a gun or two would clatter to the ground, but each time, it was quickly replaced by another one in the same doorway.

"We're getting nowhere fast," Jenkins said. "We need a new plan."

***

JENNIFER Sanderson, Sydney, and a team of special forces snipers ran quickly through the tunnels to the control room.

When they arrived, they saw Admiral Jenkins on the screen, unable to move forward onto the second floor. A few seconds later, they saw a security camera inside the elevator shaft showing an unknown team of soldiers at subbasement three and climbing.

"At this rate, they will reach Admiral Jenkins in three or four minutes," Sydney said. "We have to do something."

"Like what?" Jen asked. "There isn't any other way in."

"What if there is?" Sydney asked.

***

"MILLER, Stephenson, Franks, Justman, keep them pinned," Admiral Jenkins said. "We're going to circle around through the first floor, climb the steps in the rotunda, and surprise them from behind."

Four men took positions on either side of the door and began periodically firing shots into the hallway while the rest of the troops followed Admiral Jenkins down the steps.

Jenkins sent a small contingent of soldiers ahead to check each room along the hall on the first floor. Upon confirming that the last rooms were clear, he led the rest of the troops to join them, and they emerged into the rotunda.

Suddenly, the front doors flew open, and hundreds of troops rushed in, weapons drawn.

Oh. Crap.

***

JENNIFER and the rest of the assault team followed Sydney at a fast clip through the winding tunnels and steel badge-access doors. After what seemed like hours, they emerged at a T-shaped junction.

Sydney pointed one direction towards a doorway. "That's the coast," she said.

Jennifer looked, and sure enough, saw sand slowly seeping through gaps around the door.

"That way," she continued, "leads to the emergency exit stairs."

They continued their jog until they reached the bottom of a long, stone staircase that wound its way up the outside of a curved wall.

"Those are the emergency exit stairs," Sydney said. "If you pull that lever to the right, a section of wall swings outwards into the upstairs floor of the rotunda. You should leave half your forces here. If things get ugly, they can go in and surprise everyone."

"And the rest of us?" Jen asked, puzzled.

Sydney pointed beyond the curved stairs. A small, wooden door greeted them. Sydney opened it, revealing a passage barely tall enough to crawl through.

"You've got to be kidding me," Jen said.

***

"Fall back!" Jenkins shouted, but as they turned around, they found their escape blocked by another forty men. And when Jenkins turned back, he saw that half of the troops at the door were now facing backwards with weapons at the ready, and another team of troops—*probably secret service,* he suspected—stood behind them, also with weapons drawn.

And so they all stood there, paralyzed, silent, still, until the sound of one man clapping broke the silence. Slowly, mockingly, he clapped as he descended the left side of the rotunda staircase.

Admiral Ramirez, Jenkins noted.

"What we have here," Ramirez said slyly, "is a Mexican standoff."

Jenkins grimaced.

"Ah, Admiral Jenkins, I presume," Ramirez said, staring right at him.

Admiral Jenkins dropped the veil. Several soldiers gasped in surprise.

"Now drop yours," Jenkins said.

The fleet admiral chuckled.

"Ah. Very clever, Admiral," Ramirez replied, "but you should know that I am not wearing one. After all, you are the spy in our midst, not me."

Admiral Jenkins tilted his head.

"It is just as I have told you," Ramirez said. "See! The traitors walk among us, masquerading as us, spreading lies and disinformation."

Admiral Jenkins simply stood there, jaw agape.

Chapter Thirty-four

When Sydney and Jennifer reached the door at the other end of the tunnel, Sydney swung it open, revealing a long, sloping passage made of polished granite. Recessed rectangular lights dotted the stone walls every few feet at waist level, and the stone on the floor was well worn.

"What is this?" Jennifer asked.

"This is the speakers' corridor," Sydney replied, pointing down the hall. "That way leads to a door in the rotunda on the first floor. The first floor is highly guarded, so don't go that way."

"And this way?" Jennifer replied, pointing.

"Eventually, it takes you to stairs that lead up to the back of the hall, but first, it leads to the front grill of the dais," Sydney replied.

"Perfect...."

***

"You see, Admiral," Ramirez said, "your actions have revealed your treachery more clearly than I ever could. I particularly liked when you masqueraded as Admiral Skylarov and tried to kill the prime minister. It's just fortunate that we injured you and prevented you from killing him."

"Liar!" Jenkins shouted. "Skylarov was an alien! *You* are the one who has infiltrated our military. *You* have lied and masqueraded as one of our own. And *you* tried to kill the prime minister. Oh, and you also destroyed the Aenid!"

Ramirez laughed. "Do you not see how absurd you look, admiral? Aliens? And it was your forces who destroyed the Aenid. We have video evidence."

"No!" Admiral Jenkins shouted. "You destroyed the Aenid last April. The ship you were flying today was the Constitution."

"Semantics, my dear admiral," Ramirez replied. "The name on the hull is the Aenid, so it is the Aenid. Surely you don't expect us to believe that a simple clerical error is evidence of some giant alien conspiracy."

Admiral Jenkins pondered this for a moment, then shook his head.

Now I know how Pierre felt.

***

JENNIFER crawled up the ladder towards a trapdoor, then at the last second, pulled herself into a crawlspace between the subfloor and the raised dais.

She looked out across the floor of the upper hall of parliament, scanning every nook and cranny for enemy troops, but saw none.

Jennifer then stuck her head up through the trapdoor and looked around again.

"I think we're clear," she said, and motioned for the others to follow. They scurried up the ladder, then walked to the front of the stage, down the steps, and up the center aisle to the giant doors that led to the second floor balcony of the rotunda.

“Franklin, Stevens, you’re on point,” Jennifer said. “First priority is to get to the upstairs hall in the west wing and take out those enemy soldiers.”

Sydney slid aside a panel next to the door. Behind it, a two-way mirror allowed her to see into the rotunda.

Jennifer reached for the door.

“Wait!” Sydney said.

Jennifer looked at her, and Sydney motioned for her to take a look.

“That doesn’t look good,” Jennifer said. “Okay, Fleet Admiral Ramirez is standing on the stairs. Our first priority is taking him out.”

Sydney shook her head.

“Do you have something to add?” Jennifer asked.

“If you kill him, it will turn into a bloodbath,” Sydney replied. “If you destroy his veil with a careful shot, the enemy soldiers will see him for what he is, and they will refuse to follow his orders.”

Jennifer nodded slowly. “It’s risky. How do we know where the veil is? I thought they said it could be planted anywhere on the person.”

Sydney nodded, then closed her eyes, engrossed in thought.

“I couldn’t see anything out of the ordinary with my eyes,” Laura said, “but when I used the thermal imaging camera, I could see a tail.”

Thermal imaging.

“Do you have a thermal imaging camera?” Sydney asked.

Jennifer shook her head.

“Night vision,” Sydney said. “Do you have night vision goggles?”

Jennifer’s eyes widened. “Yes, in my pack.”

“Good enough,” Sydney replied, grabbing the goggles.

Sydney used the goggles to look through the viewing slot, carefully covering the IR emitter with her finger. She could just make out a dark shadow where the admiral's natural body heat was blocked by the metal box.

"There," Sydney said. "It's on his left arm."

Sydney handed the goggles to Jennifer, but she shook her head.

"Night scope," Jennifer explained as she attached one to her rifle.

Sydney nodded.

Jennifer took careful aim, then lowered her weapon.

"Sydney, you're a civilian," she said. "Get out of here. We have this covered. Thanks for your help."

"No problem," Sydney replied.

Jennifer waited for her to run back to the trapdoor and close it before she lined up the shot again.

Two shots—one for the glass, one for the Admiral. Just two shots.

***

"What I can't understand," Admiral Jenkins said, "is this: what do you get out of all of this?"

"Isn't it obvious?" Fleet Admiral Ramirez replied, stepping down from the stairs onto the floor of the rotunda and walking across to his counterpart. "We eliminate the threat from Colonial spies."

"What the hell are you talking about?" Admiral Jenkins shouted. "The war is over! Any colonial spies already received a full pardon from the prime minister of Earth!"

"Except," Ramirez interrupted, "for those who continue to do harm against the Terran Alliance. Gentlemen, this man is a traitor. Ready! Take Aim!"

Suddenly, the crash of a shattering sheet of plate glass echoed through the hall.

The entire room erupted into chaos, with everyone glancing around wildly looking for the source of the sound.

A moment later, the whiz of a single bullet cut through the air, and Fleet Admiral Ramirez clutched his arm.

"NO!" he shouted as he began to shimmer.

One of the soldiers shouted, "Alien! Shoot him!"

Suddenly, Admiral Ramirez, now a full-on alien, took advantage of his triple-jointed legs to jump about eight feet vertically. He flipped himself over the banister, and ran up the stairs, grabbing a ceremonial sword from beside the entrance to the upper hall of parliament as he crashed through the doors.

"He's mine!" Admiral Jenkins shouted as he ran after him. He, too, grabbed a sword as he ran through the now-broken doors, then nearly tripped over Jennifer, who was sitting on the floor nursing a hurt leg.

"Hey, Jen," he said. "Where did he go? Oh, and are you okay?"

"I'm fine," she replied, pointing towards the back left corner of the auditorium. "That way."

Jenkins ran, sword in hand.

***

SYDNEY stared through the grille on the front of the stage at the alien running towards her.

Please don't let him see me, she thought as she ducked out of sight and climbed the rest of the way down the ladder to the speakers' corridor below.

When she got to the ground, Sydney ran, and did not stop until she stepped through the door into the rotunda. As she did so, twenty men with rifles pointed them at her.

"Whoa, guys!" she said, pointing at her head. "Hat?"

The soldiers began snickering.

Sydney ignored them as she looked for anyone she knew. Eventually, her eyes met those of Captain Schoeffield standing on the balcony above her.

"Captain Schoeffield, I need your rifle," she shouted.

Captain Schoeffield dropped it over the edge, and she caught it easily.

"Thanks!" she shouted.

She checked to make sure the rifle was loaded before ducking back inside the speakers' corridor.

***

As Admiral Jenkins stepped through the doorway, the alien struck its first blow. Jenkins jumped backwards as its sword ripped a large hunk of wood out of the doorframe.

Jenkins swung back, but the alien jumped backwards, and his blow fell short. Their swords clashed repeatedly as he drove the alien down the steps to the floor of the speakers' corridor.

Suddenly, the alien jumped back up onto the stairs. Admiral Jenkins spun, but not before the alien jumped back down between him and the exit. Suddenly, he was on the defensive as the alien drove him backwards down the hall.

Down near the floor, Jenkins saw a small door hanging open.

This must be how Jen got here, he thought as he ducked inside.

After a few feet of fighting, the darkness of the tunnel made seeing impossible, so Admiral Jenkins moved as quickly as he could without looking back. As he neared the other end, the alien swung at him and missed. He spun around and swung back before backing through the small door into the emergency exit corridor.

They continued to swing at one another as they progressed down the hall, with sparks flying as their blades collided with the gas lamps and the stone walls that held them, with the floor, with the ceiling, and (occasionally) with each other, until finally they reached a T-shaped intersection in the hallway.

Left, Admiral Jenkins wondered, *or straight?*

The slash of the alien's blade blocking the path to the left made the decision much easier.

Straight.

Admiral Jenkins quickly backed down the other corridor, but after about a hundred feet, he reached the end. A few steps led up to a door, but the door looked heavy, and around it he could see....

Sand?

He pressed his back against the door, continuing to deflect the alien's relatively poor swordplay, but it would not budge... until...

...it budged...

...and Admiral Jenkins and the alien were knocked to the ground as several hundred kilograms of sand came crashing down on top of them.

***

"CAN you walk?" James Moore asked as he stepped into the upper hall of parliament.

Jennifer nodded and pulled herself up to her feet.

"The alien ran out through the left doorway at the back of the hall," Jennifer said. "Admiral Jenkins followed him. And we have a civilian down there somewhere, too. Can you help?"

"We're too busy searching the buildings and rounding up rogue soldiers," Mr. Moore replied. "It's going to be up to you."

Jennifer sighed as she turned towards the back of the hall. She walked quickly down the aisle, through the curtains at stage right, and down the steps to the speakers' corridor. When she arrived at the other end and opened the door, she saw Captain Schoeffield standing at the entrance.

"Sanderson," Captain Schoeffield said, feigning surprise, then shaking his head. "I should have known that only one person in the universe could have made that shot."

Jen chuckled.

"Where are Sydney and Admiral Jenkins?" Schoeffield asked.

"I thought they came this way," Jen replied.

Captain Schoeffield shook his head. "She was here for a minute, but then she went back in."

Damn, she thought. *That means....*

Jen ran out the front door, dragging Captain Schoeffield along behind her by his sleeve.

***

ADMIRAL Jenkins groaned.

I haven't hurt like this since my wife gave birth, he thought, *and then kicked me in the groin to show me what it felt like.*

The alien stirred.

Admiral Jenkins tried to pull himself to his feet, but he could tell just by looking that his left leg was broken, and the rest of him didn't feel much better.

A few feet away, the alien drew its sword. Admiral Jenkins felt around madly for its mate, but it was hopelessly buried in two feet of sand.

Slowly, the alien approached him, sword drawn.

"It's over," Jenkins said. "You can't win."

The alien began laughing in a deep, guttural voice.

"I already have," the alien replied. "Just a few steps from here, there are landing craft, and you have Skylarov's veil. No one will ask any questions."

Jenkins gulped.

"Give me one good reason why I shouldn't kill you now," the alien asked.

"I'll give you three," a girl's voice shouted.

The alien spun, dropping the sword in the process, its head facing the source of the sound just in time to see Sydney Caruthers fire three shots from her rifle squarely into its chest.

The alien angrily roared.

That's when the rifle jammed.

"Shit!" Sydney shouted.

The alien seized that moment of distraction to rip the veil from the admiral's chest and run through the door out onto the sandy beach.

It made it about three steps before Jennifer grounded it again with a running tackle.

As soon as she saw it fall, Sydney ran up after it with her rifle. When she arrived, she stood over the alien and spat in its face.

"This," Sydney shouted as she hit the alien with the butt of the rifle, "is for all the people you killed!"

"This is for the hell you put Admiral Jenkins through!" she shouted, hitting it a second time.

"This," Captain Schoeffield shouted as he kicked the alien, "is for blowing up Terran Command Station!"

"This is for the last year of my life!" Sydney shouted as she hit him with the rifle again.

"And this," Jen shouted, stepping on a sensitive part of the alien's anatomy, "is for Amanda, you son of a bitch!"

With that, Jen pulled out her sidearm and put four bullets into the alien's skull.

"We could have questioned him," Sydney suggested.

Jen shrugged. "He wouldn't have told us anything anyway. Sometimes it's okay to shoot first and ask questions later. Just saying."

They chuckled, then walked back to help Admiral Jenkins. As they disappeared into the tunnel, Sydney turned to Jen.

"Ooh," Sydney said. "I just thought of something."

"What's that?" Jen asked.

"Did anybody go get Laura?"

Epilogue:

A few days later.

Joseph sat at Amanda's bedside with Jennifer. Marc sat with his little sister, Anna in chairs across the room.

"You know," he said to Jennifer, "it's kind of creepy with her dad in the next bed."

Jennifer laughed.

Amanda's eyes blinked. "Oh, hey Jen."

Jennifer looked at Joseph. "You mean she's awake?"

"Yeah," Joseph replied. "She regained consciousness about an hour after you folded out of Triton."

Jennifer smiled. "Hey, Amanda. It's good to see you."

"Good to see you, too," Amanda replied. She turned towards her dad, then back to Jennifer. "It's going to be a long six weeks."

Her father chuckled.

"So," Amanda asked, "what happened after the sand fell on you?"

"Everything's kind of fuzzy after that," he replied.

Joseph Kurtz chuckled a bit. A moment later, he noticed the incoming message light on his data pad blinking, and he sighed. He tapped the screen a few times, then frowned.

"What is it?" Jennifer asked.

"I'm not sure," Joseph replied.

That's when his concentration was broken abruptly by Admiral Jameson stepping into the room.

"Admiral Jameson," Joseph said, standing immediately at attention.

Jennifer followed his lead. Amanda and Admiral Jenkins merely feigned a salute.

"As you were," Jameson said, then snorted when he saw that Admiral Jenkins had placed his salute hand somewhere near his ear.

"I have an announcement to make," he continued, "but first...."

He walked over to the window and slid it open as far as it would go. Then, he walked to the door and opened it.

A moment later, Sydney and Laura emerged, followed shortly thereafter by a reporter with a camera. As the reporter looked around the hopelessly cramped hospital room, he found no adequate space to set up his gear, so he folded the legs of his tripod together and leaned the entire rig precariously in the corner.

"Fifteen *hours* of elevator music," Laura grumbled.

Sydney just rolled her eyes and smiled an impish grin.

"And I wrote ten thousand words!" Laura shout-whispered.

"Are we on?" Jameson asked impatiently.

The nod from the cameraman confirmed that they were broadcasting live on TANN.

"In the Terran Alliance," Jameson began, "every officer is expected to show bravery in the face of danger. Every officer is expected to do his duty to protect our alliance from threats, both foreign and domestic. Once in a while, though, an officer goes above and beyond that duty."

As he said this, a band outside began playing the Terran Alliance anthem.

"Today, it is my great pleasure to stand in the midst of such an officer," he continued. "Admiral Thomas Jenkins, for your exceptional bravery, I am proud to honor you with our top military honor, the Terran Medal of Bravery."

Admiral Jameson then withdrew a medal from his pocket and pinned it to the admiral's shirt pocket.

"Likewise," he continued, "as a citizen of the Terran Alliance, we all pledge our loyalty to the alliance and to its people, but every so often, a civilian shows inner strength and courage that defies reason in defense of our great alliance. For these brave men and women, we reserve our highest civilian honor, the Terran Medal of Liberty. I'm particularly proud, then, in what is, I believe, a historical first, to present two such awards on the same day."

Admiral Jenkins and his daughter tried their best to turn their heads in his direction to watch history unfold before their eyes.

"Laura Rodolfo and Sydney Caruthers," Jameson intoned, "it is my privilege, on behalf of Prime Minister Hardy, to present you both with the Terran Medal of Liberty."

The room and the crowd outside erupted simultaneously in applause, yet over the din, they could just make out a singer singing the Terran Alliance anthem through the public address system.

Hail, Terra, victorious,
greatest planet of them[2] all.
Brave, valiant, and glorious
for your nations, we fall.
Rise, Terra, in justice
as new worlds we explore,
that in freedom may prosper
Terra evermore.

After the reporter had left and the chaos had died down a bit, Joseph picked up his data pad and looked at the message he had received earlier.

"Hey guys," Joseph said, "there's something I think you all need to see."

As they turned their attention towards him, Joseph walked over to the viewscreen, turned it on, and routed the data pad's output through it.

[2]In the original poem, and in some early musical settings, the word "them" is omitted.

Admiral Jenkins perked up and turned to face the screen.

"Fleet Admiral Ramirez left some... private records encrypted and under key escrow to be released in the event of his death," Joseph said. "Call it a technological 'poison pill', if you will. Now that he is dead, he's going to take down a lot of people with him."

With that, Joseph tapped a button and selected a file entitled *PlanetFire*.

"Here's the bit you should see," Joseph continued.

The viewscreen lit up suddenly and revealed an image that they could barely identify at first, but after a few seconds, Admiral Jenkins recognized it as the prime minister's office on Earth. Three figures stood before him: Fleet Admiral Ramirez, the Prime Minister, and...

Admiral Jameson? he thought, puzzled.

Joseph read the date stamp burned into the image for the benefit of the Jenkins family. Then, they watched in silence.

December 7, 2390

"We need to test project PlanetFire on a populated world," Admiral Ramirez insisted.

"I'm tending to agree," the prime minister replied, "but the people may need some convincing."

"Are you both out of your minds?" Jameson replied. "We can't just kill millions of innocent civilians. Hostilities are dying down! This war could end soon."

"Fair enough," the prime minister replied. "We'll hold off on testing for now. Fleet Admiral Ramirez? Convince me."

Admiral Jenkins frowned. "So Ramirez has been an alien for at least a couple of months. Nothing surprising there."

"That's not the good part," Joseph replied. "Keep watching."

A moment later, the screen changed to a different date. Admiral Jameson was gone, leaving only Fleet Admiral Ramirez and the prime minister.

December 25, 2390

"We have just received some intelligence that suggests a possible terrorist plot to crash a ship into Terran Command Station on or around the first of the year," the prime minister said matter-of-factly.

Fleet Admiral Ramirez was momentarily speechless.

"What do you think we should do about it?" the prime minister asked.

"Sir," Fleet Admiral Ramirez replied, "I recommend that we do nothing."

"Really?" the prime minister asked. "Seems like it should be a high priority."

Ramirez shook his head. "I assume we can blame it on the Colonial Alliance?"

The prime minister nodded. "Probably."

"Well, then, there's not a problem," Ramirez replied. "I'll start getting our PlanetFire project ready to deploy against Kinji in retaliation. We'll strike at the heart of the Colonial Alliance and take out dozens of terrorist groups in a single blow."

"Estimated casualties?" the prime minister asked.

"Of the PlanetFire? All of them."

"No, no," the prime minister corrected him. "Estimated casualties on Terran Command Station?"

"Oh," Ramirez replied. "Anywhere from a few hundred up to twelve thousand, depending on the day of the week."

With that, the prime minister looked at him for a moment, then looked down at the papers in front of him.

"I suppose," the prime minister said after a few moments, "that it's a small price to pay for uniting an alliance."

Closing Thoughts:

There was a moment there, after Pierre and the girls met, when I thought, "Oh, crap. The two cast groups just came together, and now I can't cut away to anything." It really wasn't obvious where it was going to go from there.

So I cut back to the present time when Pierre was telling the story to Amanda's dad. This served four distinct purposes. First, it cemented in the reader's mind that this character had to live to tell the tale. Second, it gave a further hint that we'd be returning to the original Traitors cast towards the end of the story, and that the stories would end up merging. Third, it gave me an "out" for the "no cutaway" problem. Fourth, it foreshadowed the fact that they were about to try to "replace" Pierre. All in all, an amazing amount of "win" for such a short passage, I think.

I tried to make it also be an "Oh crap" moment for the reader, so at least I got to pass on the sentiment. The passage is particularly fun because the double negatives earlier (not, not crazy) and here (not, not true) suggest that he might be crazy and that he might, in fact have done it. Of course, he didn't, but this means that they at least attempted to "replace" him once and might try it again....

Then, just a few short scenes later, I needed for them to get together so that the girls could find out what Pierre knew. At that point, it was going to be another awkward problem when they went their separate ways, so I needed another means of a cutaway. This time, I decided to have somebody try to rub out Pierre. That always seemed like a possibility as far as getting him to cooperate, and the idea of the girls interfering and saving his life accidentally was also something I had been pondering, but this gave me a reason to actually do it.

Originally, I had planned for Klern to be wearing Pierre's face at the time, but then he wouldn't have been surprised to find out that they tried to replace him when talking with Amanda's dad, so that wouldn't do. This required adding further complication—the notion that the aliens could fairly rapidly change "skins".

And then, things got messy again. Fortunately, while all this was happening, Amanda's dad was busy doing stuff, and periodically interacting with Skylarov, so that made for another good cutaway.

Another horrifying moment was the point at which I realized that the original cast believed Skylarov had died and had been replaced 25 years earlier. I wanted, however, for Skylarov to become suddenly evil when he was "replaced" for two reasons. First, he was a character that Amanda's dad would presumably interact with on a regular basis. Skylarov's sudden personality change is a really useful device for getting Amanda's dad to believe Pierre. Second, I needed to replace a character. Graphically. And Skylarov was already a character that nobody cared much for, and more to the point, his character wasn't important to this plot line, per se.

So I punted. Turns out that they tried to temporarily replace Skylarov once before. It didn't work because the experiment blew up, but the important thing was that nobody knew about it (and even if they had succeeded, no one would have known)... at least for 28 years. This actually has the benefit of making it even easier for Jenkins to believe Pierre, hence the reason he orders Pierre to be released, and the reason Pierre shoots and destroys the mechlizard sent to kill Admiral Jenkins, allowing Jenkins to fake his own death and use the veil himself to pose as someone else. It also gives Admiral Skylarov another motive for eliminating anyone involved in the mission to Lenora Prime.

***

Station Structure:

THE outer ring and arms have two levels. The central nexus has 42 1/2 levels (and a few hidden half levels).

Level 1:

At the top, with a raised observation deck in the center (C&C) and a short lift near one side that goes down to the first full-width level.

Levels 2-4: (3 levels)

Large, windowed areas. The outer portions are an observation deck for the crew. The inner portions are recreation facilities, medical facilities, and crew eateries.

Levels 5-17: (13 levels)

Central nexus above the arms.

Levels 18-19: (2 levels)

Central nexus, arms, outer ring.

Levels 20-32: (13 levels)

Central nexus below the arms.

Levels 33-35: (3 levels)

Smaller section at the bottom.

Levels 36-42: (7 levels)

> A small vertical shaft primarily used to space antennas away from the body of the station.

See the front cover of Traitors in Waiting for a picture of Terran Command Station.

***

I hope you've enjoyed the initial trilogy of the Patriots series of books. I hope to expand on the stories of various minor characters (and some of the major ones), in various other stories—some concurrent with the stories in this trilogy, some not.

Join me for the next book in the series, *Carpe Universum*, in which they blow up the moon.

Just kidding.

Or am I?

About the Author:

David is an avid musician, writer, photographer, videographer, musical composer, and hard-core geek with a Master's degree in computer science and a Bachelor's degree in communications (broadcasting) and computer science.

In addition to writing this book, David also created various workflow tools used in its production, did all of the content production and design, redesigned many of the fonts, and drew the cover art.

His choral music has been performed by the Diocesan Choir of Monterey, California and the contemporary choir at Holy Cross Catholic Church in Santa Cruz, CA. He spends much of his spare time performing with musical ensembles in the greater Santa Cruz area.

http://www.patriotsbooks.com/

www.ingramcontent.com/pod-product-compliance
Lightning Source LLC
Chambersburg PA
CBHW021623030826
48979CB00036B/1918/J

* 9 7 8 1 9 4 0 8 0 9 0 5 2 *